Sweet
Little
Lies

Also by Michele Grant

Heard It All Before

Published by Kensington Publishing Corp.

Sweet Little Lies

MICHELE GRANT

KENSINGTON PUBLISHING CORP.
www.kensingtonbooks.com

DAFINA BOOKS are published by

Kensington Publishing Corp.
119 West 40th Street
New York, NY 10018

All Kensington titles, imprints, and distributed lines are available at special quantity discounts for bulk purchases for sales promotion, premiums, fund-raising, educational, or institutional use.

Special book excerpts or customized printings can also be created to fit specific needs. For details, write or phone the office of the Kensington Special Sales Manager: Kensington Publishing Corp., 119 West 40th Street, New York, NY 10018. Attn. Special Sales Department. Phone: 1-800-221-2647.

Dafina and the Dafina logo Reg. U.S. Pat. & TM Off.

ISBN-13: 978-0-7582-4221-1
ISBN-10: 0-7582-4221-2

First Kensington Trade Paperback Printing: February 2011
10 9 8 7 6 5 4 3 2 1

Printed in the United States of America

This book is dedicated to my sister
Melissa, who is living her life like it's golden.
Make that platinum. She's co-captain,
cheerleader, sponsor, and coach for Team
Michele. This book is for all the other single,
successful sisters who are holding down
their own and living fab while doing it.
Stay real, stay up, stay focused . . . but dream big!

Courage allows the successful woman to fail and learn powerful lessons—from the failure— so that in the end, she didn't fail at all.

—Maya Angelou

ACKNOWLEDGMENTS

The past year has been a whirlwind of new experiences, humbling lessons, and teachable moments. I would like to thank all of my friends and family for sticking by me. Since I listed you in *Heard It All Before,* you know who you are! Always, I have to give a shout-out to Selena and Katie for their patience.

One of the most incredible things to come out of the past eighteen months has been my introduction and love affair with social media. I created a Web site, MicheleGrant.net; a blog, www.blacknbougie.com (affectionately known as BougieLand); two Twitter accounts, @OneChele and @MgrantAuthor; as well as Facebook pages and a BlogTalkRadio show: the BnB Radio Network.

Not only have Facebook, Twitter, and the blogosphere been great marketing and networking tools, they have also allowed me to meet a great variety of fantastic people whom I consider to be friends, both virtual and in real life.

So I'd like to take a moment to acknowledge the people who were a major help, influence, sounding board, and inspiration for me (in no particular order): Deidre Berry, Cheris Hodges, Tiffany Trotter-Mack, Lisa Bobbitt, Ashley Smith, Corey Ponder, David Parrish, Jay Anderson, Max Reddick, Joseph Duncan, Cheri Paris Edwards, Patrick Phillips, Glen Palmer, Rich Owens, Ghadeer Morris, BB Waite, Leon Rogers, Jayme Carter, Damon Smith, Eronica King, Michael Davis, J. H. Merrick, Carolyn Edgar, Yvonne Bynoe, Paul Brunson, and Glen Jasper. To all the folks at RWA/DARA and LitChat, you've been lifesavers!

I'm positive I'm forgetting people, and of course there are some I know only by your virtual names, so for all the BougieLand faithful and even those who just bothered to say "Hi!" . . . this one's for you.

How It Began

1

Days Like This

Christina—Thursday, August 13, 10:47 p.m.

"Christina, girl," my grandmother used to say, "timing is everything...and yours is always a day late and a dollar short." Grammy Vi was freaking prophetic.

The plane was parked at the gate. I was seated next to a testy black man whose last name I didn't know and whose first name I couldn't remember. I had to wonder at the circumstances that brought me here, to this moment. Thinking back to eight days ago, I asked myself the following questions:

Would I have been more lucid and less homicidal if I'd drunk my morning coffee first? Would I have been more rational if I hadn't been caught standing there with wet hair, trying to hold on to the post–shower sex glow? Would it have made a difference if this hadn't happened three days before my wedding?

I'll never know. Here's how I got from there to here:

Christina—Wednesday, August 4, 9:34 a.m.

It was Wednesday—a warm, sunny, late summer morning. The kind of morning you only get in the Bay Area. The sun was beaming through the last of the fog, with a slight breeze coming off the water. The wind softly rustled the teal silk drapes hanging across the one open window in my bedroom.

All was right in my little piece of real estate on Harbor Bay Island. Alameda was literally a hop, skip, and jump from San Francisco, nestled on an island and backing up to Oakland. My two-bedroom, two-and-a-half-bath house wasn't huge, but it was big enough for the two of us who would live here after my wedding in a few days. The best thing about the house was a view of the Bay Bridge with San Francisco twinkling like a magical jewel beyond. My bills were paid, my man was near, and my spirit was happy.

I woke up late, a rare treat. I had taken the rest of the week off to prepare for my wedding. My fiancé, Jay, was spooned to my back, his arm possessively wrapped around my waist, his thigh wedged between mine. Another rare treat, since he traveled so frequently. I lay next to him for a minute just...living. Black love, y'all. I smiled to myself before I slowly eased out of his hold and headed for the bathroom.

Midway through my shower, the etched-glass door opened and he stepped in. Very quickly, the shower went from rated R (hot and sudsy) to rated X (wet and steamy). We went from zero to sixty and back to zero in fifteen minutes' time. Another few minutes of actual showering and I stepped out to face the day. I silently apologized to my ruined hair and yanked on the fluffy robe and slippers before padding toward the kitchen.

So it was 10:02 a.m. according to the coffeemaker. I stood pouring my expensive Guatemalan whole beans into the grinder when Jay said his first real words of the day. ("Like that right there, baby" didn't count.)

"Listen, sweetheart, about the wedding..."

I paused in the pouring of the beans and ever so slowly turned my head to look at Jay. Jay, my third (yes, I know) fiancé. I paused because I knew the tone. That hesitant, I-hate-to-tell-you-this tone. I had heard the tone before.

Twice before, to be exact. The first fiancé used the tone in the car on our way back from my final wedding gown fitting. Cedric wanted me to listen while he explained that he accidentally married his college sweetheart a month before our wedding. Accidentally. Boys' night out, ran into her. One drink led to another which led to Vegas, which led to me calling 175 friends and associates with the news, assuring them that yes, I would be sending those thoughtful gifts back and no, we were not just going to have a big party anyway.

The second fiancé used the tone at a charming Italian restaurant on the Bay across the wharf from Jack London Square. Perry wanted me to listen while he explained that he was confused about his sexuality. His what? I shrieked! Yes, his sexuality. He had been living a lie and wanted me to know (two weeks before our wedding) that he wasn't sure who he was or what he wanted. Well, if he didn't know, I certainly had no clue. He was kind enough to call half of the 125 friends and associates.

So yes, when my third...THIRD...fiancé stood naked in my kitchen with that look on his face and tone in his voice...I froze before biting out, "What about the wedding?" I had a tone of my own: cold, suspicious, pissed off.

He paused before answering. Jay was a 6'1" dark chocolate, bodyguard-build kind of brother. Square jawed, former marine, short-cropped fro with a razor-sharp line, laser-beam eyes so dark brown, they appeared black. A nose that would've been Grecian had it not been broken twice, and lips that would look pouty on anyone not so unapologetically masculine. Not an ounce of fat on his faithfully maintained body. Well proportioned, he was a man who moved stealthily on his long limbs, large feet, large hands, large...well—everything. As I said, well proportioned. When he smiled, he was an engaging teddy bear of a man. When he didn't, he was the kind of brother who seemed intimidating, even frightening. He stood there looking like a Zulu king in need of a loincloth. But right now, he was the one who looked scared. "Now, Chris, let me just say—"

I put down the beans—no need for $15.95 of imported goodness to get ruined. I decided to employ a little psychology. I walked over to him calmly, put my hands on his broad chest, and smiled encouragingly. "Just tell me, baby. Whatever it is, it'll be okay. Just say it all at once. I'll just close my eyes and listen." I closed my eyes.

He sighed and relaxed slightly, rubbing his cheek against my forehead. "You're so sweet. The thing is . . . I'm really not Jayson Day. My real name is David Washington. I'm an undercover operative with the NSA and I've been out here on assignment for the past two years. I shouldn't have let things get this far, but when I met you, you were just so sweet and sexy. I couldn't help myself."

I opened my eyes slowly and took a step back. "What are you talking about? I had your background checked! You work in corporate security for TeleTech and you grew up in Oakland! I've met your parents, for Christ's sake!"

He gave me a look of smug amusement that did not sit well at all. Not at all. "I know. They told me someone was checking my cover. I thought it was cute. Those people you met were actors. The thing is, baby, I would marry you in a heartbeat, but . . . I'm already married."

I stood with my mouth open, trying to figure out what to digest and what to reject. Cute, actors, NSA, already married— *what?* "I'm sorry. I must have misunderstood. You're what?"

"Um-hmm, married—with two kids back in Denver. Daughters Dina and Daisy. They're seven and twelve." Why he felt the need to share details was lost on me.

"Kids?! Did you just say you have kids?" I really did not know what to say. I was tempted to look around for the hidden cameras. Was I on *Punk'd*?

"I can show you pictures. . . ."

The word "pictures" was still floating in the air when the

doorbell rang. In the middle of crisis situations, I tend to go on autopilot. I just take the next logical step to get to the next logical place. So for no other reason than autopilot, I answered the front door. Yes, I did. I forgot I was rocking the robe, with my wet hair turning into a Chaka Khan fro and my naked fiancé (ex-fiancé?) standing in the foyer.

"Parcel servi—" The young black delivery guy paused at the sight that we presented: Me, cute of face and slight of body, 5'5", a cocoa-colored and petite package wrapped in a huge, fluffy pink robe, matching slippers, and a scowl on my face as I cut the side-eye to the dark chocolate naked guy. Eyes the color of milk chocolate, thickly lashed and normally tilted up with good humor, were currently squinted and shooting virtual fire. Bow-shaped lips normally painted a shade of peach were bare, naked, and pursed tightly.

"Hey." I released my death grip on the door handle.

To his credit, he recovered quickly. "I have some more packages for you, Ms. Brinsley. Looks like more wedding gifts. A few of these require an adult's signature. If you don't mind my asking, are you okay?" This guy had been delivering all manner of packages related to the wedding for over ten months now. He was a cute, dreadlocked, kind of baby-faced, toffee-skinned tall guy, probably in his midtwenties, and I didn't have a clue what his name was. On the occasions when I was home for his deliveries, we made small talk about the weather. I said clever things like "Working hard out here in all this rain?" He would smile, all flashing dimples and twinkling sage green eyes, and reply "Gotta earn a living." And now, he was bearing witness to one of my top ten worst life events…okay, top five. I was determined to maintain a shred of dignity.

Before I could respond, Jay…David…Jay/David spoke up. "Man, do we look okay? Can't you just leave those and go?"

Why was he speaking to my delivery guy? Why was he speaking at all? "Don't speak to him that way. At least he's concerned about my well-being. As a matter of fact, just don't speak at all."

Delivery Guy shuffled from one foot to the other, clearly wishing he was anywhere else but here. I could relate. "Ms. Brinsley, seriously—are you okay?" I found it interesting that of the two men in the room, the one I *wasn't* supposed to marry this week was more worried about my well-being. Duly noted.

Forcing a smile, I reached for the little plastic pen. "Sure, why wouldn't I be?" I scrawled across the electronic signature box with a flourish before handing it back to him.

He read what I wrote, paused with brow raised, and read it again. "Did you mean to sign this 'Just shoot me now'?"

My lips twisted. "Does it matter?"

Making a sound that was a mix between a snort and a laugh, he headed to the rear of the truck. "I guess not."

I kept my eyes on Delivery Guy. Just looking at him was soothing to me. He was a lean and corded young man. His skin poured over his fit frame with the color of toasted almonds. And he hadn't just broken my heart. I watched in detached fascination as he lifted packages and placed them on a dolly. Without turning my head even an inch in his direction, I hissed out instructions to Jay / David. "Put some clothes on and get out."

"Christina . . . we need to talk about this," Jay / David said.

Finally glancing in his direction, I adopted my "disgusted" pose. Hand on one hip, size 7 foot tapping, head tilted ever so slightly to the right. "Think you've said enough."

"I don't want you to think that this, what we have—isn't real."

Was he kidding me with this? He wanted to talk about what was real, when quite possibly everything he had said to me for close to three years was clearly a damn lie. "Oh, it's real. It's real jacked up."

"Christina, I really wanted to marry you."

I didn't want to hear another word. Not. One. More. Word. "But you're not going to...because you can't...riiight."

"Would you rather I didn't say anything and let you live a lie?"

"I would rather you hadn't lied for the past two or three years. For all I know, you're lying now. As a matter of fact, of *course* you are lying. Who are you supposed to be? Undercover Brother...puh-leeze! Give me some credit. You could have at least come up with something believable. Why not just feed me sweet little lies? You don't want to marry me, so be it. What was this, some sort of elaborate con? I don't know what to think. I don't know what to do with this. What I *do* know is that you waited until three days—*three days* before our wedding, but exactly fifteen minutes after you made sure to get you a little morning nookie—to drop whatever this is on me. Go put some clothes on your lying ass and get out!"

He made a move to reach for me and probably realized that any point he was going to make would be far more effectively delivered when he was clothed. Turning, he walked hurriedly back to the bedroom.

My house was built in the shape of a semicircle, with the kitchen, office nook, and dining area on one side; foyer, living room, and half bath in the middle; and two bedrooms and two baths on the other side. It was designed and decorated to maximize the view of the Bay. Rich woods and shades of blue and green. But it also meant that from the front door you could pretty much see everything going on in the house.

Delivery Guy wheeled the dolly to the front door and peeked in nervously before tapping on the door frame. "Uh, you want me to bring these in or leave them out here?"

What to do with the wedding presents? Now that it seriously appeared that there would be no wedding...again. It was all too much to process. "Might as well bring them in—uh, what's your name?"

He shot me a look at the very moment I realized it was stitched onto his uniform. We spoke simultaneously. "Steven."

Shrugging, I gave a wry grin. He would have to forgive my lack of attention to detail. My life was in the process of going to hell in a handbasket...again. "Sorry, Steven. Can you just set everything on the table?" I gestured toward a circular mahogany table behind me.

"Sure, not a problem." He transferred packages with the haste of one dying to be done and on his way. It occurred to me that this was probably as awkward a moment for young Steven as it was for me.

Jay/David came back out with some sweatpants hastily yanked on, pulling a T-shirt over his head. "You ready to talk?"

"I'm ready for you to go." Funny, in a not so humorous way, how your entire world can tilt in the blink of an eye. Not twenty minutes ago, I was wrapped around this man, planning to have years and years of the same. Now I couldn't stand to look at him.

"But I think we should..." When he took a step toward me, I put my hand up in the universal back-up-off-me sign. Poor Steven stood there with a what-the-hell-have-I-walked-into look on his face.

"Jayson, David—whatever your name is! Please!" I just couldn't take anymore. I needed to process and I needed to be alone to do it.

"Christina, I know you. If I leave without trying to fix this, you'll never let me back in."

"You don't need to get back in here, you need to get back to your *wife*...and Dina and Daisy, was it? Whatever, *I cannot believe this.*"

He looked at me, face all pitiful, like I should be concerned about making him feel better.

I looked at him, mad as hell, wondering how this happened to me...again.

Steven took the last box off the dolly and turned toward

the door with understandable haste. I lived here, and I was ready to be somewhere else my damn self.

Jay / David reached for my hand, only for me to yank it back. He reached again, encircling my wrist and tightening enough to hurt. "Jay, that hurts."

"Just listen to me for just one second." Meeting his eyes at that moment, I realized that I had no idea who he really was, and that made me panic.

Hissing at him, I tugged again. "Let me go."

He pulled me toward him roughly. "I just need you to listen."

"Please stop, you're scaring me and I want you to go."

Steven stopped dead in his tracks on his way to the door. He let the cart handle clatter to the floor, turned, and stepped to Jay / David all in one fast motion. "Hey, man, I think you oughta do what the lady says and just go."

Jay / David looked incredulous. I was a little stunned myself. But Steven took a no-nonsense posture. Chest out, legs planted firmly, slightly apart. Looking back and forth between them, I noted the contrasts. Where Jay / David was broad and thick, Steven was all taut lines and sleek muscles. Jay / David had about twenty-five more pounds on his frame, but Steven was about two inches taller. While Jay / David looked like he'd seen military combat, I'd lay odds Steven had seen street combat. Personally, in a dark alley, I wouldn't have wanted to battle with either one of them. They stood staring each other down like Serengeti lions from an Animal Planet documentary. Too much testosterone in the room.

Jay / David's nostrils flared and he snarled, "Punk, don't make me—"

"What?" Steven asked, raising his chin and flexing one hand.

Yanking my wrist away, I stepped in between the men. "Fellas. Separate corners. Both of you can go." With my back to Jay / David I mouthed the words to Steven: "Thank you."

They moved apart from each other a step at a time. Jay /
David picked up his keys from the table. Steven lifted the dolly
handle off the floor where he'd left it.

"I'll be back," Jay / David said before storming out the back
door.

Steven reached past me before handing me something.
Looking down, I realized it was a Kleenex. I tilted my head
and looked at him. "Why—"

"You're crying." His voice was soft and gentle. He exited
my front door, closing it with a quiet click behind him.

Reaching up to touch my face, I realized it was true. I had
tears streaming down my face and I hadn't even known.
"Thanks again," I said belatedly to the empty room before
sinking into my easy chair to cry in earnest.

2

You're *That* Chick

Christina—Thursday, August 13, 10:47 p.m.

"**C**an you tell me how I got bamboozled into taking this trip?" Talking quietly into my phone, I rested my chin on my right hand while clutching my BlackBerry in the left. The view out the window from seat 6A on a red-eye flight bound from San Francisco to New York's LaGuardia Airport was unremarkable. It was dark, partly cloudy, and the runway was still busy with the arrival and departure of planes. Really, my question was rhetorical, but Jackie, my best friend, would provide some sort of smart-ass answer.

"Grey Goose hangover, girl. I told you to put the bottle down, but you gotta do things the hard way." Smart-ass answer, as expected. Jackie and Lynne, acting in true homegirl solidarity, came over to my house eight nights ago with the universal breakup kit—junk food, ice cream, a liter of Grey Goose, and the quintessential nineties Black Love DVD three-pack: *Love Jones*, *Soul Food*, and *Waiting to Exhale*. All it did was remind me that apparently I was destined to hold my breath a little while longer.

The fallout from the Jay / David pronouncement had been

swift and ugly. Locksmiths and threats of restraining orders were brought into play. Jay / David did not go quietly. But go he did, once threatened with legal action and bodily harm.

My mother, the ever-dramatic Joanna Brinsley, went into a rant of epic proportions. (Not. Very. Helpful.) My father died when I was very young and my mother had never remarried. She was left financially comfortable but emotionally needy. I was the youngest of her three children and she tended to cling...far more than I liked. I had to dispatch my older brothers, Clarke and Collin, to talk her down—that was after I talked them out of hunting down Jay / David solely for the purpose of smashing his face in. (He would have destroyed both of their bougie behinds, but that's neither here nor there).

Collin's wife, Celia, was a pretty and perky perfectionist who believed in silver linings, rainbows, and unicorns. I wish I was kidding. When she showed up on my doorstep with a cupcake bouquet and chamomile tea, I sent her over to Mom's as well. I wasn't in the mood for rainbow-infused, it-will-all-work-out speeches. I kept the cupcakes though; turned out they went really well with vanilla vodka. A lot of vanilla vodka.

The next morning, Jackie and Lynne loaded me up with Ugandan premium roast (I had tossed the Guatemalan blend), and urged me out of the house so they could clear it of all things wedding related. While they called the seventy-five friends and family members with the news, I went to work. Somehow in the hour and a half I spent in my office at Valiant Publications, near the wharf in the Embarcadero area of San Francisco, I managed to volunteer to write a series on a new hip-hop label that was launching in midtown Manhattan, started by a California transplant.

So here I was over a week later, miserable and bone weary, on an all-night flight to New York. "Jackie, you couldn't have stopped me?" Admittedly, I was beginning to whine a little bit. I was tired of being tired, as well.

"Buck up, *chica*. Maybe you'll meet someone cute."

I rolled my eyes. Cute guys were the last thing I needed. Guys of any sort were the last thing I needed right now. As a matter of fact, I was planning on taking a long-overdue man break and started to tell her as much. "Heaven forbid. The last thing I need is—" I stopped speaking as I watched the next passenger enter the plane. "It's you!"

"It's who?" Jackie's voice was high-pitched and loud.

The delivery guy, witness to the latest worst moment in my life, had paused in row six. My row. His dreads weren't tied back today but hung loose to his shoulders. Outside of the dull brown uniform, he had an air of self-confidence about him that I hadn't noticed before. Checking his ticket, he looked from the seat to me and back again. "Ms. Brinsley." He started stowing carry-ons and getting settled in.

"It's who?" Jackie raised her voice as if I hadn't heard her the first time. She was loud enough that he could hear . . . easily. He turned those pale green eyes on me and waited for my response.

"My delivery guy," I answered, meeting his gaze. He pulled a book out of his laptop case. It was a murder mystery by an author I was familiar with and liked a lot. I had the same book on my bedside table at home. I pulled the phone away from my ear to find the volume control. Part of the Jay / David fallout involved me getting a new phone number. I had taken the opportunity to upgrade my phone and I had no idea how to work it.

"The yummy young guy? Hot bod, sexy eyes, Denzel smile?" Again, she was loud enough that he heard. I watched a slow smile spread from his lips, across his cheeks, and into his eyes. He smiled with his entire face.

I pressed what I really hoped was the VOLUME DOWN button and put the phone back to my ear. Jackie had a way of saying whatever she thought, regardless of who she embarrassed. "Jax, were you paying that close attention?"

"Weren't you? You were engaged, not dead. That young

fella is the hotness. He could ring my doorbell anytime he wanted." As I was saying, Jackie was a bit of an over-sharer. My cheeks reddened slightly, I frantically pressed the other button, trying to lower the volume, and closed my eyes.

"Jax, please."

"What? Oh, is he right there? Hey, hottie! What's he wearing? He looked good in the uniform, so I *know* he looks good out of it." How was it possible that she got louder?

Keeping my eyes closed, I acknowledged that my life was never dull. "You know what? I'll call you when I land. Okay?"

"Aw, girl, you need to loosen up. Life is short."

"Shorter by the minute, Jax. I'll talk to you in the morning." When I opened my eyes, he was still watching me. He kinda *was* the hotness. He was a beautiful man. He was lean and cut, like a man in his prime and comfortable there. His hands were large, with long, almost graceful fingers. He wore jeans and a long-sleeve shirt well. He had that kind of frame that clothes complimented. His jeans hugged and creased in all the right places.

"Okay, girl. Hey—why don't you get drunk on the plane and make an inappropriate proposition to Mr. Deliveryman? See what kind of package he's working with. Getcha some rebound d—" I pressed and held the VOLUME DOWN button to cut off the rest of that sentence.

His brows shot up and his grin twisted a little as he held back the laughter that was twinkling in his eyes. His eyes were a hazel color that could look either green or brown depending on mood and lighting. Right now they were brown and amused.

"Girl, 'bye!" I cut her off and hit the END button before she could add any more detail to her X-rated suggestion. I made a production out of turning the phone off and tucking it away, buying myself some time before I had to actually speak. Finally, I looked at him and gave a weak smile. "So, out of all the flights going to all the cities in the world, you appear on mine...."

He smiled at my variation of the line from *Casablanca.* "Here's looking at you, Ms. Brinsley."

A man who knew his Bogart movies? "Call me Christina."

"Hey, Christina." His voice had a warm, melodic tone.

"Hey, um—hey." I cast around in my memory for his name. I knew it started with an *S.*

"Oh, okay—you're *that* chick."

"What chick?"

"The I'm-too-bougie-to-remember-service-personnel-names chick. That high-maintenance chick. You know the one."

"I do not! I am not!" Like I needed the criticism right now? Delivery Guy was kinda nervy.

"So my name is—"

C'mon now, Christina, think! It was stitched right on the uniform. The pep talk did not work and I was drawing a complete blank. He did not look amused. I was saved from admitting total ignorance by the arrival of the flight attendant. "Can I get you something to drink, Ms. Brinsley?"

"Bloody Mary, please." *And quickly,* I wanted to add.

"Mr. Williams?"

"Water, no ice, please." The flight attendant nodded and moved away.

We were sitting in stilted silence when suddenly it came to me. "Samuel, Scott, Stefan...no—Steven!"

He gave me a serious, tart side-eye. "Fourth time's the charm."

Well, sue me for not remembering. I've had a few damn things on my mind. I was more irritated than the situation warranted, and that caused me to be abruptly rude. "What are you doing in first class, anyway?"

"Wow, you really *are* that chick." Sliding a quick, disappointed look my way, he popped open his book and shifted so his back was angled to me, in the classic I'm-ignoring-your-existence pose.

Inexplicably, I was intrigued. Irritation aside, I wondered, Who *is* this *guy?* Delivery guy two weeks ago, first-class urbanite on his way to New York today? I sensed hidden depths. Jacked up as my life was as this point, I welcomed the diversion of a puzzle. And did I relate that he really was the hotness? I just wanted a little more information. "I'm really not that chick. Really. But the last time I saw you, you were in a brown uniform delivering packages to my front door. None of that screams 'first-class traveler'—forgive me for stereotyping."

"Forgiven." He was gracious.

"So what takes you to New York?"

"Grad school."

"Grad school?" Okay, I was still having trouble reconciling Delivery Dude and this guy as the same person.

He slapped his book closed. "Damn! A brother can't be educated? You see a fella delivering packages and that's all you see? No wonder your fiancé bailed."

Oh no, he didn't! Ouch. Like salt-in-a-fresh-wound ouch. Now that was just uncalled-for. Okay, I was rude first, but that was a low blow. Without uttering a word, I opened my book and shifted toward the window. Averting my face, I reached down for my iPod.

"So I guess you don't want to talk anymore? Conversation gets a little tough for you and you're done?" His snarky sarcasm was of the advanced variety.

"You know what? I don't really know you. I am not required to talk to you. Enjoy your flight. Have a nice life." My tone indicated I was done.

"You know what? You may be gorgeous, but you are on that extra for real." His tone wasn't that warm anymore either.

"On that extra? Extra what? What does that even mean?" Damn youngsters today just made up phrases.

His eyes narrowed. "Means you are just a little bit more than what's needed."

"Is that right?" Again, like I needed character analysis from the delivery guy?

"From what I can see so far? Yeah. Extra."

Now my eyes narrowed. "You know what? You may be fine, but your manners could use some work."

He opened his mouth to reply, but the captain began delivering his take-off spiel. By the time the attendant did her emergency exit speech, we had settled into a hostile silence.

3

You're Allowed to Be Impressed

I was giving old girl the side-eye as she downed her second Bloody Mary and started in on the red wine. Sure, I felt a little bad for that line about her ex, but it irked me that she couldn't remember my name. I mean, c'mon now...I've been to her house every day for at least six months straight.

The first time she opened the door, I thought, *Okay, wow*. Little thing came to below my shoulder even in heels. Beautiful chocolate brown skin stretched over a tight little body. Girl was all legs, and gently curved where a woman should be. Classically beautiful face, oval shaped with big cocoa-colored eyes and a slightly upturned nose. Jet black straight hair falling past her shoulders. Lips worthy of a second glance, full on the bottom with a pouty bow on top. Her every emotion showed on her expressive face. I enjoyed our little exchanges and generally thought she was a woman who had it all going for her.

Witnessing the implosion of her engagement was as uncomfortable for me as it was painful for her. I had no experience with that kind of personal betrayal, so I couldn't imagine what it would take to bounce back from that.

I didn't know how to describe the general vibe of her, except to say she was the kind of girl you want to scoop up and protect...until she opened that pretty mouth today. Wow, lethal weapon. I watched as she leaned into the window, staring out into the inky sky. She glanced down at her hand, which up until a few days ago held a man's promise to her. With a sigh, she balled her hand into a fist and closed her eyes.

I couldn't help but feel for her. The urge to rush in and try to make it all better ran deep. But really, it was none of my business.

Just stay out of it, Steve, I told myself. This girl had "high maintenance on the verge of a breakdown" stamped all over her. I ordered a scotch and sipped slowly. I had thoughts of my own to deal with. I had family back home depending on me to do well in school and well in life. I was the first of my family to even think of getting an advanced degree. A lot of sacrifices were made to get me where I was. I'd come way too far to let anybody down. I had no time or interest in distractions. I had the next ten years of my life planned out. Seeing Christina huddled over by the window reminded me of why romance was way down on my priority list. I couldn't afford to hit a wall like the one she ran smack into. I took another sip and then another. By the time I finished the drink, I was in a much mellower frame of mind and empathized with her. I'm sure at one time she had her next ten years planned out as well. Surely, she hadn't factored this in. The next time she shifted, I took the opportunity to speak. "So you think I'm fine, huh?" I kept my tone diplomatically light.

An unwilling smile circled the edges of her lovely mouth. "Did I use the word 'fine'? I don't recall saying that."

"Good. That means you don't recall any of the other less-than-polite stuff we said earlier. Apologies all around?" I tilted my cocktail glass toward hers as a conciliatory gesture. After a slight pause, she touched her glass to mine.

"Apologies all around. I'm really not at my best."

After a few moments of companionable silence, I decided to address the pink elephant dancing around the first-class cabin. "You want to talk about it?"

"The wedding death?"

"Is that what you call it?"

She shrugged. "Seems accurate."

"Okay...wanna talk about the wedding death?"

She shrugged again. "You are pretty much caught up. He said what he said, you did what you did, I said what I said, and that was that."

"You haven't heard from him since?" I caught her gaze and held it.

"We—my brothers and I—had some difficulty getting him to remove himself and his things from my house. From my life. But we prevailed in the end."

"Did you have his ass kicked?" If ever a man deserved a foot in the ass, her ex did.

"We decided to skip the ass-kicking, but it was a thought. Still is, really."

"Is he still calling?"

"I don't know—new phone number, new phone." She looked back at me unflinchingly.

I liked that about her. Even after the hellish week she'd had, she still looked a brother in the eye to let him know she was a little bent but not broken. "So what's next for you?"

"What do you mean?"

"I mean, what will you do to move on?"

"All I can do is put one foot in front of the other and keep moving. My company, Valiant Publications, is a start-up, but we're starting to create some buzz, so now seems like a good time to concentrate on my career."

"Valiant?" I thought for a second. "They do online magazines?"

"Yeah, *Shades* and *Webinista 2.0.*"

"You're a writer?"

Christina smiled. "Writer and editor, among other things. I wear a few hats. That's why they pay me the medium-sized bucks. So what are you going back to school for?"

"Joint master's and PhD program in transportation science."

"From NYU?"

"Columbia."

She raised her brows. "Am I being insulting if I say I'm impressed?"

I laughed. "No, you are allowed to be impressed."

"So what exactly is transportation science?"

"Simplified, it's the engineering behind moving people, energy, and things around."

She nodded and smiled. "That's really all delivery is then... transporting things from place A to place B. Hence the career, presumably to save up to go back to school?"

I nodded. "Exactly."

"So will you be trying to design highways or subway systems?"

I found it refreshing to talk to a sister on an intellectual level. Not that ladies aren't about their education.... I've just met one too many who would rather discuss the latest Drake video. If they asked about my ambitions, it was usually followed by not-so-subtle questions about how much paper I would stack in the long run. "I want to concentrate on energy-efficient, high-speed rail."

"Wow. Statewide?"

"Nationwide."

"Converting current systems to light-rail or staying with the old infrastructure?"

I kind of goggled at her. Usually when I started talking transportation science, people nodded politely and changed the subject quickly. She was genuinely interested. "It's going to depend on who underwrites the project. Generally, government wants to piggyback on what's already there. Private-sector funding would allow for more flexibility of design."

Christina smiled. "So now you seem surprised."

"I am. It's a rare treat to talk engineering with a sister."

"Now who's making assumptions?"

I put my hands up. "Guilty. You are clearly an articulate woman to be reckoned with."

"Recognize!" she teased, before changing the subject. "What's the in-flight movie?"

"Latest Bruce Willis action flick." We shared an eye-roll.

"I have an old Spike Lee joint on my laptop if you care to watch?" she offered.

I raised a brow. "Why did I think you were more of a Tyler Perry girl?"

She pursed her lips and tilted her head. "Is this payback for me thinking you were a non-degreed delivery dude who couldn't afford first class?"

I laughed. "Maybe a little bit. Okay—pact. No more assumptions."

"Sold." She opened her laptop, handed me a set of headphones, plugged in her own, and started the movie.

4

It's Just Breakfast

Christina—Friday, August 14, 8:30 a.m.

"Ladies and gentlemen, in preparation for our landing at New York's LaGuardia Airport, we ask you to turn off all electrical devices, return your carry-on items to under your seat or the overhead bin, stow your tray tables and place your seat backs in the upright position."

I jolted awake at the end of the flight attendant's spiel announcing that we would land in about thirty minutes. There was a stitch in my left side, my neck was at an odd angle, and my hand was resting on something warm and solid. Something warm and solid…that moved. I flinched slightly as a large hand covered mine and patted soothingly.

"It's okay, baby, leave it there," a deep and sleepy voice said.

I blinked and focused. I was leaning into Steven's side, my head resting on his shoulder, my hand on his chest. His arm was around me. His eyes were still closed and a slight smile was on his face. He really was gorgeous to look at.

"Steven," I said quietly.

"Hmm?" He turned his chin and kissed my forehead. "Time to wake up?"

His lips were very, very soft. I was tempted to nuzzle him back just for a minute. No. Uh-uh. Absolutely not. Jay / David's face popped up in my head and I remembered my pledge—No. More. Men. My official man hiatus could not be derailed by this cutie. "Steven," I said more firmly, and moved away.

His eyes flew open. He looked at me, frowned for a second, then moved his arm and straightened up. "Well, that was interesting. Did I maul you? Should I apologize?"

"Not in the least. We're all good and we're about to land." I used my most crisp, no-nonsense voice and did not meet his eyes.

He nodded curtly and we both started tucking our belongings away. Where moments ago we had been cuddled together, now there was a distance between us that had nothing to do with the armrests. It was a little awkward.

"So," he said tentatively.

"Yes?"

"Do you have to rush somewhere when we land, or do you want to grab some breakfast?"

I paused. Then I said, "Man hiatus."

"Beg pardon?"

"I'm on a man hiatus," I repeated firmly.

He burst out laughing...heartily. So much so that others around craned their necks to see what was so funny.

"Why is that funny?" I asked indignantly.

"Girl, it's pancakes. I swear I won't propose."

I rolled my eyes. "But to what end?"

"Um, nourishment? A little company with your nourishment."

I narrowed my eyes. "As long as you know it's just breakfast. I'm not interested in starting anything."

"Healthy ego. Modest girl."

"Cautious girl. I'm so off the market right now."

"Understood. I would never presume anything else. Especially since you're fresh out of a relationship, you're heading back to the Bay and I'm staying here, and you've given no indication of being swept off your feet by me."

A laugh escaped before I could tamp it down. "Just so we're clear."

"I will try to avoid falling in love with you over bacon."

A thought occurred to me. "How old are you, anyway?"

"Twenty-six. Why?"

I groaned. He was a baby. "I'm thirty-two!"

"Is there an age requirement to split a ham and cheese omelet? Some waffle fries? It's *just* breakfast, right?"

"Right," I agreed with conviction. While my inner voice thought, *What are you doing? Just get your bags, go to the hotel, and be done.*

He looked at me like he knew exactly what I was thinking. "Okay then. Shall we?"

Ten minutes later, we stood by the conveyor belt waiting for our bags. We stood in another awkward silence, staring intently at the baggage hutch as if that would make the bags come any faster. Finally, they started sliding out. He pulled a basic black twenty-inch case on wheels off the belt and looked at me. "I'm guessing red."

"I beg your pardon?"

"I'm guessing your suitcase will be red."

How did he know that? "Insightful." I leaned forward to grab a red crocodile-leather bag; he reached around me to get it.

"C'mon now, I'm a gentleman." He turned toward the exit door and I followed.

"Are you now?" Hadn't seen one of those in a while.

"Most definitely. Ask my twin sister."

"Twin sister? What's that like? Any superpowers or telepathy?"

He barked out a laugh. "Just twins, not superheroes."

We stepped into the taxi line. "Savannah? Sabrina? Sarah?"

"Stefani."

"Steven and Stefani . . ." I'd forgotten his last name.

"Williams."

"Okay, Steven Williams, where are we having breakfast?"

"Madeline's—midtown. Where are you staying?"

"Doubletree Metropolitan—midtown. Are you from New York?"

"Oh no, I'm a Midwest boy. Chi-town. You're a California girl, right?"

"Yessir. So how did a Chicago guy end up delivering packages in Alameda, California?"

He smiled down at me. "That's a whole lot of interest for someone determined to keep this 'just breakfast.'"

Okay, he has me on that one. "Maybe I'm the kind of girl who wants to know who I'm getting in a cab and eating with."

"Yeah, you're that girl all right." We stepped forward in line.

"So where's the rest of your stuff?"

He looked around. "What stuff?"

"You're moving here for the next three...four years?"

"Hopefully three."

"Where's all your stuff?"

He smiled at me in a way that told me I was missing something. "I shipped it."

"You shipped...of course you did." I sighed. "I need coffee."

We stepped forward again. "We're getting there. You still need to know my life story first?"

Before I could answer, my cell phone rang. It was Lisa, my counterpart (nemesis) in the East Coast office. We both started at Valiant at the same time, in the same position. We were determined not to let the other get a step ahead. From Day One it had been an East Coast / West Coast battle to see who could get the better assignments and hold the attention of our senior editor, Jeri. I held up a finger to indicate I needed one second and plastered a fake smile on my face. "Hi, Lisa. What's going on?"

In an equally fake voice she responded, "Hey, girl, just checking to see if you made it in."

Rolling my eyes, I answered, "Of course. Standing in the taxi line now. What's up?"

"The Js want to know if you can swing by for a quick meeting." Our senior editor was Jeri, she reported to Janet (editor in chief), who co-owned the company with Jennifer (CEO / CFO). It had become easier to refer to the entire senior management team as the Js.

Swallowing a sigh, I looked at Steven. He was smiling down at me in the cutest way. He had that youthful, optimistic eye-twinkle thing working. I wondered when the last time was that I had looked that content in the moment. That thought gave me some pause, and a small furrow appeared between my brows.

Steven dialed back the cute twinkle a little and tilted his head to the side. "Problem?" he mouthed.

I shrugged one shoulder and nodded...still in pause mode. Enough pause that Lisa started talking again. "I understand if you don't want to come in, what with your personal drama and all. I'm sure I can handle whatever they need."

That snapped me out of my pause and I answered tartly, "You know what? I'm actually great. What time is the meeting?" Steven and I were next in line.

"As soon as you get here."

Our taxi was up. Climbing into the backseat with Steven right behind me, I checked my watch. "Tell them I'll be there in forty, depending on traffic." I disconnected, gave the driver the address to my office building, and sighed. "Duty calls—so much for waffle fries."

Steven smiled easily at me. "How about dinner instead?"

That suggestion made me a little uneasy. I turned my head

and looked at him consideringly—the eye twinkle was back. "Dinner?"

"Yes, ma'am. The last meal of the day . . . that thing one partakes of prior to retiring for the eve? Retiring separately. To our own domiciles. To sleep. Alone presumably, but not with each other. Does that allay your suspicions?"

"Ha, ha, ha, sir. You know what I mean. Dinner is different from breakfast."

"Besides the time of day you eat, in what way exactly? Kindly elaborate."

Now I was getting exasperated. I hated having to explain myself. I stewed silently for a few moments.

He waited silently with one brow raised.

"Don't play stupid. Breakfast is oh-we-just-got-off-the-plane-let's-catch-a-meal. Dinner, especially on a Friday night, is pumps and lip gloss with all appearances of being a date."

"Ms. Brinsley, dinner is what you make of it."

"What are you trying to make of it?"

"You brought up the pumps and lip gloss . . . not me."

He had a point. I was more than a little gun-shy, but I enjoyed his company and it would be nice to have a no-strings conversational partner who was easy on the eyes across a dinner table. Truthfully, I wouldn't mind the ego stroke of his admiring glances and smiling attention. Okay, dammit, I wanted to bask in the twinkle just a little while longer. As long as I kept it casual, it shouldn't be a problem. "So, Steven, what did you have in mind?"

"What kind of man would ask you out on a date when you've just broken up with your fiancé?"

"Third fiancé."

"Third? Good Lord, woman!" He looked at me like I was a science project to be dissected.

I sighed. "Long story, but you can understand my need for the man break."

"Completely. But c'mon now...I'm not *that* guy. You're in Manhattan, I'm in Manhattan—let's catch a meal. Period."

"Um-hmm," I answered skeptically. Steven seemed like a nice enough guy, but I really wasn't trying to start anything. I wasn't trying to do anything but get through this day and the next and the one after that. My thoughts were all over the place. That damn Jay/David had me questioning things that just weren't that complicated. One minute I wanted the twinkle, the next minute I didn't want to be bothered. I was a mess. A hot mess, to be exact. With a deep sigh, I leaned back. "Sorry, I'm just so tired." Physically and emotionally, I was running on fumes.

He nodded slowly. "That's why I thought dinner. You have time to go to your meeting, get settled into your hotel, get a nap, and meet me later. But it's no big deal, Christina. I'm a big boy. If this makes you uncomfortable or stresses you out, we can do it another time. Or we can shake hands, say 'nice to know you,' and walk away."

And with those words, I felt good again. I threw my hands up. "What the hell, right? It's dinner in Manhattan. I'm in. No harm, no foul?"

"No victim, no crime."

I laughed. "No body, no autopsy? What word game is this?"

He shrugged. "No woman, no cry? I don't know. I was going with the flow."

He was good at that. "Okay. Eight-thirty. Meet me in the lobby of the Doubletree?"

His smiled widened. "You're a puzzle, Christina Brinsley. And yes, I'll see you this evening."

The taxi pulled up outside the building on Lexington Avenue and I climbed out with my luggage, laptop case, and purse. I reached in my purse to dig out money for my part of the fare, and he waved me off.

"We're good. Knock 'em dead in there."

"Thanks." I took a few steps forward and looked back. "Seriously, Steven—thanks."

"Seriously, you're welcome, and hey—don't let Lisa get under your skin."

"How did you—" I smiled. Steven was observant and smart. "Gotcha. See ya later."

"Looking forward to it."

I was too, though I would never admit it to him or myself.

5

You Two Will Play Nice, Won't You?

Christina—Friday, August 14, 10:14 a.m.

Stepping off the elevator on the forty-third floor, a thought suddenly occurred to me: From the time Steven and I agreed to watch the movie to right this very minute, I had only thought of Jay / David once. The Jay / David fiasco had not been far from my thoughts for the last week. I kept going over and over it in my mind, wondering what I missed, what I should have seen, what I should have done differently.

Because of my two previous serious-relationship disasters, I took dating very casually. It took a long time for me to agree to a second and then a third date. It took twice as long for me to get physical. If there is a speed between slow and a full standstill, that's the speed at which I allowed the relationship between me and Jay / David to progress. I checked his background. I met his parents, his friends, his coworkers. I had a key to his house and knew what was in every nook and cranny. There had not been a single clue that pointed to Jay / David's being the lying, treacherous, two-timing dog I had planned to marry and spend the rest of my life with.

That shook me more than anything else. Now, not only

would I have to learn to trust men again (not likely), I had to regain my trust in my own judgment. I clearly had to have missed something along the way. Right?

"Hey, Christina!" Jeri called out from down the hallway, waving happily. Jeri was tall and thin with a razor-cut bob and pale, pale skin. She was all sharp angles and lines with the exception of huge green eyes, which she lined heavily. Though she didn't look it, Jeri was the corporate cheerleader, bless her heart. I tabled my introspection for later... after I survived the shark tank that was an editorial meeting at Valiant. I pulled my shoulders back, pasted on my best it's-all-good smile, and headed toward the conference room.

The New York Valiant office was designed like an old-school newspaper office but sleeker: rows of desks with low glass separators, offices along the walls with glass enclosures, open pit areas at each end. The color scheme was very simplistic, all primary colors with emphasis on blue. I followed the low-pile navy carpet through rows of cubes, smiling at co-workers as I walked through.

"Hey, Jeri," I said cheerfully as I paused to drop my suitcase and carry-on in the visitors' office. I nodded and waved at a couple of staff members before I stepped into the conference room. There were six women and two men gathered around the table. They all looked at me with varying degrees of curiosity.

"How are you?" Janet asked in that tentative, super-concerned tone people use when they suspect someone is suffering from post-traumatic stress. Janet was blond, sleek, and always looked like someone from *Vogue* styled her every morning.

Jeri, Janet, and Jennifer formed a semicircle at the head of the table. Jennifer was a light-skinned sister who resembled Vanessa Williams but dressed conservatively like Condoleezza Rice. Lisa sat to her left. Lisa had some sort of mixed-race heritage, was slightly overweight, wore her long wavy hair in a ponytail every day, and dressed straight out of the Banana Republic catalog.

Our Web designer / IT guy, Thomas, sat next to her. He was short, perpetually orange from the self-tanning lotion he was clearly addicted to, which clashed terribly with his shock of orangish red hair and light blue eyes. Next was our advertising operations manager, my girl, Carey. Carey had that cool, earthy sister vibe about her. Only slightly taller than me, she had the same complexion, long natural hair, dangly earrings, and loose, flowing clothes. Carey and I had attended Berkeley together (so many years ago) and had met outside the football players' dorm waiting on the same guy. We both dumped him and had been friends ever since.

Across from Carey was our research editor, Brandon. Given half a minute, Brandon would explain why he was the answer to every single sister's prayers. Brandon was a Morehouse alum and self-proclaimed chic geek. To his credit, he was a tall, fine brother but always admired himself before anyone else got a chance to. Staring at him adoringly was young Rita, perpetually tanned and talkative, with chestnut hair and hazel eyes and the figure only girls under twenty-five have with no effort. Rita was our resident floater, who acted as administrative assistant, writer, copy editor, travel department, and whatever else the Js dreamed up. Rita was already a high-strung sort, and she looked ready to hyperventilate at any moment.

I decided the best approach was a direct cut to the chase. "Okay, everyone can stop looking at me like I'm going to break for the window and jump. Yes, my engagement went to hell in a handbasket, but believe me when I say I dodged a bullet there. Besides, the longer you guys keep looking at me, the longer it will take to get this meeting done. And I have a date tonight." Yep, after spending all that time making sure Steven knew this wasn't a date, I invoked the "d" word for my own protection.

Everyone's face relaxed instantly. "Wow." "Way to get back

on the horse." "Oh, we're so glad." The chorus of glad tidings followed me as I took the empty seat between Carey and Brandon. Smiling so hard my jaw ached, I sat down and powered on my laptop.

"So what's up, New Yorkers?" I asked.

Jennifer nodded. "Let's get started. We have a lot to cover."

Four hours later, I was wiped out but exhilarated. Gratefully, I snatched a turkey sandwich from the deli tray they were passing around. I had missed breakfast and we'd had no breaks in the meeting.

The meeting was fast paced and information filled. Thanks to some savvy partnership agreements, Valiant Publications was about to expand in a major way. The influx of cash would mean updated Web design with server storage to match. All the fun ideas we had tossed around for the past three years to increase readership could actually get serious consideration. We were going to add staff, which meant all of us could quit wearing multiple hats and there would be more than three of us in the West Coast office.

I was relieved. It looked like the gamble I took three years ago by accepting a job with Valiant instead of going to one of the more established publications was going to pay off. At least *something* in my life was working out the way I'd hoped. Okay, enough of that. I picked up my turkey on wheat with swiss and took a bite, tuning back in just in time for Jennifer to say, "So Lisa will be moving to San Francisco and she will share management of our West Coast operations with Christina."

I choked and reached for my water, taking a large swig. My eyes met Lisa's across the table and she looked just as pleased as I was . . . not so much.

The Js looked back and forth between the two of us. Janet asked, "Is that going to be a problem?"

"Absolutely not," I stated with as much ebullience as I could muster. I raised a brow at Lisa, daring her to say the same.

"Well, if you all think that Christina can't handle it alone, what with her emotional upheaval and all—of course I'm happy to bolster her up."

Jeri spoke before I could rise to the bait. "Christina hardly needs bolstering and you know it, Lisa. Truth is, we're hoping to expand into TV down the line, so we have more than enough to keep both of you occupied for a while. You two will play nice, won't you?"

I smiled innocently. "I don't know any other way to play."

"Great. So that's settled," Jennifer said. "Let's go over content and advertising for the next few weeks."

One more hour later I was definitely fading. My energy was dipping below the reserve level when Janet called my name. "Christina, do you have your outline for the Halo Records article with you?"

Clicking a few keys, I said, "Just sent it to you along with my research and interview schedule."

Brandon spoke up. "Look at you—I see you're going to Yung T's record launch party tomorrow night. That's the hottest ticket in town. Gotta date? You know I'll take one for the team if you need me to pinch-hit." Yeah, Brandon had the tendency to come across condescending and a little icky from time to time.

I rolled my eyes. "Depends on how tonight's date goes. You can keep your bat sheathed for now, thanks." Everyone but Brandon laughed. He shot an irritated glance in my direction.

"And on that note . . . meeting adjourned," Jennifer said.

Thank God. I could not wait to get to the hotel room, spin twice in the shower and dive face-first into the bed. It seemed like forever and a day since I catnapped against Steven's shoulder. Smiling slightly thinking about it, I walked into the visitors' office to get my suitcase. Carey was right behind me and closed the door.

"Okay, spill. What the hell happened with Jay, and who is

tonight's rebound date? When did you find time to pick up a date in New York? And most importantly... how are you?" She flung her arms out in a come-to-mama gesture.

Laughing, I leaned into her and we shared a squeeze. I backed up and perched on the edge of the desk with a sigh. "Girl, I don't have the energy to explain the Jay / David debacle to you right now."

"Jay / David?"

"Um-hmm. Seems he's either one or the other. Maybe neither—who knows? Oh, I know who knows—his wife and his two kids: Dina and Daisy!"

"The *hell?*"

"Again, I'll have to catch you up at brunch on Sunday. But I think I'll be taking some time off from men."

"Another of the famed Christina man-hiatus thingies?"

Okay, I might have sworn to take man breaks before... and they never seemed to work out. "This time I mean it."

"I hear you talking. How is the family taking it?"

"Joanna has gone all high-strung matriarch on me. Collin and Clarke threatened to kick his ass."

"I can't see Clarke kicking anyone's ass. It might wrinkle his Italian silk."

I had to snort out a laugh. Her description was dead-on accurate. Clarke Brinsley did not rumble. And for some reason, he and Carey had never gotten along. "Okay—well, he would've hired the best in the business to kick his ass, then."

"There you go. What's the story on tonight's date?"

"Oh, it's not a date. It's dinner with my delivery guy."

"I'm sorry, did you just say deliveryman? What is Christina Bougie Brinsley doing dating the deliveryman? Is it that bad out there?"

Pursing my lips, I shot her my patented you-are-so-not-funny look. "There's nothing wrong with dating the deliveryman, snob. But he's not my delivery guy anymore. He's a graduate student at Columbia. Anyway, it's just dinner. No date. I really just said that to quell the poor-Christina looks I was getting."

"Grad student? Go cougar, get your prowl on. How old is he?"

"He's twenty-six."

She treated me to her I-don't-believe-a-word-you-are-saying look. "What is grad student's name?"

"Steven." Twinkly, sparkly Steven.

"Um-hmm. If you could see what your face just did when you said his name."

"What did it do?"

"It went all soft. This is a date."

"It's not a date! I'm just getting out of a doozy of a relationship, if you recall."

"Oh, I recall."

"All right then. It's just dinner."

"Got it. This makes sense. You're having dinner on a Friday night with a young man who makes your face go fuzzy and it's not a date. How long have you known this guy?"

"Seriously—he was my package-delivery guy for close to a year."

"And all he was delivering was boxes and envelopes, right? He wasn't slipping you an afternoon express every once in a while?"

I laughed. "Get your mind out of the gutter, Carey Elizabeth Jaymes. Yes, he delivered mail-sanctioned packages. That is all. He happened to be on the same red-eye last night. We were gonna go grab breakfast, but the meeting was called so we rain-checked for dinner."

"Dinner on a Friday night in Manhattan with a young man? Less than ten days after what was apparently a disastrous implosion of your engagement to Dina and Daisy's daddy? Christina Violet Tempest Brinsley: This is a date."

I threw my hands up. I clearly wasn't going to convince her. "Think what you like. I've got to go get some sleep."

"Yeah, beauty sleep so you look all sexy for your hot date tonight."

"Carey!"

She grinned evilly. "Huh?"

I shook my head and leaned forward to hug her again. "It's so great to see you. We're still on for Sunday?"

"Oh, I wouldn't miss this for the world. Bring your new man. Oh, you probably don't want to talk about the Jay thing in front of him."

"He saw the whole thing go down. But he's not my young man, so I won't be seeing him again after tonight." With that I grabbed up my stuff, swerved around her, and started wheeling out the door. Quickly.

"He what?! But how? Now you know I need details." Carey was racing along, chasing behind me to the elevator as I waved and said my see-you-laters to the team. "I'm not going to be able to wait until Sunday!"

"What's on Sunday?" Lisa called out as we whizzed by. We both ignored her.

Finally I reached the elevator and pushed the DOWN button. "You're going to have to, unless you want to come out with me tomorrow—but I know how Bryan plans your weekends down to the minute." Bryan had been Carey's boyfriend for over six years now. He was a bit of a control freak and seemed disinclined to formalize their relationship beyond moving in and planning their every moment.

Carey's smiled faded a little bit. "Okay, we'll talk Sunday."

Concerned, I put my hand on her arm. "Are you okay? Are you and Bryan okay?"

"We are exactly the same."

"Oh." The elevator dinged. "Listen, I can call off this dinner if you want to come to the hotel and have a room service slumber party tonight?"

She pushed me toward the elevator. "What? Have you miss out on the non-date date with the hot delivery guy?"

"Who told you he was hot?" I stepped on the elevator and turned around.

She threw back her head with laughter. "You just did. Have a good time."

With that, the elevator doors closed.

6

Is This Still Not a Date?

Steven—Friday, August 14, 8:32 p.m.

I switched my weight from foot to foot as I waited for Christina to come down to the hotel lobby. When I called up to her room, she said she'd be right down. I kept my eyes on the elevator doors but hadn't seen her. But there was this one woman...an absolute knockout. And then I froze.

I did not recognize Christina when she first got off the elevator. I had seen Christina in business suits and sweats (and that last bathrobe incident). Never had I seen her look like this. She had on a short, light green sleeveless dress that fit everywhere it was supposed to. Showed off incredibly smooth brown skin and long legs. She had on high-heeled shoes with her toes peeking out. Her long black hair was curly; her lips were glossy and tinted a purple-pink color. Something pretty twinkled on her ears and throat. My mouth went dry and then so wet I had to swallow. I had thought she was a cute girl. She was a beautiful woman. A really beautiful woman.

She walked toward me with a brow raised. "What is the matter with you? Why are you looking at me like that?"

I tried to regain some composure. "Like what?"

"Like you've never seen me before."

I ran my eyes up and down her once more. "I've never seen you look like this. You look amazing."

She grinned. "I clean up well, and thank you."

"That's putting it mildly."

She took a moment and looked me over. I knew I was on point. Tailored tan slacks, crisp white shirt, white linen jacket. She nodded. "You know you look good, youngster."

I smiled. "I'm a youngster now, hmm? Okay, I see you. Is this still not a date?"

"Definitely not a date." She was firm.

"Even though you have on the pumps and gloss?" I couldn't resist teasing her.

"I'm being polite. When you called, you said to dress for someplace nice. I didn't want to shame you."

"I so very much appreciate your efforts on my behalf. Shall we go?" I gestured toward the revolving doors.

"Have a great evening, folks!" the doorman called out as we stepped out into the hot and humid night. I was really going to miss my mild Bay Area weather.

"Thanks!" I answered, and turned left. "Do you mind walking? It's not very far."

"Sure, why not?" she said easily.

As we stepped forward, I moved her to the inside so I was closer to the street and reached for her hand to clasp it in mine. She stopped dead in her tracks. I looked over. "What?"

"That was a very datelike thing you just did. Taking the street side and holding my hand."

I glanced at our linked fingers. "Christina, how many times do I have to tell you? I am a gentleman. And I'm not trying to date you." I really wouldn't mind sleeping with her; but as prickly as she was—no way would I make that move. I couldn't blame her. But she was mighty skittish. I definitely didn't notice her releasing my hand either.

She squeezed my hand for a quick second. "Still not a date."

I squeezed back and we continued walking. "Got it. No date here. And a good thing, too."

"Why do you say that?"

"Oh, if this was a date you'd be in trouble tonight, Ms. Brinsley."

"Oh yeah?"

"Most definitely. I'd be trying out some of my best moves on you."

She snorted. "What makes you think I'm interested in seeing your moves, Mr. Williams?"

"You don't wear a dress like that and shoes like those without expecting a brother to pant a little, try a little sumthin'. C'mon now."

"Are you panting a little?"

"Just a little. You know I'm smooth with mine."

"Those smooth moves, do they work for you?"

"More often than you'd think."

She sent me a side-eye. "I'll just bet. Good thing, then."

"Like I said. I'm a gentleman. Man of my word and all."

"You're a rare breed."

"I thought you knew."

Christina laughed. "Ha! You talk a good game, I'll give you that."

"Again, I thought you knew."

"I actually don't know you at all."

I slid her a glance. "I thought you wanted to keep it that way."

"Excellent point."

For someone who proclaimed not to be on a date, she sure looked the part and did the flirty banter well. We walked in companionable silence the rest of the way to the restaurant. Cutting past the people waiting outside, I went straight to the maître d' station. "Williams, party of two."

"Right this way, sir. Madam. Is this your first time at Pesca?"

Christina said yes as I said no. He led us to a booth on the side wall and seated us. Handing us the menus, he snatched the Reserved sign and snapped his fingers. A large bottle of San Pellegrino water was placed on the table. "Your server, Jason, will be out momentarily to get your drink orders and answer any questions about the menu. Chef David has asked to be informed when you arrived, so I'll go tell him now. Enjoy."

I smiled and nodded as I opened the menu. A brother was starving. I never had my omelet and waffle fries this morning. I had settled into the apartment I was going to share with three other people and promptly fallen asleep. By the time I woke up, grabbed a slice of pizza, ran over to campus to register, and introduced myself to a few professors, it was time to run home and get ready for this non-date. The surf and turf was looking good. In the midst of contemplating rib eye vs. porterhouse, I felt Christina's eyes on me. I closed the menu and leaned back in the booth. "Okay, now you are looking at me some kind of way.... What's up?"

She opened her pretty mouth and then shut it again, shaking her head. I watched as her hair bounced and settled against her shoulders.

"No, now. Might as well spill it," I said.

"You're going to accuse me of being 'that chick' again," she said.

"Why?"

"Because I want to know how a delivery-guy-turned-grad-student gets a reserved table at a Manhattan restaurant with less than twelve hours' notice *and* warrants a visit from Chef David."

I took my time, poured us both some expensive bubbly water before I answered. "Chef David is a friend of mine from Chicago. He opened this place about six months ago. I called him today to tell him I was in town and he insisted I come through."

"You are friends with a celebrity chef," she stated slowly, as if getting used to the idea.

She cracked me up. Hard as she tried to put me in a box, I kept climbing back out. I could tell she was dying to ask questions but couldn't quite bring herself to do it. Heaven forbid she should sound datelike. I just nodded with a little smile.

"Oo-kay."

I couldn't help it, I had to laugh. "It's killing you, isn't it?"

"What?"

"You're dying to ask about my background, but you don't want to act like you care because after dinner I'm supposed to be dismissed from your world, never to be heard from again. Am I right?"

She leaned back, squinted a little before sighing. "You got me. I really don't want to start anything, so can I just be a little curious about you without it meaning anything more than that?"

"Would it make you feel better if I said I don't have time for any sort of entanglements now myself? I start graduate school in less than two weeks and plan to completely immerse myself in that. Besides, you seem like a woman who needs a lot of time and attention. I don't have either of those to give. You can stop worrying about me stalking you after our non-date is done, no matter how good you look tonight." She had this great expression when she was deciding whether to be irritated or amused. She had worn it often since I sat down next to her on the airplane last night. Was that just last night?

She smirked. "That was both complimentary and insulting at the same time. Are you calling me high maintenance?"

"Girly, I saw those wedding presents. I know you're high maintenance," I reminded her.

She nodded her head. "Point taken." She sighed. "Those were some nice gifts."

"No doubt. But easy come, easy go—right?"

She made a moving forward motion with her hand. "On to the next."

We sat smiling at each other with the candlelight dancing between us when Chef David walked up. "Hey, S. Dub, what's good?" I got up and clapped him on the back.

"Dave Roget, Christina Brinsley. Christina, this is Chef David."

Dave was a 5'9" light-skinned brother with a great smile and just enough glossy sophistication to cover his South Side Chicago roots. He took one look at Christina, leaned in to take her hand, and flashed the smile. "Christina, a pleasure. A true pleasure. Welcome to my little bistro." He squeezed one of her hands between his and looked at me. "Nice, son."

"Thank you for having us on such short notice," Christina replied while trying to pull her hand away.

"Not a problem at all. Thanks for gracing my humble establishment with your presence."

"Down, son. Unhand the girl," I teased and sat back down.

"Oh, sorry. So do we want to talk about how you two know each other and whether Christina wants to be my first ex-wife, or get straight to the menu tonight?"

Christina laughed. "No, thank you. And menu, please."

Dave put his hand on my shoulder. "S. Dub, you trust me?"

I nodded. "With everything but her, sure."

"I'll send you guys some stuff I'm working on, then. This one's on me. You two just sit back and enjoy your date."

"It's not a date!" we both said at the same time. Adamant and in unison.

Dave looked from me to Christina and back again. "I . . . see."

Christina folded her arms and looked at me. I looked back, saying nothing.

"All right then. We'll be sending out some wine pairings with each course, unless you want something stronger?"

I tilted my head to Christina, indicating that the decision was up to her.

"Wine sounds lovely. Thank you, Dave."

"Great, great. I'll be back out to check on you." He leaned down to whisper in my ear. "Can't wait to hear the story on this one. *Cannot* wait." He walked back toward the kitchen, laughing.

"What did he say?" Christina asked.

"He just welcomed me to New York."

"I'll bet he did. S. Dub?" She said it with a scrunch of her nose.

"Steven W. equals S. Dub. What, you have no childhood nickname that followed you into adulthood?"

Our server, Jason, brought wine and a basket of artisan breads. Christina picked up a small roll, broke it in half, and reached for the butter. "I could tell you, but then I'd have to kill you."

"You're never going to see me again after tonight, so what does it matter?"

She held the roll up and gave me a considering glance. "True. Okay. My family calls me Ti-Ti."

I burst out laughing; she was not a Ti-Ti at all. "I can't see it. You are very Christina Brinsley. Not Ti-Ti B. Where did they get it from?"

She shrugged. "ChrisTIna Violet T. Brinsley . . . Ti-Ti."

"Never Christy or Tina or Chrissy?"

"No, sir."

"And what does the *T* stand for?"

"Oh, that's not something I'd share with someone I wasn't dating," she said firmly and bit into the roll. She groaned and her eyelids drifted shut. "Oh my God. That's amazing." Her face was a study of bliss as she licked some melted butter off her upper lip.

Wow. That was sexy. Unexpectedly so. Watching her tongue trail after the butter sent a jolt straight to places that had no business anticipating attention. She wasn't even trying and I was lusting in a bad way, just that quickly. I reached for the wine and took a generous swallow. *Nope, still wanted her. Dammit.* She opened her eyes and caught the expression on my face before I could school my features. She went very still.

"What?" she asked in a quiet voice.

"Right now, you look like a Ti-Ti. Testing temptation. Teasing and tantalizing."

A pulse was beating visibly at the base of her neck. It wasn't just me. She felt it, too. She took a deep breath and exhaled. "You have a creative side."

"I have many sides."

"You're flirting with me."

"I'll stop." *Stop it, Steve,* I scolded myself. *Stop looking, stop lusting. Just eat, talk, and go.* But it was too late. That man/woman thing was out of the bag between us, and I wasn't sure either of us wanted to put it back. When Jason brought a dish of chopped shrimp and scallops in a fragrant sauce, we both picked up our forks gratefully. We were hungry and in need of a diversion.

1

I've Got All Night

Afer I licked the butter off my lip, the evening took a turn. It went from light and flirty to tense and tingly. Dammit. I didn't need tingles. I needed light jokes and easy conversation and absolutely nothing complicated. When I looked up into Steven's eyes, it felt complicated. So I concentrated on the food and the wine and made light conversation.

I found out his close friends call him Steve. His father was a mail carrier, his mother was a teacher. His twin sister was also a teacher and there was a wide net of extended family: cousins and aunts and uncles. He had grown up modestly and tried his hand at thug life for a short stint in his early teens. He decided he didn't like it and concentrated his energy on schoolwork after a close brush with the law. He went to UCLA on a full educational scholarship and afterward moved to San Francisco. He started in the operations department of the delivery service and tried to get exposure to each department in the two years he worked there.

When David came back out with wafer-thin slices of beef, he shared that he had lived with Steven's family for a while when his own home life wasn't very stable. He told a story of Steven not letting him watch TV in the evening until he'd finished his homework and Steven being the only person who truly encouraged him to follow his passion in culinary arts. He called Steven the brother he never had.

Well, damn. The problem was, I had hoped to use the twenty-questions-style chatter to distract me from being attracted to Steven. Instead, the more I found out—the more I liked. I lost track of how many courses and wines were brought out. It was all delicious. But my head was spinning and my stomach was full. "Steven, I've had enough," I announced when Jason came back with what he described as a palate-cleansing sparkling dessert wine. I was peeking at the label when Steven spoke.

"You've tasted your fill, huh?" Something in his inflection made me look up. I raised a brow at him.

"Are you flirting again?" I took one sip. It was liquid ambrosia, but I set it aside.

"Do you want me to?" He took one sip and set it aside as well.

I paused. He smiled. I answered him. "No. I'm stuffed. Let's call it a night."

He nodded. "As you wish."

David came back out of the kitchen and we said our goodbyes. Stepping out into the night, I realized that I'd had quite a bit to drink in the last twenty-four hours and not so very much sleep. I was a little off balance but all of sudden inexplicably energetic. I took a quick step forward and teetered slightly. His hand was there to steady me.

"You okay?"

"A little light-headed but I feel great. You want to walk for a little while?"

He gave me a strange look. "I thought you were ready to get rid of me."

I took a step back. "Are you in a hurry? Do you need to get home?"

"I'm a grown-ass man, Ti-Ti. I've got all night."

Uh-oh. I shook my head at him. "Let's just walk, S. Dub. Let's just walk."

So we walked. Block after block, making easy conversation along the way. We had walked for quite a ways when I heard salsa music playing. As we neared the club, I paused and did a quick step. He reached for my arm and spun me around to complete the step and fell in beside me. I smiled up at him. "You know salsa?"

He cut another step and grinned. "You tell me. You game?"

I laughed. "Oh hell, why not?"

As we walked in, he said in my ear, "Still not a date though, right?"

"Definitely not."

"Just checking." When I reached in my purse to pay the cover charge, he frowned and shook his head. Handing money over to the hostess, he said, "Okay, let's see what you got, Ti-Ti."

The song was changing as we stepped to the small dance floor, the music started, and I smiled in recognition. "Oh, it's a Willie Colón song."

"Tito Puente did it better though." He slid his arm around my waist and we started moving together. "And close your mouth, Ti-Ti. A brother knows music, too."

My last thought before he spun it out of my head was that it was a shame I wouldn't know him for much longer. He was the most interesting guy I'd met in years.

I had no more time for stray thoughts. I had to concentrate on keeping up. This boy could move, and he had a flair for the dramatic. He spun me and dipped me and danced me backwards and in a swirl. When the music turned slow and dreamy, he pulled me close and we swayed. When it switched to a reggaeton beat, he stepped back and we kept moving.

They say you can tell a lot about somebody by the way they dance. If that is at all true, Steven was the smoothest brother I had ever come across. He had moves I couldn't keep up with, and I could cut me a step. He had the nerve to look good doing it, too. Effortless. I watched him and he watched me right back. It had been ages since I danced like this. We kept it going until the band took a break. He took my hand and led me off the dance floor. We paused by the bar for a second and he ordered something.

"Whew!" I dug a lone Kleenex out of my tiny handbag and dabbed at my face.

"You ready to go?" he asked.

I nodded and gratefully accepted the bottle of water he handed me. I opened it and took a deep swig as we started walking. My head was spinning, I was hot and my feet were killing me, but I felt better than I had in ten days. Suddenly I stopped.

"What? Did we forget something?"

"No. I just realized—I haven't thought about Jay / David once tonight. Not once."

He grinned. "That's a good thing."

I shook my head. "That's a great thing!"

"Well, all right then. So you had fun tonight?"

"I had fun."

"Then I've succeeded. Glad to be of service."

We started walking again and I tugged at his hand. He stopped and looked down at me. "Yes, Ms. Brinsley? What can I do for you?"

I took a step closer and looked up at him. "Steven, thank you. What a great night." I stretched up on my tiptoes and kissed him on the cheek.

"That's a thank-you?" he teased.

I moved a half inch over and kissed a little closer to his mouth. "Thank you," I said in a softer voice, rubbing my cheek against his.

"You're almost welcome."

Laughing, I placed my lips against his and pressed once and then kissed softly. "Thank you," I whispered, letting my eyes flutter shut.

He kissed back, nibbling my lips and licking in between. "You're welcome."

I raised my lashes a little bit to gauge his expression. "Oh, to hell with it." I put one arm around his neck, arched into him and dove into his mouth for a real kiss.

It was all the invitation he needed, wrapping me up in both arms and matching my tongue strokes with bolder moves of his own. One of his hands came up to clasp the back of my head and angle me gently where he wanted me to be. Damn, if he wasn't really good at this. No, I mean really talented. An actual shiver raced down my spine. I wanted more. I whimpered a little and tried to get closer when a taxi honked from the street.

"Hey you two—get a room!"

I leaned back in his arms and I suddenly had no qualms and no indecision. "I have a room," I said and met his eyes directly.

His gaze was level and his voice was gravelly when he answered, "Yes, you do."

"Would you like to . . . visit?"

"By visit do you mean coming back to your room, stripping you naked, and learning every single thing that makes you shiver and groan like you just did?"

I swallowed. He was observant. "Yes, that is exactly what I mean. So would you care to?"

"You know, I believe I would."

"Let's go."

"Taxi!"

8

Room 2018

It was all I could do not to grope her in the cab like a teenager. The ride was less than three minutes, but it felt like we were moving in slow motion. When the cab finally stopped, I flung money at the driver, hopped out, and dragged Christina along behind me. I was a man on a mission.

The elevator came immediately. After she pushed the button for the twentieth floor, I backed her into the corner, lifted her up and pressed against her. With my hands under her thighs, I held her open and ground gently against her with my hips moving in a slow circle—once, before easing back. Just as gently, I bit down on the pulsing vein in her neck and licked once and then twice. She squealed.

"You're killing me. That feels incredible. Do it again." She breathed out. Her head was flung back and her breath came quickly.

"As much as you can take. That's all for you, baby. Whatever you want, whatever you need." My vocabulary had turned to Marvin Gaye love-speak and I didn't care. As the bell dinged and the doors slid open, I set her down reluctantly, so she could dig out her room key.

"Room 2018." She handed me the key and turned hastily to the left.

We got there quickly. I opened the door, ushered her in, and paused. Whatever came next was her decision.

Tossing her tiny purse toward the desk, she launched herself at me with a decision apparently made. Catching her at her waist, I lifted her easily. Her long legs wrapped around my hips. Pivoting, I braced her against the door and hitched my hips closer. I was steel against her softness, and the air around us heated up a few degrees. We were sloppy and eager. Tongues roaming, hands sliding, moaning and gasping for air. I wanted to touch her everywhere, all at once, as soon as possible. Her tiny shifts and breathy moans told me she felt the exact same way. I just knew I wanted more Christina right now. But I'd made a sorta kinda promise at the beginning of the evening. Reluctantly, I stilled my hands and hips, untangled thighs and lips, eventually slowing to a stop. Placing my hands on her waist, I set her down.

Backing up a step, I rested my forehead against hers and waited until she opened her eyes. Her lids came up slowly and I gave her a chance to decline. "Christina, yes or no?"

She closed her eyes for a second and smiled slightly. When she reopened them, the answer was right there swimming in the chocolate depths, but still I needed the words. "Christina? You have to say it."

"Yes. Please. And the sooner the better, thank you."

Good words and definitely the ones I wanted to hear. With those words, the mood shifted from frantic and urgent to slow and sensual. I slid my hands from the small of her back around to the swells of her breasts, stroking softly before moving along to the curve of her rear. She sighed against my lips and looped her hands around my neck. Even in high heels she barely came to my shoulder. I pulled her in close, wanting to feel as much of her against me as possible. She was soft, warm, and smelled faintly of vanilla frosting.

As if still dancing, we turned and stepped in unison toward the bed. Dipping her backwards slowly, I followed her down and took a minute. I was horizontal on a bed in New York with Christina Brinsley. It felt good. I looked down at her face. She had a faintly dreamy smile floating around the edges of her lips, her eyelids were at half-mast, but the expression in them caught and held me. A combination of trust and admiration with a sprinkle of excitement and a lot of desire; it was the sexiest thing I had ever seen. My voice was husky as I voiced my thought. "I'm glad we're doing this, but don't thank me yet. It's about to get a whole lot better."

"Cocky young thing, aren't you?" she teased, but I saw that pulse at the base of her neck flutter faster.

"You tell me later if I've earned it or not, okay?" Sliding down the zipper of her dress, I reminded myself to go slow. To savor. To seduce. As I brought my hand around to release the front clasp on her bra, she caught my hand.

"Just so we're clear—this is just a thing, for the moment... right?"

"Definitely. You're heading back to the Bay. I'm staying here."

"No muss, no fuss."

"No victim, no crime. No harm, no foul." However many ways she wanted me to say it, I would.

"Still not a date."

"Clearly not. May I continue?"

"Please do, Mr. Williams."

I peeled back her clothes and undergarments as if unwrapping a valued gift, stopping to tease, taste, and touch along the way. Her breathy sighs turned to throaty moans as I discarded her lacy panties and explored the liquid warmth waiting for me there. Parting her slowly, I replaced my fingers with my mouth. Before I could relish her flavor, her nails dug into my back. "Steven!"

"Hmm?"

"I've no need of teasing foreplay...seriously. I'm good."

"You're very good but—" My words strangled in my throat as she reached between us to stroke me determinedly. Before I could finish my sentence, my pants were unzipped and shoved downward. "I wanted to go slow."

"Next time."

"Next time? I thought we were for the moment."

"Steven, you want to debate my word choice or do you want to get naked and do this?"

When she put it that way... "Let's do this."

"Baby, I'm waiting on you." Her eyes glinted challenge.

I was up to it. Quickly, I stepped back and sent my clothes flying, keeping my eyes on her. Damn, she looked good. She lay on the bed in nothing but those sky-high sandals. I fished a condom out of my wallet before I flung my pants to the side. "Christina," I said as I rolled the condom on.

She watched me with a hunger that made my hands shake a little. "Hmm?" Now she was the one with her eyes glued on me.

I repositioned her on the bed. Standing over her, I slid a finger and then a second between her legs to test her readiness. Her groan and her heated moisture told me she was ready. Lying over her I slid forward, slowly breaching her opening and sinking deep. She was snug, pulsing and warm. We both groaned and shuddered. Her arms and legs came up to pull me closer. I sunk in a little deeper. "In case I forget to tell you..."

"Yes?" She shifted slightly and squeezed her internal muscles around me.

I sucked in a breath and had to concentrate on what I was trying to say. "In case I forget to tell you later...this is the best non-date I've ever had." I slid back a little bit and sunk back in, rotating my hips.

"Umm, Steven—shut up and don't date me some more."

I shut up and got down to business.

9

We Kiss and Say Good-bye

Christina—Saturday, August 15, 10:18 a.m.

It took me a second to figure out where I was when my eyes opened. Squinting against a bright light, I blinked a few times. I was naked, in bed, in a hotel room. I blinked some more to focus. I was...in New York City. I turned my head. For the second time in as many days, I found myself waking with my head on Steven's shoulder and my hand on his...oh! That was not his chest—considerably south of that but also with a pulse of its own. I started to lift my hand away when his hand covered mine.

"It's okay, baby, leave it there," he said in a deep and sleepy voice.

It was the exact same thing he had said yesterday. "Déjà vu?"

"This is much, much better." He kissed my forehead.

I lifted my gaze to meet his. "Hey, you."

"Hey. Are you freaking out yet?" He traced his index finger along my hairline and down my cheek.

"Should I be?" Really, I was more worried about what my hair looked like.

"We had dinner, we went dancing, we..."

"Burned up some sheets?" Casually, I stroked upward with my hand. I loved the heavy weight of him. He was long, thick, and smooth. Amazing how much pleasure those inches of flesh could provide. Stroking down and back up, I smiled with the memories of the night. He twitched, growing firmer and warmer in my hand. Fascinated, I squeezed along every inch from base to tip and flicked lightly across the head with my thumb.

"Dear God, that's good. You have the hands of a...anyway, yes, we set the sheets aflame. Three times at my last count. I think we broke all your non-date rules." His finger moved down the side of my neck to my shoulder.

"Are you in love with me?" I shivered a little at his touch, switching strokes to teasing flicks with my fingertips.

He pulled in a deep breath as his finger slid from my shoulder to my chest. "I'm in love with your left hand right now. That's all I can attest to."

"Well then, I think we're still okay. It's only the men who profess to love me that cause me problems." I slowed my tempo to match his lazy touches.

"Are you in love with *me?*" His finger grazed my right nipple as if by accident and then circled, pressed, and moved to the left.

"There are a few parts of you that I am growing mighty fond of." I slid on top of him and looked my fill. He was smooth muscles covered with honey-kissed skin. He was long lines and aroused-male scent. I sat up, wriggling my hips a little.

"You better watch yourself, girl. You are asking for it."

"I just might be. Are you going to give it to me?"

He put his hands on my hips and arched up. I was so liquid, his hardness slid back and forth making wet noises. "Only if you ask me nicely."

I leaned down and sucked his bottom lip into my mouth. "Steven, I'm wet."

"I noticed that."

"I'm wet, I'm sticky, my hair is all over my head, I don't know what kind of breath I'm working with, and I quite frankly need to pee."

He went completely still for a second and then dissolved into laughter. I joined him for a second and then climbed off him and out of the bed. Still giggling, I ran to the bathroom and shut the door, taking care of business before stepping up to the sink. Flicking on the light, I looked into the mirror.

"Ahh!" I screamed at my reflection. Last night's curly do was a frizzy fro. We're talking eighties Chaka Khan hair. What was left of my mascara was ringing under my eyes in splotches. Speaking of eyes, mine were of the bloodshot variety.

"You look fine!" he shouted from the bedroom.

"Fine for roadkill," I muttered. Grabbing emergency hair serum and a brush, I tamed the beast and twisted it into a tight bun. I brushed my teeth and scrubbed my face. I opened the door a crack and announced, "I'm going to take a shower." Shutting the door, I switched on the tap and set the shower temperature to a shade below scalding. Grabbing a washcloth and a bottle of body wash, I climbed in the shower.

A minute later I heard the door open. "Do not be offended. I have to pee."

"Do what you need to do." A flush later and the curtain opened.

"You know New York City is under strict water conservation laws."

"I think I read that somewhere."

"You would only be doing your civic duty to share the water."

"Far be it from me to shirk my civic duty. Come on in." He climbed in behind me and I saw him place a foil packet on the soap ledge. "You need an umbrella in the shower, S. Dub?"

"I am just that civic-minded, Ti-Ti." He took the wash-cloth from my hand, knelt down, and began to lather me in stroking circles. He started at my feet and ankles and worked his way up the front, down the back, and along my sides. By the time he stood back behind me, I was a panting bundle of nerves and sensations. He adjusted the spray to hit the side wall and whispered, "Lean forward."

"Oh my God," I breathed, leaning forward and bracing my arms on the tile in front of me. The sound of the foil packet tearing took what was left of my breath away. I closed my eyes, widened my stance, and waited for his entry. Instead of the gentle, incremental slide I was used to, he slammed into me, filling me deep and quick in one confident stroke. I screamed out and my knees buckled.

"I got you," he said, holding me around the waist. "You okay?"

"Do it again." Pulling all the way out, he slammed back in, touching places I did not know existed.

"Just like that?"

"Again," I whispered, needing everything he had to give me. He stroked again and again, somehow with different angles and depth. With his free hand, he reached up and flicked that long finger against my sensitive nipple. It was more than I could take. With a sharp, keening cry, I exploded, and wave after wave poured through me. Unsteadily, I pushed his arms from around me, turned and dropped to my knees. Before he knew what I had in mind, I took him in my mouth and sucked.

"Oh, sweet mother of... Oh." He swore under his breath and locked his knees as I used my mouth to express my appre-ciation for his talent and attention to detail. With a free hand, I cupped him and squeezed while still applying suction. That's all it took. He moaned low and long, threw back his head, and released. I stroked him through it and just as he was finishing, I sucked one more time. "Christina!" He gave up a little more before I let him go. He sunk down to the tub floor next to me. "Wow."

"Exactly," I responded without meeting his eyes.

He sighed and leaned his forehead against mine. "What is it now?"

I shrugged and whispered, "How did you know?"

"What? That you would like it like that?"

I nodded.

"I see the depths in you. You aren't near as buttoned-up and proper as you would have people think."

Humph. This guy knew more about me in thirty-six hours than my three idiot fiancés had figured out in years. That was scary.

He stood up and dragged me along with him. "So now are you freaking out?"

Again, he was too damn intuitive. I didn't say anything and reached for the washcloth.

" 'Cause I'm still not in love with you and this is still not a date."

"What is it, then?"

"Depends. Are you kicking me out after this shower, or can a brother finally get an omelet?" His tone was light and unconcerned.

I enjoyed his ability to defuse my neuroses with humor. I followed his lead and responded lightly. "You are go for omelets."

"Then this is a weekend fling."

"I don't leave until Tuesday night." Oops. Now that sounded like I wanted him to stick around until Tuesday.

He laughed. "Then this is a five-day fling. After which we kiss and say good-bye. Agreed?"

"Agreed."

10

Riding the Wave

Steven—Saturday, August 15, 7:43 p.m.

Christina was in the living room playing Xbox with two of my roommates. I was rifling through my suitcase in my bedroom. The apartment in Morningside Heights was a three bedroom, spacious by New York standards. It was in a prewar building with exposed brick, refurbished hardwoods, and wonder of wonders—new plumbing. I don't like to think about how much of my savings I sunk into the down payment on this place. As it was, I had found three roommates to split expenses with. Jimmy, a fast-talking brother, was one of them. He was talking my ear off now.

"Man, she's gotta have a single friend or two in the city she can hook us up with!?"

I was beginning to think that swinging by my apartment with Christina in tow was not a good idea. The fellas were clowning. You would think they hadn't seen a pretty girl with brains and personality before. "I told you she's just out here a few days, and then she's heading back to the Bay Area. She's about business, not hooking you knuckleheads up."

"Just sayin' it wouldn't kill you to ask." Jimmy was also

starting at Columbia as an MBA candidate. He was also a
Midwest guy, from St. Louis, and we liked each other immediately when we'd met at the preview weekend months ago. He
wasn't the best-looking brother in the bunch, but he had that
personality and sense of humor that won over people easily.

"Please act like you've seen a good-looking girl before." I
opened up a second suitcase, trying to find something suitable
to wear to this party Christina invited me to. Record industry,
rap stars, finance folks. I was thinking dark jeans and long-
sleeve, lightweight shirt. Casual without trying too hard.

"Plenty of those—this here's a woman who has her act together. We could use some upgraded femininity around these
parts."

I wondered how Christina would take being referred to as
"upgraded femininity." She would probably launch a scathing
comeback and then laugh about it. "Oh I see, this is about you
trying to get on that come-up with a pimp move. Nice."

"Pimpin' ain't easy. Easiest way to reach the top is by getting a hand up, my brother."

I clapped Jimmy on the back. "Good luck with that. Listen,
she and I are just hanging for a few days. So I'll be right out
there with you forging my own come-up as well."

"Y'all just hanging out, you say?"

"Yes, sir."

"That's not the vibe I'm tracking, young Steven."

"What is it you think you know, son?"

He wiggled his shoulders and wagged his brows. "I ain't
Dr. Phil or nothing, just saying you two feel like more than a
bump and run."

"Well, tuck your feelings away there, Oprah. This is what it
is." I tossed a few more things in a garment bag and was turning toward the door when Christina walked in from the living
room. When a woman makes you want, and she's wearing
shorts and a T-shirt, you know you're in trouble.

"S. Dub. It took me zero time at all to beat down your boys

in Madden. Are you in here sewing apparel from scratch? What's the holdup?" She put her hand on her hip and smiled.

"Oprah here wanted to talk about feelings and the like." I gestured to Jimmy.

"Is that right? What's he coming with?"

"He says we have a vibe," I teased, and walked toward her.

"You and me?"

"Me and you."

"Hmm. Interesting. And he based this on the thirty minutes since we walked in the door?"

"Apparently."

"That's impressive. Listen, you two boys wanna light some aromatherapy candles and watch *Sex and the City* reruns, or you want to go to the hottest party in town tonight?"

Jimmy hopped up. "Wait a minute, C-Money. I'm invited, too?"

She raised a brow at me and I nodded. Why not?

"If you promise never to call me C-Money again, can snatch something to change into in the next two minutes, you're in."

Jimmy twirled around. "Score! What I tell you, Steezy? On that come-up! Hey, you think I'll meet some of the rap groupies? My God, I'm about to slay at the party. Y'all not even knowing! Don't leave without me!" He ran down the hall to his room.

"You already regret inviting him, don't you?"

"I do. But hey, it's only for one night."

I sat on the edge of the bed. "You're very live-in-the-moment these days, aren't you?"

She perched on my lap. "I guess I am. I'm not thinking about it."

"Going with the flow?" I ran my lips up the side of her neck to just below her ear.

She leaned into me. "Riding the wave."

"Come what may." I nibbled across her jaw to her mouth.

"Gotta problem with that?" She turned to meet my lips.

We kissed once and then twice before I pulled back. "Since I'm the direct recipient of your wave riding...no. I have no problems with it at all."

"Good answer."

"You like that?" I smiled against her lips.

"You know I do." Her lips curved upward.

"Ah hell, naw!" Jimmy's voice interrupted some definite plans I had for the next few minutes. "Are you two going be slobbing each other up all night? 'Cause I could stay home and watch cable for that!"

"Your boy's an idiot," Christina said as she hopped up from my lap.

"This is true."

"But in a mostly harmless way."

"Let's hope so."

"Come on now, good people." Jimmy raised his arms up and started shaking his behind. "Let's go booty bump with the beautiful people."

"This living-in-the-moment thing may have a repercussion or two," Christina said as she followed Jimmy's gyrating ass down the hallway.

"Wait a second!" Rob, the youngest of my roommates, called out as we marched past. Rob was a baby-faced, light-skinned, heavyset senior from upstate New York. He was a double major—computer science and graphic design—and planned to blaze a trail in the world of computer gaming after graduation. If Jimmy was the clown, Rob was the cool nerd. The term "geek chic" was invented to describe guys like Rob. "Where you headed?"

Christina and I exchanged glances. I shrugged. It was up to her.

With a sigh, she reached in her purse. "This is my last pass to the party. You can come and bring one friend only. Do not embarrass me or make me regret inviting you."

I nodded. "What she said. And wear something other than jeans and a sci-fi movie T-shirt, please."

Rob looked at the invite. "Dude. You need to keep her around. She is useful."

"I'm outta here on Tuesday, so you have to enjoy me for the moment," Christina said.

I smiled. "I am—I definitely am."

A slow smile spread across her face. "Let's go, then."

"Let's get it!" Jimmy nodded and bounced out the door.

"I may regret this," Christina sighed.

"Just remember this was your idea, Ti-Ti." I shut the door behind me.

11

These Things Sometimes Happen

Christina—Sunday, August 16, 11:47 a.m.

Carey already had a table on the sidewalk when Steven and I strolled up. We were a little bit late, but we didn't seem to be able to get up out of bed and dressed in the morning without taking a little pause for the cause. This would explain the huge smiles on both our faces as we made our way down the street.

"Hey, Carey!" I called out, and when she looked up I waved. She waved back and then her mouth fell open. Not subtle at all. I could not blame her. Steven looked amazing. He could look good in a hotel towel. Hell, he *did* look good in a hotel towel. But today, with the dreads hanging free and his mouth curved up in a smile and the eye-twinkle going on, he was especially easy on the eyes. Not to mention the cargo shorts and navy tee showing off the bedroom physique. He was oozing the sexy today; we'd received enough admiring looks from the females on our way here for me to know he had that thing going on.

"Hey, girl!" she called back, finally closing her mouth.

We walked around the railing and she stood up. "Carey Jaymes, Steven Williams."

"So this is Young Steven." She was cheesing so hard, I was afraid she could chip a tooth. They shook hands enthusiastically and she took her time letting go.

I sent her a side-eye she completely ignored. "Yes. I believe that's what I just said. This is Steven."

He nudged me. "Be nice, Ti-Ti. Pleasure to meet you, Carey. I love your hair. It's beautiful."

"Yours, too."

"Mutual natural hair care love," I teased.

"You should let yours grow out natural," Carey said.

"You really should. Then you wouldn't be as spastic about it getting wet in the shower," Steven said.

"Do tell?" Carey said, giving me the eye.

"Sit your nosy ass down," I scolded, and turned to Steven. "So I'll see you later?"

He leaned down and whispered in my ear. "As much as you want as soon as you want me."

I actually had to reach back and put my hand on the table for support. Good Lord, the things he made me feel. "I was just going to have you meet me at the hotel later on."

Carey said, "But why doesn't he meet us back here in an hour and a half? We can all hang out."

"Unless you have other stuff you need to do today?" I asked, giving him an out if he wanted it.

"What did I just say?" He hit me with the look.

I inhaled a deep, shaky breath. "So ninety minutes, right back here."

He dropped a kiss on my open mouth, so full of promise it was all I could do not to drag him back to the hotel right then and there. He stepped back and let go of my hand. "See you then." He smiled down at Carey. "I'll look forward to talking to you some more." He lifted one hand in a wave and headed down the street.

I sank into the chair and we both watched him walk away, going as far as leaning out over the rail to keep him in sight.

"Um-um-um, he looks just as good going as he did coming. Day-um!" Carey said.

"Amen." I nodded, still watching.

At the end of the block he turned back around and caught me looking. He grinned before pointing at me. "Okay, I see you." Then he disappeared around the corner.

"Christina!" Carey called out and I blinked.

"Hmm?" I righted myself in the chair and focused in on what she was saying.

"Obviously, it was a bit more than dinner."

"Girl..." I didn't even know where to start.

"Hold on, hold that thought." She lifted her hand for the waiter. "Can we get two pomegranate mojitos and an appetizer platter? Thanks." She turned back to me. "Okay, spill."

"I don't even know where to start," I admitted out loud.

"Why don't you start with how you ended up naked with Young Steven?"

"Who said anything about naked?"

"So now I'm stupid? You shower with your clothes on? Did I not just see the look he gave you, the juicy kiss? Steam is still rising off your hot ass."

I sighed. "What can I tell you? These things sometimes happen."

"Not to you—not in years. Are you rebounding?"

"Probably."

"Does he know you're in major rebound mode?"

"Oh! I forgot that you don't know the tale. Let me give you the quick and dirty version of how Jayson Day became Jay / David." I launched into an abbreviated version of the tale. Even as I was telling it, I couldn't believe how off-the-wall it sounded.

Carey felt the same way. "So who the hell is he exactly?"

"Beyond a married man with children, I don't know."

"Do you even know if that's true?"

Huh. I hadn't thought about it. Truthfully, once he spun his tale—what was I supposed to do with that? It no longer mattered whether he was married, a spy, a technician, a father. He was no longer who I thought he was and definitely not my fiancé. "I honestly don't know."

She paused while the waiter set down our drinks and appetizers. "Well, do you think you should get an explanation?"

"To what end? I mean, there's nowhere to go once someone tells you their entire life is a lie. I'm done." Saying it out loud, I realized it was true. I had nothing else to say to Jay / David and didn't feel I needed to hear anything else out of him.

She lifted her glass in a toast. "On to the next, then. Is that where Young Steven comes in?"

"Oh no—this is just a fling," I reassured her, or myself. "There's no future here. We're just having fun."

"Christina, be careful. You two have a chemistry that's obvious. Just make sure that he knows it's just a fling."

"He knows. He's the one who came up with the term 'fling.' I didn't know what to call it."

"All right," Carey warned. "I'm just going to say for the record that Young Steven doesn't look at you like a man who's having a fling."

"Carey—believe me. We have gone over this. He starts an intensive master's / PhD program next week. He has goals and plans and no time for some thrice-spurned, burned-out older chick from way across the country."

"Is that what you are now? Thrice spurned and burned out?"

I shrugged. "I kinda am." How depressing was that?

"Christina." She reached across the table to touch my hand.

I squeezed back. "I know…this too shall pass. Enough about me. What's going on with you and Bryan?"

Now she was the one who looked sad. "Well, it's not getting better. How sober do you need to be when Steven shows up?"

"Oh—uh, it's a three-mojito story?"

"Definitely."

"Steven is ever so resourceful. He'll pour us into cabs if he has to. Drink up and start talking."

"Shouldn't I be lifting your spirits?"

"I'll be okay."

Carey pursed her lips. "I forgot, you've got Young Steven to, um—elevate your mood."

"Now, now—don't be hatin'."

"No hate, but brunch is on you."

We settled in to catch up.

12

Someday Maybe, but Not Today

Steven—Tuesday, August 17, 7:24 p.m.

Sitting in the airport lounge across from Christina, I was still debating whether I should really just let her go. Yeah, yeah... I know what we agreed, but that was five days ago. It seemed like a whirlwind and a lifetime ago.

For the past five days we had spent twenty-two out of every twenty-four hours together. And it never got old, awkward, or uncomfortable. The very cool thing about Christina: She remained the same person, no matter where we went or who we were around. And I liked who that person was. Straightforward, funny, complicated, and sexy as hell.

We talked a lot. About any and every thing. She told me about her ex-fiancés, and my regard for her grew. She had been reckless with her heart, but she was a survivor. I felt honored to be spending time with her.

We went to a music industry party, brunch with her friends, a visit to her office, another visit to my apartment to hang out with the roommates, back to dinner with Chef David, and dancing again. It was all so effortless. There was a flow and symmetry to our togetherness that was instantly addictive. Speaking of addictive—the bed game was ridiculous. Chemistry kicked up another forty degrees. How often did all of that come together? I had spent time with a woman or two in my life, and nothing had ever felt like this.

Just looking at her now in jeans and a T-shirt, I felt the attraction. Did she really not feel it?

"Steven," she said in the voice that I now knew meant she was serious about something.

"What?"

"You have to just go. You have to get up and walk away. We agreed."

"I know we agreed. I just can't remember why right now. Why did we decide we can't be together?"

"I live there, you live here. I just got out of my third failed engagement. You have a master's and a PhD to obtain. You are twenty-six, I am thirty-two. Do you need any more reasons?"

"What if we just stay in touch, be friends, see what develops later on?"

"That's just going to make it harder. You know that."

I did know that. "Okay, okay—just answer me one thing honestly."

"Just one thing."

"Did it feel like just a fling to you, or did it feel like the start of something?"

The fact that she couldn't or wouldn't look me in the eye told me what I needed to know.

"What difference does it make?"

"You said you'd answer honestly."

"Honestly, I've never had a fling before, so I don't know. Maybe this is what one feels like."

"Cop-out."

"Best I can do."

"Not by a long stretch, Christina Brinsley. You can do better in your sleep with one hand behind your back. In fact, you did...just this morning."

She closed her eyes. "Low. Okay, listen. Maybe..."

"Maybe?"

"Maybe...if things were different I would give it a try, but it's not fair to you or to me right now. Neither one of us can put in the time and attention we deserve to make this into something. So let's just cut it off here. It's already hard enough."

So she did feel something. "Is this where you give me the speech about 'if this was another time and another place'?"

"No. This is where I say...someday you'll look back and realize that I am right."

"Someday maybe...but not today. Today it just feels like you are running away."

"That's because I am."

I had to know one other thing. "Did you feel like this before...with them?"

"I don't know what I felt. I don't know what I'm feeling. I don't know how much is you and me, how much is rebound, how much is just lust. I don't know anything right now. That's why we made the pact, the promise, whatever it was."

We sat in stony silence for another moment or two.

She leaned toward me. "C'mon, Steven. No fuss, no muss. Right?"

I knew when to give up, but I didn't have to like it. "Right."

A few more minutes passed before she checked her watch. "Now stand up, kiss me good-bye, and walk away."

"I'm not going to beg you."

"I don't want you to. I really don't. I'm not sure I wouldn't give in. Don't put me through that." For the first time since we'd been together, she looked tortured. I definitely did not want to be the cause of her distress. She had been through enough.

"Okay. We agreed. My bad. It is what it is."

"Don't be bitter."

"Now that's funny coming from you."

"Don't be ugly either."

"Yes, ma'am. We'll do this your way." I put my hand behind her neck, leaned down, and kissed her with all the emotion I wanted to display but wouldn't. Her lips clung to mine when I finally lifted my head.

"Wow. That did not help."

Wasn't supposed to. I took a step backwards. "You're gonna miss me, Ti-Ti. You really are." I took one step backwards and then another.

I was only a few steps back when I heard her. She quietly said, "Dammit, I know."

I nodded, pivoted, and walked away quickly without looking back. I knew she stood watching me. I really wanted to glance back for one last look. But what would it change? This was what we agreed to do. Maybe someday I would think it was for the best. For now, I just needed to keep walking.

B

Nobody Gave Me Anything on a Silver Platter

Christina—Tuesday, August 17, 8:17 p.m.

The flight heading east had gone by in a quick blur. The flight back home, not so much. Sometime after the first half hour, I found myself fighting fatigue. It was a mental tired though, the kind that sleep can't solve. I set my iPod to an unobtrusive instrumental jazz mix, closed my eyes, and just let the thoughts run free. My mind was a jumbled mess and there was a vague ache in my heart that I couldn't pin down.

You know that feeling you get when you suspect you have really screwed something up? Yep, that's what it was.

Christina, you're being melodramatic and stupid.

Maybe I was, but in the past seven years I'd been through three fiancés and now an ill-timed fling with my deliveryman. The look on his face as he backed away from me was one I wouldn't soon forget. I never wanted to be responsible for making a person look like that, like they weren't good enough and there was nothing they could do about it.

That really wasn't my intent. I'd intended to spare both of us a lot of drama and heartache. Hell, I'd intended to just go to dinner with him and go about my life. I couldn't justify why I let it go on, knowing both of us were going too far too fast. But I hadn't felt that good in ages. Not just physically but mentally. There was an energy between me and Steven that buoyed me and made me feel like the world was an exciting place where exciting things were waiting right around the corner. And whatever those things were, I could handle them, especially with a man like him by my side.

I hadn't felt that way, supercharged by life, since I left for college. College was an escape from my mother's clinginess and my brothers' overprotectiveness. With my father dying when I was so young, my mother and brothers always felt they had to overcompensate and fill that void. But they never understood that I wanted to feel the void and learn how to live with the empty space instead of filling it with substitutes.

Growing up, I was the girl everything came easily to. Or so it seemed. I worked my ass off for every A, to make head cheerleader, to be fourth in my class, to get that full tuition scholarship to Berkeley and the internship at the *Chronicle*. Graduate school, then the job at Valiant. I started out writing four-line commentaries as filler on the Web pages. From the outside looking in, I get that it looked easy.

No, I never had to worry about whether the bills were paid or where my next meal came from, and I recognized that for the blessing it was. But nobody gave me anything on a silver platter. I was taught that if you worked hard and you really wanted it, eventually you would reap the rewards.

Funny how that didn't seem to work in my private life. Cedric was my college sweetheart. He was literally the boy next door in my coed dorm. He was your all-around good guy. Smart, ambitious, and good-looking in a generically handsome way. We came from similar socio-economic backgrounds and had the same goals. We understood each other. We were friends first. He was taking forever to make a move, so I nudged him along. And though it wasn't all magic and moonbeams, it was nice and exactly what I expected. Things moved very quickly after that. We went from friends to fiancés in no time flat. Everyone loved Cedric. He was articulate, steady; you knew what you were getting with Cedric. Or so I thought. He was the very last person I thought would hurt or betray me. But he did. When he announced that he married someone else in the middle of our engagement, I was angry at him, of course, but I was livid with myself that I hadn't even noticed that anything was wrong. It took months before I even thought about dating again, let alone letting it get serious.

When Perry came along, he was like a balm to my wounded spirit. He said all the right things, liked all the things I liked, and was by far the easiest man to get along with in the world. He was flashy and spontaneous and went with his heart instead of his head. We had ridiculous arguments, we agreed on nothing but the fact that we were committed to each other. There were days where he felt more like a good friend than a lover, but I counted that as a positive. He was Cedric's polar opposite. I never knew what to expect from Perry from one day to the next. But the unpredictability was exciting... right up until it bit me in the ass. Again, I was left to wonder what signs I'd missed and why.

Jay / David was supposed to be one who proved (to me and everyone else) that I could get it right. I took my time with him, I was cautious and watchful. The chemistry was there; we had fun together. Jay / David was steady but not dull. He laughed a lot and was great for delivering the grand gesture. He was about the thirty-six roses on a Wednesday afternoon for no reason. Spontaneous trips to Napa just because. Proposing in the middle of a Golden State Warriors game on the jumbotron. That was Jay / David. And I just realized while looking back that that was all I knew to be 100 percent true about him. For all I knew everything else was fabricated.

In fact, chances were that I knew more about Steven, having spent five days with him, than I ever knew about Jay / David over the course of three years. And that depressed me all the more and it made me angry. Yes, extremely angry. I sent Steven packing because I couldn't trust my feelings or my judgment any more. I couldn't trust that what seemed like the best sex I ever had wasn't on account of my rebounding, übervulnerable emotions. I was angry that I couldn't trust that feeling I had, strolling around Manhattan holding hands with Steven. That feeling that I'd found something worth holding on to. Couldn't trust it, so I ran away. Or rather, pushed a nice guy away. A nice guy who had done nothing to deserve that look on his face.

What in the hell am I doing with my life?

That was it. No more men. Not on the serious tip, anyway. All casual, all the time. Clearly, what I was good at was career-building, investigative reporting, journalism—that was it. That was my world. From now on . . . I was Christina, strong yet driven, successful yet detached, single yet determined. I went to New York broken and tired. I was coming back just as tired but with my new attitude serving as Band-Aids, holding me together. I was, above all, a survivor.

How It Began Again

(Five years later)

14

The Business of the Day

Christina—Thursday, October 9, 10:18 a.m.

The West Coast offices of Valiant News Network reflected the eclectic tastes of the area. The floor was designed in a funky loft-style with exposed ductwork and polished concrete. Steel and leather furniture meshed with twill fabrics in burgundy, teal, and gray.

"Christina, you're back on the air in three...two...one." The red light on cameras one and two went on.

"Welcome back to VNN, where your news is what counts. Following up on the story of the day, Congressman Walker is being investigated for allegedly pocketing funds earmarked for researching the viability of building a cross-country, high-speed rail system. The project, nicknamed Mercury, was supposed to launch two years ago but fell apart due to lack of funding. Did that funding finance Congressman Walker's lavish lifestyle? Stay with us on the Valiant News Network. We'll be getting to the bottom of this story. Next up, sports. Which Bay Area team is heading to the play-offs without its marquee star? Let's check in with Vic to find out. Vic, what can you tell us?"

As the camera cut away to Vic, my assistant ran up to the

desk. "Your mother's holding on line two. She said to smile more. Lisa's waiting to video chat, and your brother is waiting in your office."

Typical Mom stuff, and unfortunately typical Lisa stuff. "Thanks, Diane. Tell my mom I'll call her back. Lisa knows I'm on air live, and which brother?"

"Collin."

Curious. Collin was not a drop-by-the-office kind of guy. "Okay, he can come out to the newsroom. Has Carey landed yet?" Carey was transferring to the San Francisco office after finally (finally!) breaking free of her boyfriend, Bryan, a little over six months ago.

"Not yet. I'll go get Collin."

I finished my 10:00 a.m. updates, handed over the anchor desk to Tracey, and stepped down off the podium. I walked over to Collin. My oldest brother was a tall, dark, überpreppy man, well aware of his attractiveness. He had the Buppie-with-bank look down cold. Collin had the same chocolate skin tone as me and wore his hair closely cropped to his head with a razor-sharp line. He was right at six feet tall with the build of a man who was vain enough to stay in the gym. Generally suited in Tom Ford and flawlessly groomed, today he seemed a little rumpled.

Leaning in to give him a hug, I noticed he wasn't wearing his customary all-is-right-with-my-world, don't-you-wish-you-were-me look. "What's wrong?"

"Great job as always. Are you ever going to take over a whole show, or just stay special correspondent?"

Hmm, he wasn't answering a direct question. "Collin, you already know I don't want to anchor. I'm already producing, directing, editing, and doing investigative reports—that's enough. What's going on?"

His shoulders fell. "In your office."

This couldn't be good. Grabbing two bottles of water, I handed one to him as we sat on my tiny sofa. Collin was normally talkative, garrulous even, with a personality that filled a room effortlessly. Quiet, subdued Collin was troubling, but I let him take his time opening up.

"Celia's cheating on me."

Perky, perfect Celia? "Not a chance in hell."

"She is! She's been taking these classes at Bayside U and her hours are getting more erratic, she's evasive about her whereabouts, not answering her phone, and..."

"What?"

He looked around as if making sure we weren't overheard. "We're off schedule."

"Off schedule?" I had no idea what he was talking about.

"Yes. We schedule things, Christina, and the schedule is off." He narrowed his eyes as if willing me to understand.

"What things? It's just the two of you—what could you possibly be scheduling?"

He huffed. "Intimate man-wife things."

I couldn't help it. My mouth fell open and I had to clap a hand over it to hold the laughter in. Knowing he was not appreciating my amusement, I struggled to contain myself. Minutes later, I was adequately composed. "Are you telling me you schedule sex? How often? For how long? Do you request certain acts in advance? Do you track it with reminders in your BlackBerry?"

"Christina. I'm serious here."

"Okay, okay. Sorry. On further reflection, I probably really don't need the details anyway. So you're off schedule. By days or weeks?"

"Months."

"Months! Did you talk to her about it?"

"We don't discuss that sort of thing in detail."

"Say what now?" What married couple without kids was skipping sex for months and not calling each other out about it?

"Christina, not all of us are passing it out with double

coupons and keeping some sort of scorecard by the bed, okay? Some of us are happy to be in committed, mature relationships."

Well, ouch. Granted, I had given up on the happily-ever-after thing. And okay, maybe I had a fairly lengthy list of rotating FwBs (Friends with Benefits). But I was a busy woman and in no frame of mind to have to nurture and support somebody who was ultimately going to walk away carrying what was left of my heart when he went. My needs were attended to as I saw fit, on my playing field, by my rules. Still, no reason for my own brother to call me all measure of slutty. "Collin, you are rapidly losing my sympathy. What can I do to help?"

"Sorry, Ti. Just, you know—it's been five years since the Jay / David debacle. We kinda hoped you would be back in the relationship saddle by now."

"We?" I didn't like the thought that I was fodder for family gossip. But now wasn't the time to have that discussion. "Never mind, this isn't about me. What do you want me to do about Celia?"

"Do you mind sniffing around campus a little? Just let me know if I'm way off base or not?"

"Are you sure? Take it from me, this is the kinda thing that once you know—you can't ignore it."

"I need to know." My confident Collin sounded as unsure as I'd ever heard him.

"Okay, but I gotta tell you—even with your schedule slippage, I find it hard to believe that Celia is stepping out. She adores you... to a fault."

"I don't know. I've been on the EVP track and not paying her as much attention as I used to."

"What VP track?" Collin worked as a hedge funds manager for a financial services company. I had no idea what that meant, except that I gave him my savings and he turned it into more savings. Collin had been successful and comfortable for so long that it honestly never occurred to me to wonder what his ultimate goals and aspirations were. Though now that he mentioned it, an executive vice presidency before the age of fifty sounded very much like Collin. For all our faults, the Brinsleys were all madly ambitious.

"Again, Ti—you haven't been very plugged in. Anyway, I was hoping you could find a way to just discreetly see what's going on and let me know."

"I'll see what I can do, Collin. Don't even worry about it."

"Thanks, baby sis." He gave me a one-armed hug. "Sorry about the coupon thing. I know you're dealing in your own way."

Somehow that actually made me feel worse. I almost would rather have his disapproval than his pity. I hugged him back and sent him on his way before sliding behind my desk and adjusting the monitor. Clicking a few keys on the keyboard, I opened the video conferencing software and found the call that was waiting in the queue.

"Hey, Lisa, what's up in the Southland today?" Lisa and I had battled it out to head West Coast operations. For two years we had grappled for assignments, one-upping each other. With the exception of a *Dynasty*-style catfight in the middle of the newsroom, we battled. Whether through sheer perserverance or the fact that I refused to take the low road and I never griped about it, I won the leadership position in the West. This was something she never got over, even after she was given the entertainment desk down in Los Angeles.

Valiant had grown significantly in scope over the past five years. Becoming less of a Web magazine and blogger hangout, Valiant morphed into more of a crossover media vehicle. Our channel, Valiant News Network (VNN), was driven by those bloggers and Web enthusiasts who first started following our online magazines. Our popularity was based on the fact that our content was viewer driven. We showed the stories they wanted to see, not whatever the mainstream media thought was hot. Our one concession to pop culture was the daily one-hour segment concentrating on entertainment news. Thankfully, that was Lisa's domain.

"I needed you to sign off for the award season expenditures." Lisa had been requesting what amounted to one-fourth of the entire quarterly budget so she could "properly" cover award shows and parties in LA.

"You didn't send any justifications, Lisa. You sent me the e-mail equivalent of a blank check and asked me to sign it."

"Exactly. I know what I need; you don't—just find a way to get me the funds."

I eyeballed the image on the monitor. "What do you really think the probability of that happening is?"

"You aren't confident enough in your leadership to let go of the purse strings."

Seven years in this company and she still thought she could manipulate me. Truthfully, this position would be a lot closer to perfect if it wasn't for the constant Lisa shenanigans I was forced to deal with. "Send me the budget requests, complete with details, and we'll see what we can get from New York, okay?"

"Why don't I just call New York directly and tell them you don't understand this side of the business."

"Good luck with that, Lisa. Have a good day." I disconnected and turned my chair around to face the window. It was 11:00 a.m. and I was already exhausted. Valiant still ran lean. That meant that I had to be reporter, anchor, producer, director, manager, and finance person all at once. They paid me handsomely, but days like today made me wonder if it was worth it. That was one of the reasons I was so glad they were sending Carey out. She was going to be my second-in-command and a person I could trust not to run tattling back to headquarters every time I did something the least bit unorthodox... which was often.

My intercom buzzed. "Carey is on her way in from the airport, your mother is back on the line, and Brandon says he has a contact over at Bayside U who can give you some background on your Project Mercury story."

"At Bayside?" This would be a great opportunity for me to kill two birds with one stone.

"Yeah, some professor over there leads a research foundation called Chi-Wind. Brandon wants to know if you want him to call first, or if you'll just go in cold."

"I'll go in cold. Tell him to e-mail me the details; I'll take a look and go over them first thing tomorrow. Can you pull whatever we have on high-speed rail, wind energy, and green initiatives and forward it to me? Oh, and go ahead and put my mom through." Taking the top off the bottled water, I reached with my right hand into the top drawer for the Advil I kept there. Taking a deep breath, I hit the button for line two. "Hi, Mom."

"What was your brother doing there? Why did you wear green on camera, baby? You know it washes you out. Did I tell you I met a young man you might be interested in dating?" It was a quintessential Joanna Brinsley conversation. Quick, question laden, and the slightest bit accusatory. Swallowing the two Advil, I rested my head against the back of the chair. It was shaping up to be one of those days.

"Visiting, I wear what Wardrobe puts me in, I'm not interested in young men right now—don't you have a luncheon for spina bifida today?"

"Spinal-cord injuries and stem-cell research, Christina."

Whatever. Joanna was a lady who lunched. I had given up knowing the cause of the day years ago. "Sorry, Mom, I'm in a terrible rush. Carey is coming in and we have a ton of work to cover before we can get her settled in."

"Once she's settled in, you'll be able to relax and have a real social life again, won't you?"

Wow, second jab from family today about my social life.

They clearly were not appreciating my no-muss-no-fuss approach to dating. I was keeping my encounters light. Why was that anybody's business but mine? I also knew better than to rise to the bait.

"Most definitely. Maybe I'll even meet that young man you've got lined up."

"Good, good—oh, I told your brother Clarke to treat you and Casey to dinner tonight."

Why my mother still felt I needed a man to buy my meals was beyond me. "It's Carey, Mom. Not Casey. And I'll check with her—she may just want a quiet evening at the house."

"Oh, baby, don't become a recluse. You know that's why Jackie and Lynne are married and you are still single. You've become a workaholic recluse."

Rolling my eyes, I bit back what I wanted to say. Jackie was married to a man she met online and was now expecting her first child. Lynne was married (at long last) to her longtime boyfriend. I caught up with them when our schedules permitted, but it seemed there just weren't enough hours in the day to get everything in as it was. I thought about explaining this but decided it was easier to tell her what she wanted to hear. "Okay, Mom, I'll check in with Clarke in a few minutes."

That seemed to pacify her enough to move her along to the end of her conversational thread. Hanging up, I could finally get down to the business of the day. I turned on the TV to see how Tracey was doing on the desk. Prayerfully, it was a slow news morning and we could fill with pretaped human interest stories. Valiant News Network came across as a lighter, friendlier channel. Somewhere in between a HLN and a full-on CNN. Our major stories broke from the New York office, but we handled just about everything else here in San Francisco, with the exception of the team we had in Los Angeles. So while we kept a live anchor on desk, we repeated major stories throughout the day. Since I wore so many hats, this allowed my associate news director to stay on breaking news while I dealt with station business.

I was reviewing the pitches for upcoming stories when the phone buzzed again. "Yes, Diane?"

"Carey's on her way back and Jeri's on line three."

"Send her back, and thanks." Digging through the piles on my desk to get to the folder holding the information I thought Jeri would want to talk about, I pushed the blinking red button by line three. "Hey, Jeri."

"Have you seen these costs from Lisa?" Jeri's voice was screechy and she rarely did screechy. I quickly scanned my e-mail to see if Lisa had copied me on the e-mail. Nope.

"Jeri, she forgot to copy me on the e-mail." I wasn't one to throw a colleague (no matter how trifling) under the bus.

"You mean she went around you, thinking she'd get more if she sent it to all of us and left you out of the loop."

Diplomatically, I said nothing. Jeri continued her rant. A movement in the doorway caught my attention and I looked up to see Carey standing just outside the door. She was in a travel-ready outfit of black pants, white shirt, and suede jacket. Seeing her dialed up the happy in my life exponentially. I waved her in and pressed MUTE. "You're just in time. Lisa drama. Jeri on the warpath."

"So nothing's changed but the time zone." Carey gave me a quick hug before settling in a chair in front of the desk.

"I'm sending this to you and Carey now, and I want you to make it clear to Lisa that there is a reason we have a chain of command here and we are not made of money!"

Carey and I exchanged looks. When Jeri's feathers were ruffled, that could only mean bad things. I took the phone off mute. "Uh—are you all right?"

"Things are just a little tense. We're losing some advertisers because of our coverage of Congressman Walker—do you have any leads yet?"

"I do. I'm checking out a source tomorrow morning at Bayside U. I'm hoping to get some background on the original project and an idea of the congressman's involvement."

She gave an audible sigh of relief. "Okay. Christina?"

"Yep?"

"We need this one. Go get it."

"Done." No pressure or anything.

"Did Carey make it in yet?"

Carey leaned forward. "Hey, Jeri."

"Hey. Listen—I hate to throw you in the deep end, but I need you to take everything off Christina's plate except her morning on-air news recap, this story, and budget approvals."

"Done." Carey raised a brow. This was way beyond what was discussed when Carey decided to come West. I shrugged; I had no idea what was going on.

"Of course we'll compensate accordingly. Christina, I'll e-mail you her transfer letter with the salary bump. I gotta run. You girls make it happen." Just that abruptly, she hung up.

Carey and I listened to the dial tone for a second before she hopped up and came around behind my desk. "Well, let's look at the raise. Looks like I'm going to earn every penny."

Laughing, I scrolled through to find the e-mail and opened the attachment. We both looked at the number and then at each other.

"Well, that's a whole lot of work they're expecting from me, huh? To whom much is given, much is expected. I guess dinner's on me tonight?!" She whirled and did a little happy dance.

"Oh—about dinner."

She stopped midtwirl and looked at me. "What?"

"My mother is siccing Clarke on us."

Carey sighed. "Of course she is. Two single women couldn't possibly take themselves out to dinner. Joanna never changes."

"She never will." And at this point, I didn't really want her to. Mom was Mom.

Carey surprised me with her answer. "No problem. It could be fun, Clarke is good people."

I raised a brow; she considered Clarke to be even more of a stuffed designer shirt than Collin. I distinctly recalled during our college years when Clarke disparagingly referred to Carey as a "displaced flower child" to her face on more than one occasion. I also recalled her responding that he needed a colonic to get the stick out of his ass. But hey, who was I to bring up the past? Lord knows I never wanted to discuss mine. "If you're good with it, I'm good."

"It's all good. Let's drop my stuff off at my brand-new empty condo, pick up some lunch, and you can brief me on all the crap you're about to start shoveling my way."

Truthfully, I could use a break. "Let's get outta here for a little while."

15

Well... That Was Awkward

Christina—Thursday, October 9, 8:12 p.m.

Carey had truly come into her own since leaving Bryan. She had always had personality and style, but all of her promise seemed to blossom once she was freed of her toxic relationship.

She was more expressive, more confident, more aware of her own thoughts and opinions. I was thrilled to have her back on the West Coast. I was sitting in her brand-new empty condo, waiting on her so we could meet Clarke for dinner.

"Girl, can you come on?" I called out.

"Two seconds. I have to be cute," Carey called back.

I rolled my eyes. Carey was more of a funky, wild-child, whatever-I-feel-like dresser than one who was worried about being cute.

Which is why my mouth fell open when she walked out with smoky eyes and mauve-glossed lips. Her hair, still long and loose in a texturized natural style, hung in shiny tight curls past her shoulders. She still favored chunky, eclectic jewelry and accessories, but her clothing style had become less organic cotton and more refined silks and knits. The lines of her clothing tended to drape and flatter rather than bag and conceal. Tonight she wore a slate blue dress with a deep V-neck in front and back, falling in ruched layers to just above her knees. Chunky shades of topaz at her neck and ears and sky-high bronze pumps completed the look. "I guess the flower child is gone for good?"

"She lives inside, heffa. You don't think I lived in New York all those years and picked up nothing, did you? Close your mouth and let's go."

I glanced at my black jersey wrap dress and glossy patent boots and shrugged. It was cute but safe. "Spotlight is all yours tonight, sister."

"You're always stunning and you know it. Can you come on and feed a friend already?"

If my reaction to Carey's transformation was amusing, Clarke's was comical. He was just inside the door of the restaurant when we entered, and his faced showed his every emotion. He looked at me with a pleased smile, glanced at Carey in confusion, looked back at me, and then studied Carey more closely. His eyes widened and his brow furrowed. "Carey, what did you do to yourself?"

She stepped forward to give him a hug and whispered in his ear, "I grew up. Have you?"

Oh, really now? I watched as their hug lasted a beat longer than I expected and Clarke's hand slid slowly down her back and around her waist before releasing her. Clarke was in a severely cut black suit with a white shirt and silver tie that only the very handsome and very confident could pull off. Clarke reminded everyone of Isaiah Washington's character from *Grey's Anatomy*, Preston Burke, in both looks and demeanor. He and Collin looked quite a bit alike, though Clarke had grown an attractive thin mustache lately.

He was arrogant enough to catch your attention, good-looking and charming enough to hold it but classy enough to pull it off. Soft-spoken but strong, I never thought of Clarke as much of a player with the ladies. Where Collin was the protective brother, Clarke was more playful with me.

Clarke was an attorney who recently opened his own practice after years with a prestigious firm handling international mergers and acquisitions. He was currently looking at Carey as if he wanted to merge and acquire her...soon. The night just turned interestingly awkward.

I sent the both of them a side-eye that they missed. Finally I cleared my throat. "Don't mind the sister; I'll just stand here hungry and neglected."

They both turned to look at me and it clicked. All the snippy, snappy back-and-forth over the years made sense. Sexual tension. Just what I needed. I didn't know how I felt about my friend and my brother hooking up. But I knew one thing—I was officially out of it. One thing I had to thank the Tragic Trio (my nickname for the ex-fiancés) for was that I learned that I had no clue who made a good match or what it took to start and maintain a relationship. I no longer offered love advice to anyone, including myself. I leaned in for my hug. "Food and wine, please."

"That's the least I could do for the pleasure of the company of two such beautiful ladies this evening," Clarke said, smiling at Carey. She beamed.

Oh good. I was going to be treated to player-Clarke this evening. Sitting down, I reached for the wine list.

By the time we had placed our orders and received cocktails, I was already beyond ready to call it a night. As much as I enjoyed the company of both Carey and Clarke, I seriously would have preferred a large bottle of wine, my DVR, and an early bedtime. I thought longingly of my queen-size pillow-top Sealy as I sat in Waterfront Restaurant at Pier 7, just down from the Valiant offices. Squelching a sigh, I reached for the glass of Pinot Grigio our server had set by my left hand. Watching them banter and flirt made me nostalgic, happy, and uncomfortable all at the same time. I was officially a third wheel. I was contemplating a doggy bag and exit strategy when someone called my name.

"Good evening, Christina. You are looking particularly tasty this evening."

Dante, one of my former FwBs, was standing alongside the table. Dante was a former major-league baseball player. He wasn't terribly tall, but he had pretty-boy looks reminiscent of a sun-kissed Antonio Banderas, the smile of a charmer, and was blessed with a . . . natural athleticism. In fact, it was his penchant for insatiable, marathon bouts of naked aerobic activity that caused me to excuse him from my FwB rotation. A girl had her limits, and there was something to be said for quality over quantity. Dante was all about the quantity. He was widely known as an untamable playboy with an excessive taste for the good things in life.

He was a man who loved women and they generally loved him right back. Since I was cured of that "love" disease, he was a perfect FwB for me . . . for a while. Staying in the orbit of the sun was exhausting, and I liked to keep my distance before I was singed. Dante was not the type of man most women walked away from. He preferred to do the walking away. To say he hadn't taken my dismissal of his services well was an understatement of the highest order.

I wasn't entirely comfortable with all the intersecting tangled webs my life was weaving into this evening. I generally kept my friends away from family and my family away from my FwBs. Everyone all at the same place at the same time was putting my head in a bad space. But in typical Christina fashion, I plastered on a smile and rose from my seat to accept his outstretched hand.

"Dante, I thought you were in the Dominican Republic." I tilted my head so he could kiss my cheek.

"I was. Now I am here." He smiled with a glint in his eyes that I knew too well. He was working the whole I've-seen-you-naked-and-want-to-again vibe.

Turning back to the table, I gestured. "This is my good friend Carey Jaymes, and my brother Clarke Brinsley. This is Dante Esteban. Dante is a ... friend of mine."

Clarke rose and was in the process of shaking his hand when Dante said something really ignorant. "Oh, *querida,* I think we were more than friends, no?"

Clarke gave him the Brinsley stony-eyed glare. "That's my sister. Please watch what you say in front of the ladies."

Dante sized up Clarke and then glanced at me. Did I mention how very much I wished this day was over? All I could do was shoot accusatory beams of pisstivity in Dante's direction. What I really wanted to do was stomp my booted size 7 foot and scream "Go. Sit. Down!"

"My apologies. Do you mind if I join you for a round of drinks? As an apology for my lapse in behavior?"

Carey and Clarke looked at me. Carey's face had "how you gonna handle this one?" written all over it. I shot a glance toward the door, wondering if I could break for freedom. Damn these four-inch heels—not a chance in hell was I doing a mad dash in these babies. Add to that the fact that the whole front side of the restaurant was now eyeballing our table. I had forgotten that Dante was a crowd favorite when he played for the Oakland A's. He was something of a sports celebrity.

As the kids in the newsroom say—FML (Eff My Life). I motioned to the empty chair next to mine and reapplied the fake smile.

"Have a seat, Dante." I motioned to our waiter. "We'll take another round, thank you."

"Will Mr. Esteban be joining you for dinner?"

"Uh, no—we don't want to monopolize Mr. Esteban's time." The smile was starting to hurt my cheeks a little at this time. And speaking of cheeks, Mr. Buns of Steel was sitting a little too close for my comfort. When he handed the waiter some bills to cover the drinks, I discreetly slid my chair over an inch.

"So..." Carey tested the conversational waters. "How did you and Christina meet?"

I gratefully accepted my wine refill from the waiter and sipped deeply.

"Chrissa and I met on the set of VNN. I was there to do an interview with that sports guy..." He paused.

"Vic." I hated the name Chrissa, I really did.

"Yes, Vic, and I saw the lovely Chrissa across the room. It was, how you say? Magic, no?"

"No, not really, and it's Christina. I've told you that a million times."

He leaned over to whisper in my ear. "There were times you didn't mind."

Through clenched teeth I responded, "Times change." I sent Clarke a say-something, pleading look.

"So, Dante, how is life after baseball? What are you doing with yourself?"

Thankfully, Dante launched into a lengthy speech about himself, thus freeing the rest of us from having to make any conversation beyond a "really, how interesting" every time he paused to take a breath.

I zoned out. Crossed one leg over the other, stared out of the floor-to-ceiling windows at the inky bay water. Taking another fortifying sip of wine, I wondered just what all was in that water. Then I squinted and looked about thirty-three degrees southeast. I imagined that I could see lights on my next-door neighbor's back patio, which he seemed to have an aversion to turning off no matter the time of day.

"Isn't that right, Christina?" Dante's voice broke into the first truly peaceful moment I'd had all day.

"I'm sorry, what was that?" I blinked twice and saw both Carey and Clarke waiting expectantly for my answer.

"I was telling your brother and your friend here that the real reason I left the Bay Area was because you kicked me out of your bed and told me I wasn't welcome back again. Even when I pleaded, you still said no. Threw me out naked in the rain before tossing the car keys at my head. *Es verdad?*"

Now, bad enough that he decided to share this with Carey and Clarke, but his voice had risen dramatically and the other half of the restaurant that hadn't been eavesdropping before were now actively engaged in the conversation.

I opened my mouth to snap out a scathing reply when his hand slid under the table and landed on my thigh. That hand had the nerve to start sliding upward. *No, he didn't!* I abruptly closed my mouth. I was about to shut this nonsense down.

I turned toward him with a slow, sweet smile. I waited until a slow smile spread across his handsome face. "A lady never kicks, tosses, and tells. A gentleman would know that." With that, I allowed my right hand to accidentally knock over my water glass with the majority of icy liquid splashing directly into his lap. He leaped up as the waitstaff rushed toward him with napkins outstretched.

"Oh, *lo siento, papi,*" I apologized in Spanish. "You may want to take care of that."

He shot me a look that warned of retribution.

I nodded once and raised my wineglass in salute. "Thanks for the drink, Dante. Welcome back to the Bay."

"I'll be seeing you around, Chrissa," he announced as he marched toward the exit.

"Not if I see you first," I muttered into the wineglass that had become my best friend for the evening.

Appetizers we had not ordered appeared on a tray next to the table. "Dinner is compliments of Mr. Esteban this evening."

"In that case, you can just bring the bottle." I flashed a smile at the waiter. Turning back to Carey and Clarke, I motioned. "Well, dig in."

"Well . . ." Carey hid a giggle behind her napkin. "That was awkward."

"Shut it and eat a shrimp."

"I mean, I knew you were slaying 'em in the streets, but you are *literally* slaying dudes in the streets!" She dissolved into laughter. Clarke joined her.

"Sis, you nothing to play with. You wet down a gazillion-aire celebrity in public and still got dinner paid for." He lifted his cocktail. "Respect."

I toasted. "Recognize. Now pass me a damn crab cake."

16

Of All the Classrooms in All the World...

Christina—Friday, October 10, 11:48 a.m.

My goal for the day was simply to survive. To get through it with minimal drama and get into bed (alone). It had been a hell of a week and I flat out needed some downtime. I lost track of how many glasses of wine I self-medicated with last night. Clarke ended up driving me home. Then he drove back into the city to take Carey home. The whole night was more than I wanted to think about.

I had spent the first part of the morning battling with Lisa and trying not to look like warmed-over roadkill on the air. I prayed that Carey was ready to take the reins because I only had time to jump out of the chair, change clothes, grab my file for this interview, pick up my car from the restaurant parking lot, and make my way to Bayside. I hadn't appreciated the smirk on the valet's face when I picked up my car either. Clearly, he remembered me from the night before.

Finding an authorized visitor's parking space on Bayside University's campus was no small task. Next item up: finding the engineering quad. Of course it was nowhere near where I had parked. The morning fog had burned through the clouds, but there was still that bay breeze to contend with. With a sigh, I switched out my stilettos for cute loafers I kept in my trunk. To be safe, I dug out a suede trapeze jacket in a chestnut color, in case the breeze picked up or the temperature dropped.

Checking my reflection in the right window of my Kelly green BMW convertible (my gift to myself on my last promotion), I was glad I looked better than I felt. My dark mulberry pantsuit with crisp lilac shirt underneath, was just the right touch of professional meets trendy. My hair was contained in a sleek ponytail and the bags under my eyes were concealed with the wonders of Lancôme makeup.

Double-checking the map and building directory, I headed out. First things first, I had to do some surveillance on Celia. According to her class schedule, she was taking a class called The Movement of People, Places, and Products. I had no idea what that was about, but luckily it was in the same building where I was to meet the professor I needed to consult with today.

Entering the building, I asked a passing student for directions. "Which way to auditorium 1.178?"

"Professor Williams's class is straight ahead to the right. He's just wrapping up."

"Thanks." I found the door quickly and slipped into the first empty seat without looking up.

A familiar voice that I hadn't heard in a very long time rang out, reaching all the way to the second level of the room. It sent a shiver straight down my spine. "In a few years, more than six billion people will inhabit the world, placing enormous stress on existing air, rail, and highway transportation systems and creating the need for new ways to plan, manage, and engineer the systems of the future. What can we do, here and now? What can we engineer to avert certain transportation catastrophe? That's our challenge, that's our purpose, and that's what you need to think about. We'll pick up here next week, and don't forget your midsemester papers are due next week as well. I will not have office hours this weekend, so catch me on e-mail or make an appointment to see me next week. Thanks, everybody."

The class erupted into applause as I sat with my mouth open. Up on the dais stood S. Dub, former deliveryman, former student, former fling. All the promise of his youth had come to fruition. He had come into his own. The lean, wiry muscle had turned into solid-packed muscle. His dreads had grown down his back and he had them partially secured with a leather band. His skin was still that warmed-up honey color, but it was stretched over features that were chiseled now. The baby face was replaced with a more squared and defined jaw. The dimples were more like grooves outlining those full lips. Basically, he looked good. Really, really good.

I was completely oblivious to the students filing past me as I sat staring at him. I wondered how his life had changed, how he got from there to here in five years, and yes, I wondered if he was married. I could honestly say that out of all the man drama I had been through in my thirty-seven years, Steven was my only regret. I still thought I did the best thing for both of us, but I regretted not being brave enough to at least try. I thought back on what I knew about Steven and dug out the information from Brandon to find the name of the professor I was supposed to meet. Scanning through, my eyes fell on a name: Dr. Steven Williams, MST. MST—Master of Science in Transportation. Doctor Steven Williams—he had done it. I was extraordinarily proud...and curious to know more.

"Christina, what are you doing here?" Celia's voice yanked me out of my reflection.

I reluctantly lifted my eyes from Steven's bio to find Celia frowning down at me. Celia, bless her heart, was wearing a tailored skirt suit with pearls and boots. To a college class. My sister-in-law was a tall, willowy, dark-skinned beauty with a very proper side-part pageboy swinging just above her shoulders,

and lips that magically stayed lightly glossed in the same neutral mauve tone twenty-four hours a day. Standing to her left
was a man I guesstimated to be in his midtwenties. He was
dressed in jeans and a sweatshirt. I noticed he kept his eyes focused on Celia's lips. He was kinda cute, kinda fine, and very
young. The boy had cougar bait written all over him. Hmm.
Now *this* was interesting.

"Celia, hey!" I stood up to give her a hug. Celia and I were
never the bestest of friends. We generally kept our conversations superficial. Collin, clothes, culinary arts. "I'm here to interview Dr. Williams for a piece I'm working on. Who's your
friend?"

She paused before answering and then turned reluctantly
toward the young man. "This is Dax Fredericks, my study partner. Dax, this is—"

"Oh, cool, you are Christina Brinsley from that news
channel! You doing big things. I'm a fan." He spoke loudly and
two other students turned to look. As word rippled that a news
reporter was in the room, I held my breath. I could physically
feel the minute Steven's eyes fell on me. I literally flushed from
head to toe. My nerve endings jumped to full attention. Wow.
I hadn't felt that in quite a while. It took every bit of whatever
acting ability I ever possessed not to turn and look at him. I
was dying to know what he saw when he looked at me, what
he thought, what he felt, and if his eyes still changed from
green to brown with his mood.

Calmly, I shook Dax's hand. What the hell kind of name is
Dax Fredericks? Sounded like a porn name. But it would be
tacky to point that out, wouldn't it? "Great to meet you.
Thanks for the kind words. Celia, I didn't realize you were taking engineering classes." The story was that she was pursuing a
master's degree in business administration. So I was interested
to know exactly how transportation science fit in.

Now she looked uncomfortable. Something was definitely

going on. "I'm taking this as an elective. Steven is one of the most dynamic speakers on campus. And, of course, I'm a supporter of his research foundation."

Did she just say Steven? This gets more interesting by the minute. "Chi-Wind? That's one of the things I'm here to talk to him about. So if you'll excuse me? Great to see you." I stepped into the aisle before turning back to watch her and Dax exit together, heads close together in conversation. My urge to follow them was superseded by my urge to talk to Dr. Williams. Heading down the steps, a few students stopped me to say hello and let me know how much they enjoyed VNN. I murmured politely and made the appropriate responses, feeling like it was taking forever to get down the aisle. One student stepped out in front of me.

"Hey, do you know you're on YouTube today?"

That stopped me in my tracks. "I beg your pardon? Me?"

"You are Christina Brinsley from VNN, right?"

"Yes."

"Yep, it's you. Someone posted a video of you throwing water on Dante Esteban in a restaurant last night."

Damn this new media generation. Was nothing private? "Oh." Weak, I know, but it was the best response I could come up with on no notice.

"Wanna see?" Before I could answer yea or nay, the student had shoved his phone in my face. And sure enough, there I was in high-def. Sip, smile, splash, exit. For the whole world to see.

A young girl pushed her way through the students who now hovered around me. "Hey, did you really throw him out naked in the rain?"

Well, double damn. I had forgotten what came before the smile-n-splash. "I might have."

"A man who looks like that? Really?!"

Okay, enough of that. "Pardon me, guys. I have to interview Professor Williams."

"Cool! Have you seen him naked, too?"

As much as I wished the world to just swallow me up right then and there, I dug into my reserves of patience. "I'm interviewing him about his research foundation." See how I did that? Answered the question without answering the question—I had skills. I had paid my dues and made my way to the top (sort of) of my profession...if I could just act like it!

"Can we YouTube the interview?"

"No, you cannot, and since I just expressly forbade it, if you do—that's a problem." I threaded my way through and continued toward Steven.

When I reached the edge of the stage I looked up. Steven looked at me with no expression on his face at all. But his eyes...they spoke volumes. They were currently hazel. They said both "hello, glad to see you" and "why the hell are you here—go away" all at the same time. And I became nervous. Something that hadn't happened to me in years. I had interviewed all manner of celebrities, politicians, and bigwigs in my day, but walking up five short stairs with Dr. Steven Williams's eyes on me had my stomach in knots and my pulse skittering.

He didn't move a muscle as I strolled in a deceptively casual fashion toward him. He was perched just as casually on the edge of a tall stool with his arms crossed. When I was a foot away, I stopped and drank him in without guile. He wore flat-front gray slacks paired with a polo-style gray cashmere sweater. I noted the quality of both items before allowing my eyes to travel up to his face.

He had a brow raised at my bold head-to-toe appraisal, and the slightest shadow of a smile was chasing around the corners of his mouth.

I allowed a grin to spread across my face. Whatever thoughts or feelings he had about me, I was happy to see him. So happy to see him here, successful and well—doing exactly what he set out to do.

He stood up to his full height. "Of all the classrooms in all the world, she had to walk into mine..."

"Here's looking at you, Dr. Williams."

We stood still, sizing each other up in silence for a few more moments until we realized that the remaining students in the auditorium were all focused on us. Frankly, I was tired of having an audience for all the moments of my life. Something about the energy between me and Steven—it was a palpable, living, breathing thing. And apparently everyone could see it.

"My office." He turned and picked up a cognac-colored leather messenger bag. Without looking back to see if I followed, he slung the bag over his shoulder and exited through the back door.

Guess that puts me in my place. Hustling, I followed behind him.

17

You're Not the Same

Striding out of the building with Christina Brinsley following me, I was overcome by the most surreal feeling. It was as though I was still there, walking briskly and not saying a word, while a whole other me was witnessing this and bouncing up and down, asking, "Can you believe this?"

Christina Brinsley. If she was still Brinsley. I knew she was using it as her professional name, but for all I knew, she could be married with children by now. Though the way she ate me up with her eyes, I felt bad for the man if he existed. The vibe between her and me screamed "unfinished business."

I had been contacted by a man at VNN wanting background on Chi-Wind and the missing government funds. It never occurred to me that they would send Christina. And why hadn't it? If I had given this the slightest amount of thought, then maybe I would have been the slightest bit prepared to see her standing, gorgeous as ever, in my classroom. Just like that, there she was.

Crossing the quad to my office building, I calculated that I had about five minutes to figure out how I felt about seeing

Christina again. On the one hand, this woman had very casu-ally, almost callously, rejected the offer of any sort of relation-ship with me, boarded a plane, and never looked back. Not a call or an e-mail out of her in five years. On the other hand, she'd done me a huge favor. Thanks to those five days way back when, I wasn't willing to settle for any less than what I'd felt with her. I did not have to worry about being distracted by the women I met in New York. I was kind, even generous, but I never made promises or gave my heart. I stayed on the grind, working two jobs, carrying heavy class loads and never taking the summer off. So I guess I owed thanks to Christina. I was so focused, I finished my program in half the time and was able to quickly establish myself in the industry that interested me that much sooner.

It was actually a finance genius that I met at the party for Yung T hosted by Repo Records that Christina had taken me to that assisted me in launching the research foundation and getting it attached to this university and aligned with govern-ment sponsorship. That, plus the contacts I had made back in my delivery days put me ahead. So in a twisted act of fate, I had Christina to partially thank for my current success.

I didn't know how I felt about that either. What I did know was that she still looked *good*. A little tired but good nonetheless. It was clear she kept up her gym visits. Her skin had that same Hershey's Kiss glow. And whatever the hell that thing was between us that made me want her naked and will-ing under me...that was still there. I was still susceptible. Dammit.

Entering building 4, I turned left and climbed the stairs two at a time. Reaching the third floor, I marched to the end of the hallway only to find two students camped out. One was Sarah, an adoring young freshman who was clearly out of her depth in the engineering program and looked to me as some sort of savior. The other was Jeffrey, a grad student who re-minded me very much of myself at his age.

"No office hours today, guys. Is it crucial?"

Jeffrey spoke first. "I wanted to talk to you about my thesis."

"I was hoping to volunteer at your foundation," Sarah added softly.

I nodded at both of them. "Come by Monday between eight and ten and we'll talk about it." Unlocking my office door, I waved Christina inside.

Sarah still hovered in the hallway, looking from me to Christina and back.

"Is there something else, Sarah?"

"Um, no. Have a good weekend." One more glance and she scurried off down the hallway.

With a sigh, I closed the door. Locking it, I leaned back against it and just spent a minute adjusting to the fact that Christina Brinsley was in my office. Life was funny.

"Someone has a crush," Christina said softly.

I shrugged. "It happens."

"You never cut your hair." Her eyes swept over me again.

I shrugged. "I've developed a bit of a Samson thing with it."

"So . . . how long have you been teaching here, Professor?" Her lips curled upward as she pronounced the last word. "It thrills me to call you that. It really does."

"It thrills me to hear it." We shared a smile. The list of people who knew exactly how long and hard the road was from S. Dub to Dr. Williams was a short one. But she was on that list.

"So how long have you been at Bayside?"

"I'm in my second year."

Her eyes flashed with something unhappy. "You've been back in San Francisco for two years?",

"You sound surprised." She actually sounded hurt. I found that surprising and ironic.

"I told you to call me when you finished school."

"You told me a lot of things." A little something slipped out in my tone there, but I kept my face neutral. I was not that guy begging in the airport anymore.

She took a step backwards. "You *cannot* still be angry with me?! Look at you. Look how things turned out for you." She whirled around in a circle, gesturing to the interior of my office.

More than anything, I did not plan to have this conversation with her right now. "I'm not mad, Christina. How have you been?"

She tilted her head in a way that took me back. It reminded me of a moment when she and I were arguing over tacos near Chelsea Piers in New York. She wanted pork; I thought the chicken was a better bet. Funny how things like that come back to you. "Okay, Steven. I've been okay."

"No Mr. Christina?"

"Absolutely not."

Well, that was worded strongly. "Absolutely not?"

"Definitively not," she reiterated firmly.

"Still all about the no muss, no fuss?"

"It works for me."

"Interesting." I nodded and moved past her to my desk. I sat behind it and motioned to the chairs in front. She sat down.

"That's interesting to you? Where is Mrs. Dr. Williams?"

"Yet to be discovered."

"I see."

I sighed. We could be here all day talking around each other. "You see what?"

She rested her chin on her hand and blinked.

"You know, I've seen you use that trick on unwitting subjects in your interviews. But I'm immune to that one, Ti-Ti."

At the nickname, visible color stole across her cheeks. Apparently, I wasn't the only one feeling that chemistry thing. "You're immune to me?"

I set myself up for that one. "I'm immune to that particular trick in your arsenal."

"Is this war?"

"Never."

She met my gaze for a few beats more. "You're not the same."

"I'm not twenty-six anymore, no."

"It's not just the maturity. You've got an edge now."

"An edge?"

"Yes, like what you did just now. Five years ago you would have answered me straight, instead of deflecting the question so I had to clarify my meaning. Even though you and I both know that you catch my meaning. You have a harder shell now."

"Don't most of us have on a little more protective gear? You're pretty much the same, but maybe a little more withdrawn. Just a little more calculating." I didn't say it in a mean way, just as a matter of fact.

"I've had to fight to protect myself," she said quietly, and I wondered who she was protecting herself against. Everybody? Men? The world?

Well, I'd learned a lesson or two myself. "And I've had to learn not to give pieces of myself away."

She leaned back. "That was my fault?"

"Not completely. It was a lesson that I had to learn. So thanks for that."

"You don't sound grateful."

I wasn't. "How do I sound?"

"I'm not sure. I can't read you now."

Five years was a long time. "And?"

"I'm not sure I like it." A slight frown line appeared in the middle of her forehead.

"Well, I'm not standing in the airport begging you to give me a chance anymore. Maybe that's what you don't like?" I kept my tone deliberately light.

"Um...ouch?"

"Too much truth?"

"Too much anger."

"I told you. I'm not angry, Christina."

"So you say." She clasped her hands together in front of her and crossed one leg over the over. "So this thing..."

"This thing?"

She sent me a glowering look that I remembered all too well. "The zingy thing between you and me. That makes us banter and crackle around each other."

"Ah, yes. That thing."

"Is it going to get in the way? Tell me now, because I really need your help with this investigation."

She, on the other hand, had not changed very much at all. "Still have your priorities in order, huh?"

"This is important to me," she snapped.

"And it's still all about you, huh?"

"You know, for someone who swears they aren't angry, you do seem to be getting some zingers in."

She had a point. I might have a little hold-over resentment. In my experience, women were generally extremely interested in being whatever I wanted them to be. She was the only one to walk away...without a glance back. "We'll chalk it up to a young man's slightly bruised ego. It won't get in the way."

I must not have sounded too convincing. "I can get the channel to assign someone else if you'd be more comfortable."

I wasn't even trying to play games with Christina. I would not be giving her the satisfaction of knowing how she affected me. "Sister, you can dial back that melodrama. I have no problems working with you. We cool?"

"Yeah, brother, we cool."

"Anything else?"

"So we keep this strictly professional?"

Down this road again? I wasn't that guy anymore, and she needed to understand that...now. In one motion, I was out of my chair, around the desk, and had her up and in my arms. Before attacking her lips with mine, I realized she smelled the same. Like vanilla frosting over something fruity. It threw me, sapping the anger from my spirit and leaving nothing but the want. The reality of that scent rising from her skin unsteadied me to the point that my lips gentled as they settled against hers. With either a sigh or a gasp, her lips opened and I slid my tongue into her mouth. Her hands slipped around my neck and I tightened my arms around her waist. We both groaned. It felt like... coming home. Coming home after a long, lonely journey and finding it just as warm and welcoming as ever.

We let our lips and tongues rediscover each other slowly, then eagerly, then frantically. Like two parched souls long banished to the wilderness, we tried to slake our thirst for the taste of each other. Our tongues teased and tickled and slipped and slid against each other. And it still wasn't enough. I growled in frustration and she answered with a shudder that ran the length of her taut body.

Fighting against the need to go further, faster, now! I set my hands on her waist and lifted my head. In a move that felt way too comfortable for my liking, I rested my forehead against hers and took in deep gasps of air.

"Dammit, that still works." Her voice was achy with longing. The sound of it had me considering tossing her on the desk and just getting it out of our systems. Scratching the itch for once and for all. But I was smarter now, right? Wiser? I had an edge or a shell or whatever it was she called it. Tempting. Very, very tempting. *Pull it together, Dr. Williams.*

I cleared my throat. "Yeah, that still works well. So no more of that strictly professional bullshit, okay? I think we'll get along fine if we keep things as real as possible. Let's not play games with each other. We'll just try not to label things and put them in a box." I released her and moved back around the desk. No way was I going to sit in this office with six surfaces I could take her on, and calmly talk about wind energy and cross-country rail systems. "So, how about you come out to the Chi-Wind offices a week from Sunday around eleven in the morning and we'll get started with what you need for your story."

I would be lying if I didn't say that I was pleased to see that she looked a little unsteady and more than a little unsure about what just happened. The upper hand was something I had never enjoyed with Christina. I had to savor it for a moment.

The expression on her face was part confusion, part resignation, and all sexy. "You have most definitely changed, S. Dub. For the better or worse remains to be seen." She came around the desk and reached across me. She plucked one of my business cards from the holder. As she retreated, she caught my earlobe in her teeth, biting lightly and licking before backing away. Evil. She remembered that was a quick and easy way to get me ready to go in an instant. "See you next Sunday. I'll e-mail you for details."

With a wave she was out the door and gone before I even moved out of the chair. Damn, she retook the upper hand in less than thirty seconds. Truthfully, I wasn't entirely sure how I felt about that.

18

This Could Be Bad

Christina—Sunday, October 19, 3:43 p.m.

"So the high-speed rail in Spain is wind powered?" I asked Steven as we sat at my dining room table. We had spent the better part of the day at his foundation offices in San Jose. I was impressed. No, I was blown away. In a few hours I had learned more about trains that went over 110 mph than I ever expected. Dr. Williams was a great teacher.

I don't know why I was surprised, but I was. I was also seriously pleased that we fell back into our easy conversational cadence that we'd had in New York. When I first saw him at the university, he seemed so guarded and angry. That was replaced with something else today. Professionalism, openness and an unknown tinge of something else I couldn't put my finger on.

The Chi-Wind Foundation was housed in a two-story, postmodern building in the heart of Silicon Valley. Surrounded by global technology companies, the foundation was in a wind- and solar-powered building made entirely of recycled and refurbished materials. The final product was a brick-and-glass, sloped structure that resembled a pyramid rounded at the bottom and turned onto its side.

The interior was no less impressive and included state-of-the-art research and development facilities, a computer lab dedicated to simulating train movement, and even a small-scale railcar and track system. It was, in a word, aweinspiring.

After touring the facilities and getting an overview of the project, I met a few of the staff members, including his chief operating officer / business partner, Lance Porter. Lance was the finance guy. He resembled JFK Jr. in both looks and charisma. He knew Steven from Columbia. After scheduling a later time for me to speak with Lance, we headed back to my house to discuss the investigation in private.

"Yes, Arizona is working on one using solar power. Just about every power option associated with these trains cuts carbon emissions, so you also have to factor in the importance of creating green jobs and reducing the greenhouse effect."

Wow. Smart was the new sexy. And he just displayed a whole lot of smart there. Another sentence came out of his mouth, but I was too busy watching his lips form the words to concentrate on what was coming out of them.

"Christina? Are you listening to me?" Steven waved his hand in front of my face.

I blinked and looked down at my notes. "I got it. So your major focus is on how to make this all work?"

The slow smile that spread across his face told me that I hadn't fooled him, not one bit. He leaned back in the chair and folded his arms, causing the cotton T-shirt to stretch across his chest. He had on a pale green T-shirt and khaki pants. In the past five years, Dr. McGreen Eyes had developed a fierce six-pack, thighs of steel, and an impressive set of guns. I liked the sculpted, grown-man vibe he was giving me.

Christina, you have got to get your head out of his pants. I flushed a little at my own thoughts. I didn't mean it like that.

He was still speaking. "My job is to review the engineering it will take to make this system work nationwide using the existing railroad infrastructure."

"Oh, but I thought you once told me that your dream was to build light-rail."

"So you were listening?" I wondered what he would think if he knew I remembered every single moment we spent together.

"I was listening. Go on—what changed?"

"I had to grow up and learn a thing or two. You can't build light-rail across mountains and rivers and deserts."

"So where does the funding for all this research come from?"

"The initial influx was part of a government stimulus package under President Obama. States have to match the funds. More government money is solicited and then private entities also contribute."

"And who tracks the spending?"

He raised his arms in a "who knows?" gesture. "That's where I step out. Lance Porter, who you met earlier, handles all the money and politics. I just do the research and spit out my findings into reports that people read. Every now and then I show up at a dinner or a banquet or a seminar, share my vision of the future, and checks get written."

That gave me pause and all of a sudden I wondered if this was a much bigger story than one congressman skimming funds to enhance his lifestyle. The journalist in me woke up. "So how do you know if the money you are spending on research and payroll and the beautiful office building in San Jose is good money or bad money?"

"You lost me. What is good or bad money?"

"How do you know where the money comes from?"

"I don't."

"Doesn't that bother you?"

"It didn't until right this minute. What are you implying?"

"I'm not implying anything...yet. So you are paid by the university, right?"

"Right."

"And you also draw a salary from the foundation?"

"Yes."

"And there's no conflict?"

"What kind of conflict? I teach what I research and re-search what I teach—yes. But I also teach numerous engineer-ing principles that have nothing to do with high-speed rail. I don't think I like where you're going with this." He pushed back from the table and stood up. He started pacing. His ex-pression said he was mulling over all of this in his mind and was not happy about his conclusions.

I stood up, too. "Wait. I'm absolutely not accusing you of anything, but money is missing. Somewhere between Wash-ington and San Francisco, millions of dollars are gone. Are you the least bit concerned that your foundation may be a part of that?"

He paced along the length of the bar separating the kitchen and the living room. "Christina, there are literally hundreds of foundations and state-run agencies that received funding. Why are you so sure that my company is involved?"

"I'm not. But yours is one in the district that Congressman Walker represents. So it stands to reason..."

He sat back down with a sigh. "This could be bad."

I nodded. "But it could be good. What if we find out that Chi-Wind should actually be receiving more funds?"

"We?"

Without thinking about it, I sat down in his lap. "C'mon, Steven. You have as big if not bigger a stake in getting to the bottom of this as I do. We can help each other out here."

He put his hands on either side of my waist, lifted and turned me so I was facing him with my legs straddling his. Instinctively, I put my arms across his shoulders and leaned in. His voice was a husky rumble when he spoke.

"Don't think I don't know what you're doing, Ti-Ti."

"What am I doing?"

"You're playing me."

"I am *not!*" Maybe I was, just a little bit.

He scooted my hips closer. "You ARE. But it's okay because I'm cosigning. You need me for access to information for your story. I need you to make sure my foundation isn't entangled with anything grimy. Just be aware..." He canted his hips upward.

Hmm, he had learned a trick or two in the last few years. Like ways to turn up the heat with very little effort. I liked it. I liked the slow hum of attraction and arousal that buzzed along my veins. And I suddenly wondered if this feeling wasn't what I had been chasing with my FwBs. He shifted again, aligning the hardest part of him with the softest part of me. I struggled to recall what we were talking about as my hips started circling of their own accord. The conversation seemed far less important than how quickly he would put his hands on me.

"Be aware of what?" I asked impatiently. Work Christina was ready to shut down and let Sex Kitten Christina take over. My lips parted and my eyelids felt heavy.

He circled his hips in the opposite direction from mine, creating an impossibly addictive sensation. "Be aware that the relationship is a separate thing."

The word "relationship" was like a splash of cold water. My eyes popped open and I tried to raise myself up off of him. His hands tightened on my hips, keeping me in place. My eyes narrowed. "Relationship? I don't do relationships."

With a flash of white teeth, his smile came and went. "So I hear."

"I beg your pardon?"

"Your little YouTube adventure spawned a fleet of responses. Apparently you do just about everyone and everything else *but* relationships. But I'm not Dante Esteban, sweetheart."

"I never thought you were." As if I could ever confuse the two!

"Just making sure you can keep all your men straight. You've been through a few since I last spent time with you."

Okay, that smarted. New Grown Man Steven was more than edgy, he was mean. He had verbal weapons and he knew how to use them. "Don't you dare judge me!"

"Oh, I'm not judging you. I personally like a woman with a little worn tread on the tires...just a little, though. Just enough to make it interesting. But I'm not down to be your bed buddy."

Did this ninja just say I had worn tread *on my tires?* I wasn't sure I liked Grown Man Steven, no matter how hot he was. "I don't recall asking you to bed me, Steven."

One of his large hands spread across my back, snaking up to my neck. My body had a mind of its own, leaning into his touch, my nipples beading into points. I shivered as his hand brushed across my chest. I arched my back and he pressed his lips to the front of my shirt, nipping at the tight buds through the layers of shirt and bra. I hitched forward.

He lifted my T-shirt and nipped again. "Yet. You didn't ask me yet. Why even play the game? You know you want this."

I was a quivering moist bundle of nerves writhing away on his lap. No way could I pretend to be unaffected. I shifted so he could tease the other nipple. But I was not so blinded by lust that I had completely lost my mind. "I do want you. I want you urgently right now, in all kinds of freaky, worthy ways. But I do *not* want a relationship...ever."

He lifted my bra up and sucked the bare tip of my breast into his mouth. "Not even with me?"

"Oh my God! Not even with you."

He had a way of nibbling, with teeth and tongue alternating flicks and strokes, that completely set me aflame. "You sure?"

"That's not fair." What was it about him that made me lose all manner of resolve? I had always been a very sexual being, but he had a way of amplifying my need.

He sucked harder and tilted his pelvis at an angle that rubbed him against me in exactly the right spot. "Who said I had to play fair?"

I pressed harder against him, craving the friction. "Steven, I can't. You're gonna make me..."

"Go ahead, baby, take what you need." He opened the waistband of my pants and slipped two fingers inside. Without hesitating he stroked into my moisture, making sure his thumb and knuckles dragged against my nubbin. His mouth kept time with his fingers and within seconds I convulsed against him. He stroked me through it, sending aftershocks and tingles through me. Finally, I calmed and struggled to take in air. He righted my bra, pulled my T-shirt down and stroked my back.

I leaned into him, placing kisses along his neck and jaw. I had reached release while he was still wired and taut. "Let's do something for you." I reached for the button on his khakis and he caught my hands in his.

"I'm good."

"But you didn't finish!"

"I got what I wanted. I wanted to watch your face and listen to you make those sounds in your throat and feel your honey on my fingers." He lifted his fingers to his nose and sniffed. "I got what I wanted."

Damn, if that didn't make me hot all over again. "Steven, you make me so..."

"Horny, crazy, needy, happy? I get that. You do the same to me."

Happy? Okay, maybe I was happy to be around him. I really was, and it wasn't just the superior orgasms he seemed to be able to pull from my body at will. "You also kind of terrify me. I don't want a relationship. History shows that I suck at them. As in epic failure territory. I genuinely like you. I don't want anything to mess that up."

He lifted me off him and stood up. My eyes were drawn to the impressive erection straining for freedom at the front of his flat-front pants. "I'm up here, Christina. Focus. You may not think you want a relationship, but that's what we're getting ready to have. You want the story, the sources, the friendship, the sex? I want a relationship. All or nothing."

"Wait—are you blackmailing me into having a relationship with you?"

"I'm giving you an excuse to do what you really want to do. This way you can tell yourself sweet little lies to make yourself feel better, and we both get what we want."

Grown Man Steven was also kind of arrogant and full of himself. "You think I lie to myself?"

"I think you're in a huge state of denial, but it's sexy on you. Now I gotta go—my sister lives out here now, and I'm expected for dinner." He started gathering his files and laptop.

"Stefani is here?" I couldn't seem to do anything but ask mimicky questions.

"Yes, she's married and her husband was transferred to Walnut Creek a year ago."

As he spoke I realized I didn't know that much about his life now. And I was a little embarrassed that I hadn't asked. "Can we just talk sometime?"

"About the investigation?"

"No, about anything, everything. Just because."

A surprised and pleased smile spread slowly across his face and he seemed for a moment like Younger, Happy Steven. "Anytime you want." He leaned over and kissed me on the forehead. "You better watch out, you're starting to sound like a woman in a relationship."

"But about the investigation..."

"Ha! You could not help yourself. I'll send you over the latest income and expense documents. You can tear into those. There's also a reception in three weeks. It's formal. All of your government liaison, fundraiser, sponsor types will be there. You come with me, chitchat, see what you can see. And you can meet Stefani."

I was dying to ask him if he didn't plan on seeing me for three weeks. But I didn't want to sound pressed. One taste and I was already feenin' for the next hit. Not good if I wanted to keep my emotional distance.

"I can honestly read the thoughts flying across that pretty face of yours. Walk me out and I'll talk to you later."

I walked him to the door. "Do you ever think about the last time you were at my house?" It was the day of the Jay / David meltdown.

He looked around. "I prefer not to. Do you ever hear from him?"

"It got messy there for a minute, but now I'm in a Jay / David-free zone."

"I like the new way you decorated. What did you do, re-place everything he ever touched?"

Insightful. That was exactly what I had done. All the heavy slate tones with cherry and leather pieces had been replaced with shades of blue and green in textured chenilles with teak and bamboo. "Something like that."

He took a strand of my hair and tucked it behind my ear. "Poor baby, just running from memories."

The gentleness of his voice and touch caused tears to well up in my eyes. And I wasn't the crying type. The disconcerting thing was that technically I hadn't really known Steven for a lot of days, but I felt that he knew me better than some members of my own family. I'd have to think about what that meant. For now, I allowed him to cup my neck and draw me closer to him.

"Kiss me good-bye," he whispered against my lips, and my eyes drifted shut.

His lips were soft and firm as they moved against mine. I had thought that Steven was an excellent kisser before, but he had an element of patience and guile now that wasn't there before. It was a feeling of taking it slow, knowing we'd have all the time in the world to explore more later. This kiss was less of a good-bye than an I'll-see-you-later. He sampled and lingered and infused his kisses with a sweet emotion I could not place. With one last press of his lips, he stepped away.

"I'll call you later," he announced before letting himself out and striding down the walkway. He didn't look back, climbing into his navy blue Land Rover and pulling away.

That was how Grown Man Steven made an exit. And I didn't like it at all.

19

I Don't Need This Right Now

Steven—Sunday, October 19, 4:12 p.m.

Starting my car and driving away from Christina's house, I had to wonder if I was just a glutton for punishment. My life was exactly as I wanted it to be right now. Professionally, I was flying. Personally, I was...unencumbered. And I was happy that way. I had neither time nor interest in tap dancing around the dating scene. I hated dating. Over the years, I had become a pro at selecting women who were interested in keeping things fun, light, and superficial. Easy come, easy go. So why this need to insert Christina Brinsley into my life? This was the one and only woman to touch (and break) my heart. What was I doing getting involved with her on any level?

Okay, sure. Christina was fine, smart, accomplished, beautiful, and self-reliant. All things to admire and want in a significant other. But she was emotionally still wounded. I wasn't sure she was any more healed today than she was five years ago. And that didn't bode well.

By the time I passed through the Caldecott Tunnel on my way to Stefani's house in Walnut Creek, I had definitely begun to doubt my own intelligence. Seriously, did I need this right now? I punched on the satellite radio in time to hear Stevie telling me "don't you worry 'bout a thing." I guess we'll see about that. But I listened to some old-school R & B the rest of the fifteen-minute ride.

Stefani married a marketing executive for a large retailer and they had transferred out to the Bay Area a little over a year ago. I was happy to have her near and just as happy to swing by and grab a home-cooked meal from time to time. Though I was a fairly accomplished cook, I didn't see the point of doing it all that often for only one person. Consequently, more often than not, on a Sunday afternoon I found myself pulling up outside her neat, slate blue, two-story home in one of the more affluent suburbs of the East Bay.

Before I could even get up the front path, she swung the door open. "What's wrong?"

I smiled. "Disturbance in the twin force?" We'd always had an uncanny way of knowing when the other was upset, even over the smallest of things.

"You might as well spill it." There was no hiding the fact that Stef and I were twins. Both in action and appearance, we often came across as a matched set. She and I were both tall with slightly square jaws and the green eyes that seemed to skip a generation in the Williams family. She also wore her hair long. Though I worked out to keep a little bulk on my frame, Stefani stayed willowy and thin. Again, luck of the genetic draw. We had the same skin tone, somewhere between a beige and a caramel, and we both had the same impatient streak. Right now, hers was showing. "Just tell me."

I said two words as I walked in the door. "Christina Brinsley."

"The bitter bitch who broke my baby brother's heart?" Okay, I guess she remembered who Christina was.

"Whoa there, sis! 'Bitch' is a strong word. My heart was only bruised a little and you are only seven minutes older. Chill with that." I reached out to give her a hug. Beyond her, I looked through the neatly decorated living room to see Marcus outside on the patio, standing over a grill. "Dare I hope your husband is flaming up a thick slab of red meat for his favorite brother-in-law?"

"Don't try to change the subject. What about the Brinsley bi—girl?"

"What up, Marcus?" I raised my voice and waved. He smiled and waved the grill tongs at me. Marcus was a good, solid brother. A shade under six feet with an eagle eye, a ready smile, and generally pleasant disposition, he was one of the most genuine guys I'd ever met. Marcus had the distinction of being a truly nice guy. He wasn't flamboyant or flashy, didn't fall back or push forward, just a solid man's man who adored the ground my sister walked on. I was glad they'd found each other. He was the kind of guy I would've hung out with even if he hadn't married my twin.

"Steak, bro!" he called out with a smile on his face.

"That's what I'm talking about!" I smiled back. Stefani was a vegetarian and tended to frown on the "slaughter of animals for humans' conspicuous consumption," but Marcus put his foot down. He allowed her to decorate the house in twenty variations of what all looked like tan to me, and she allowed him fish and chicken with rare passes for red meat.

"Steven! I can still serve you a tofu burger, you know. Why are you bringing up that woman's name?" Both Stefani and I tended to get emotional, but she was all dramatic with hers. I tended to play my cards a little closer to the vest; she laid them out for all to see.

"Christina is doing a story on high-speed rail and came to see me at the university a week ago. I took her on a tour of Chi-Wind earlier today; I'm just coming from her house now."

She squinted her eyes at me. "Please, please, please tell me you are not getting involved with her on a personal level again. Please tell me you are keeping things professional."

I paused and then turned to walk into her monochromatic

kitchen. Reaching into the fridge, I pulled out a beer and set it on the countertop.

"At least tell me you haven't already unzipped and fallen on top of that woman in a week?!"

"You're gonna have to stop calling her 'that woman' and yes, I stayed zipped." That was true—I had stayed zipped. Christina on the other hand . . . well, some things a sister, even a twin sister, didn't need to know.

"Steven, I swear to God . . . do not let that—her—back in. You spent five days with her five years ago, and she completely spun your head around. Just don't get involved. You don't need this."

I sighed. "I know. I really do know. I don't need this. Not at all. I'm not even sure I want this. Whatever this is. But something about her, Stef . . . she attracts me, you know? There's a connection that hasn't gone away in all these years. I have to at least try to get her out of my system."

"Yeah, people say that about crack, too. It rarely works out well." Her tone was brittle and harsh. Not good. She was generally a sunny-outlook person.

I turned toward the back patio and held up the beer bottle in the universal "want one?" gesture to Marcus. He nodded. I retrieved another beer before I answered. "I know you don't like her because of the things I told you about her back in the day. And it's true, she and I didn't part on the best terms. But that's water under the bridge."

"Is it? Or are you trying to prove something?"

She had a valid point. "I don't know. But, Stef, you're going to have to try to be civil."

"Why? Why do I have to try to be anything at all? If you're just scratching an itch, I don't need to know anything about it. I don't need to see her."

"She's coming to the fundraiser . . . with me."

"Dammit, Steven!" She smacked me upside the head with the back of her hand.

"Hey!" It hurt a little bit.

Marcus stuck his head in the door. "Leave the boy alone and let him bring me my beer, woman."

"Marcus, mind your business," she replied.

"My beer is my business and you're keeping it from me. Come on, Steven. She can lecture you anytime—come take a look at these porterhouse I got sizzling."

I lowered my voice. "It'll be fine, Stef. You'll see. I've got it all planned out. No need to worry about me." I kissed her forehead and picked up the beer.

"That'll be the day," she muttered under her breath as I walked away.

Everything was going to be just fine.

20

More of a Lady

Christina—Saturday, October 25, 1:36 p.m.

"Christina, just try the pink dress on," my mother said from outside the dressing room in Macy's.

"Mom, when was the last time you saw me wear baby pink?" I asked from behind the door. Once every few months, Mom and I came to the Macy's at Union Square for a mother-daughter shopping pilgrimage followed by lunch on Nob Hill. It was inevitably a long and somewhat trying day. I loved my mother, adored her in fact, but we did not have the same tastes, ideas, or opinions. Especially not about me. We did not agree on what was best for me at all.

Joanna Brinsley believed that a career was what you had until you caught a husband. So my three failed attempts to make it to the altar, coupled with my continued rise at the network, completely exasperated her.

"Pink is such a feminine color, Christina—it wouldn't hurt you to soften up your image a little bit. Men like women who aren't afraid to show softness and vulnerability."

Behind the door, I rolled my eyes and sent up a prayer for patience. This was how it started. It was easier to give in and try on an overly girlish, pink knee-length sheath dress with pleated ruffles than have her start the Joanna Brinsley Lecture Series on "How Christina Can Catch and Keep a Man." I set aside the chocolate, dolman-sleeve sweaterdress that I already knew I was buying and pulled the pink monstrosity over my head. Turning back to look at my reflection in the mirror, I bit back a groan. All I needed was a string of pearls and some matching ballet flats and I was ready to join lunching soccer moms in Pleasanton. Yes, there's an actual suburb of San Francisco called Pleasanton. And yes, it's quite pleasant there.

"Well, let me see it!" she said excitedly.

Gritting my teeth, I opened the dressing room door. "Here it is."

"It's perfect." She clapped. "Maybe with some pearls and the right shoes?"

"Ballet flats?" I asked sardonically.

"Christina, you cannot catch a man in flats. How many times have I told you that? Some slingbacks with a nice heel to them should do it. Do you have a pair?"

"I do." I knew better than to argue. The pink dress would be worn once at a family gathering and then donated to a charity, never to be seen again. I had the drill down pat. I also knew how to deflect before she went in search of a matching pink cardigan. "Mom, shouldn't we get your formal for the breast cancer awareness banquet coming up?"

She lit up in the way that I remembered. It took so little to make her happy. "Yes, if you're sure we're done with you."

"What more could I need?" I asked, tongue in cheek.

She gave me a look. "I'm not completely clueless. I know you don't love the dress, but it will grow on you. Some things I actually know more about than you, Miss Thing."

I had to laugh. "Did you just call me Miss Thing?"

She giggled. "I must have heard it somewhere, but it suits you."

I resisted the eye-roll and shut the door. "Let me change and we'll go up a floor to find your formal."

"It's so nice when we spend a little girl time together, Christina. We should do this more often."

"We should," I agreed. With a smile, I kept that sentiment for the next hour and a half while we shopped and eventually found her a perfect ensemble for her event. The sentiment held as we headed to the top floor to grab a meal from The Cheescake Factory. Too hungry to go to Nob Hill. But it started sliding away as we sat perusing menus. She launched a sneak attack.

"So did you call Kenneth?"

"Who?"

"Kenneth, the young man I wanted you to meet."

"No, Mom, I didn't."

"Why not, Christina? You are not getting any younger, and I just saw this study about single, educated black women and the shrinking pool of suitable men."

I prayed silently that Jesus would appear in the form of two extra-strength Tylenol and a shot of vodka for me right this minute. Like I hadn't read the articles and blog posts? She had forwarded at least two to me in the last month alone. What could I do or say to get out of this conversational wormhole? Swinging for the fences, I announced, "Mom, I'm already seeing somebody."

"What? Who? Not that Dante character who was so crass?"

"No, Mom, not Dante Esteban. His name is Steven Williams and he's a professor at Bayside University."

"Oh, a professor! Tenured?"

"No, he's a little young for that." Oops, I let too much slip out there.

Her eyes narrowed. "How young is he?"

"Thirty-two."

She tilted her head to the side, considering. "That's not too bad, actually. Maybe a younger man with a little swagger is what you need."

"Seriously, did you just say 'swagger'?"

"I saw it on an Oprah rerun. She was interviewing Jay-Q."

"Jay-Z?"

"You know who I meant. Anyway, maybe if you had a man who was more of a man, you would be more of a lady."

My mouth opened and closed twice on that one. "I need a man to show me how to be a lady?"

"Don't get dramatic. I just mean someone you can't take the lead with, or control, or walk over."

"Is that what you think happened in the past?"

"Christina, let's not get into all that unpleasantness."

"No, you brought it up. Are you telling me that the reason Cedric married his high school sweetheart, Perry turned out to be gay, and Jay / David turned out to be a pathological liar is because I wasn't enough of a lady?" I could physically feel my blood pressure rising.

"A man needs to feel like a man, Christina. That's all I'm going to say on the subject."

I blinked at her twice.

"I used that double blink on your father, Christina. It doesn't work on me. I'm sorry you don't agree with my assessment. If it makes you feel any better, you can just tell yourself that I don't know what I'm talking about, like you usually do."

"Mom, I do not."

"Honey, you most certainly do think your mother is a flighty, flaky woman, but that's all right. I love you in spite of your flaws."

I wasn't sure if I'd just been slapped or stroked. "Umm."

"There comes a time when children think they've learned all they can from their parents. They're wrong, but they think it anyway."

I kinda did think that, but had no idea she realized it. It

gave me pause to realize that my mother was smarter than I thought she was. "Well now . . ."

"That's neither here nor there. I want to hear everything. How did you meet Steven? Where is he from? What does he look like? I know he's handsome—you like them handsome. Who are his people and when are you bringing him around? What did you wear on your first date? I hope you curled your hair."

Now this was the Joanna I was used to. I signaled the waiter we were ready to order while I gave her an abridged and edited (okay, somewhat fabricated) version of how, where, and why I came to know Steven Williams.

21

Just Tell Me How It Works

Steven—Wednesday, October 30, 4:47 p.m.

I was in my office at the foundation with Christina on the speakerphone. I hadn't seen her since the day we toured the foundation several days back. I was keeping a professional distance while getting to know her a little bit again.

It was slow going; each of us was wary of the other. She didn't trust men in general and I did not trust her, specifically. It made for a lot of guarded conversation. On her part, Christina made it clear she was interested in getting the story and getting our freak on. I was curious to see what (if anything) else was there. It would be interesting to see which of us got what we wanted first.

"Did you find the financial reports yet?" she asked me.

I rifled through the folders on the top of my desk. "I found the public statements we released to contributors, but I haven't found the detailed statements to back these numbers up yet. I'm just going to ask Lance to explain it to me."

"Well, good luck with that. He kinda talked around the details when I tried to interview him. I couldn't get past the spin."

"Okay, well—he plays wary with the press, so don't worry about it. Did you get the information on the Arizona plans?" We had been working to put together an overview of each state's future rail plans and how they were being consolidated for a nationwide program. This consolidation was part of what my foundation was funded to do.

"Yes, I got them, but some of this is too much engineer-speak for me. I'll need you to translate some of the technical terms into phrases the general public will understand."

"I can do that."

"Maybe you can swing by this evening and do that for me?"

I smiled. "Is that what you want me to come by and do for you? Really, Christina?"

She sighed. "I'm just saying. We have a lot of work to do; you might as well come by so we can do it together."

I laughed. "Are you making these double entendres on purpose?" I wasn't about to fall into the sex trap with Christina. I knew once we went there again, it would be hard to focus on anything else.

"What do you think?" Her voice was silky.

"I think you're playing games again. Listen, I know what you want. Please believe I have every intention of giving it to you. But on my timeline, in my way, okay?"

"So I see. Might I remind you that you are the one who wanted some sort of relationship? It's hard to relate without actually seeing each other."

She almost spat the word "relationship" like a curse, confirming for me that slower was better. "I think we're relating just fine. Not everything's a sprint, Christina. Some things are cross-country endurance."

"Sounds painful, tiring, and tedious."

She was trying to provoke a fight. Looking up, I saw Lance approaching my office. "Also really great when you get to the finish line. Listen, Lance is on his way in, so I'll talk to you later."

"Will you see me later?"

"I'll definitely talk to you later." I hung up on her exasperated huff and waved Lance in the door.

Lance came in, looking as always like he was ready for a Ralph Lauren photo shoot. He sat down in the chair by my desk. "Got your message. What's up?"

"It's these financials. I don't see the detailed information to back up the report. Can you tell me where to find it?"

"What?! Steven Williams asking to look at spreadsheets? Who are you and what have you done with Steven?" he joked. Lance had been in the Master of Financial Management Services program at Columbia. We met picking up the same woman for a date. She had double-booked for the same time and the same day. We were both so underwhelmed by her lack of game that we went out and got a drink. He and I had been friends ever since. Not sure whatever happened to the girl.

My dislike of economics and finance was well-known. I didn't mind doing a calculation to determine load-bearing weight or mass-to-speed ratio, but I had no desire to be a forensic accountant. That's why I had Lance.

"I know, but Christina raised some concerns over the foundation funds and I want to take a look and reassure myself everything is on the up-and-up."

He gave me a look I couldn't interpret.

"What is that look?"

"Christina has concerns, huh?"

I didn't like his tone. "In the course of her investigation, she came across a few things that are cause for concern. What point are you trying to make?"

"I'm saying, this chick hasn't been back in your life but for a hot minute and already she's got you doing backflips. Man, is it that good?"

"Don't even start. It really has nothing to do with her. If I'm going to be the face and mouthpiece of this foundation, I really should pay more attention to the inner workings anyway. Don't you think?"

"I think you're an engineer and you should stick to the engineering and let us handle the rest. That's what you've got us for."

"What about the government funding—are we all good on that? Bases covered?"

"Look, I think your reporter friend is digging up dirt where there's none to be found. It could cast suspicion where none needs to be cast. But at the end of the day, Chi-Wind is clean and we're doing good things here. Give her a few sound-bites, we'll get some good publicity, and then get on with the business of building rail systems."

I nodded. He made sense. "We're so close to making it real."

He got up and clapped me on the shoulder. "Don't sweat the small stuff, Steven. Stay brilliant and we've got your back. But seriously, tread lightly with the woman. I don't know if at the end of the day she has your best interests at heart."

He wasn't the first and probably wouldn't be the last person to tell me that. So I answered him in all honesty. "I'm a big boy now—I'm watching my back. This is just a thing with us; we both know what it is."

"You know," Lance said on his way to the door, "I would feel a whole lot better if that wasn't exactly what you said five years ago in New York. We both know how that turned out."

He had me there. "Different time, different mind-set, but thanks for the concern. I got this."

"I hope so."

I did, too.

How It Continued

22

Girls' Night In

Christina—Saturday, November 6, 10:03 p.m.

"You're just being nice because you want to get in my pants," I whispered into my cell phone. I was over at Carey's house for girls' night. Carey's condo was bohemian chic with African influences. It was very Berkeley-wild-child-meets-New-York-sophisticate. Overstuffed natural fiber chairs meshed with traditional pieces. Ebony played well with Brazilian cherry and bright jewel tones layered on her base color of chocolate. It should have been jarring, but it worked.

We had been huddled around the long tumbled-marble bar, refreshing our cocktails, when Steven called. True to his word, he called. He texted, he tweeted, he stayed in touch, but I hadn't laid eyes (or anything else) on him since he strolled away several days ago. I found myself in the strange position of eagerly awaiting his calls. Steven gave good conversation. I was curled up on the chaise lounge in Carey's guest room with my BlackBerry pressed to my ear.

"I'm being nice because I'm generally a nice guy. I've already been in your pants, if you recall?"

"You *used* to be a nice guy. Now you're edgy with a mean streak."

"Baby, ain't I been good to you?"

"Oh, now you wanna go South Side Chicago on me. Okay, I see you. The point is—I was terrible today. That was the worst I have been on camera in a while."

"And I'm telling you... you're way too critical of yourself. It was a two-minute interview and you came across as classy as you could... given the circumstances."

Earlier in the day, I was put in the unenviable position of getting interviewed by my own news channel. That stupid YouTube video of me splashing Dante had gone viral. And Dante, never one to shun the spotlight, had been milking it for all it was worth, calling me the one true love of his life and the only thing he ever wanted that he couldn't have. The story had taken on a life of its own thanks in no good part to Lisa, who was lapping up the opportunity to embarrass me. The entertainment hour had led with a Dante vs. Christina story twice in the past week. I would have squelched it if only the ratings weren't so high. But thankfully the Js stepped in and said enough is enough. As long as I agreed to do an on-air interview, they would make sure that everyone at VNN agreed to let the story die a natural death afterward. And after the bland, generic answers I gave, I expected that to be just the case.

"Well, thanks, I guess."

"I did notice your stumble over the relationship question."

"Yeah, well. You know." When asked if I was in a relationship with someone else, I froze before giving my answer: "Sort of... I'm in the process of figuring that out right now."

"For future reference, the easy and correct answer is: Yes, I am and he makes me very happy."

"I don't see all the happy-making, Professor."

"My phone calls don't make you happy? My e-mails don't make you happy? Or are you the kind of girl who's only happy when she's getting the good-n-plenty on the regular?"

I barked out a laugh and the door swung open. Before I could answer Steven I was confronted by Carey, Lynne, and a very pregnant Jackie glaring me down. "Is it girls' night or giggle-with-your-freak-of-the-week night?" Lynne said... loudly.

"There's no freaking involved. Not this week, last week. He is *so* not my freak of the week," I answered.

His voice, full of laughter, came through the speaker. "Now is the time to give your easy answer. Go ahead. I'll wait."

I rolled my eyes before reciting the words. "I'm in a relationship and he makes me very happy."

"The *hell?*" Carey shrieked.

"With *who?*" Jackie yelled.

"When did *this* happen?" Lynne asked.

"I'm gonna let you handle that. Good luck. Talk to you tomorrow." He hung up.

Why was it I was never getting the last word with this man? Damn, that was irritating. "Ladies, calm down. Let me top off the drink and I'll explain all." My phone buzzed as we walked down the hallway. It was a text from Steven. *Don't think you're getting out of answering that good-n-plenty question. To be continued.*

I texted back. *Unless you want to continue the discussion naked, hold on to it for a minute.* When I looked up, all three ladies were staring me down. Wearing various expressions of interested irritation, they made quite a sight.

Jackie was petite and olive-toned, her normally slim body rounded and in some places bloated from eight long months of pregnancy. Her dark auburn hair was cut into a short, natural curly fro that suited her face. She had stepped away from an executive-level sales job to prepare for motherhood. She was still as outrageous and opinionated as ever.

Lynne was a glamazon of generous proportions. She was over 5'9", had a gleaming caramel complexion and a true hourglass shape. Her store (aptly named Glamazonia) was an upscale boutique for plus-size women. She had riotous chestnut curls pulled back into a ponytail. Currently, her left hand was resting on her shapely size 20 hips. No doubt she had her foot tapping to match. Where Jackie was outrageous, Lynne was emotional. Lynne tended to get defensive when challenged and was a bit of an instigator.

Carey's hair was piled up on her head tonight. She, like the others, was dressed casually in sweats. "What is going on with you?" Carey remained solid, the friend who stood in your corner no matter what. She had a wicked sense of humor, and in this group she was often cast in the role of peacemaker.

"Sorry, I'm done. Muting the ringer now. See?" I set the BlackBerry down on the bar and reached for my wineglass. Circling the counter, I started opening drawers looking for the corkscrew. In the third drawer, something shiny caught my eye. It was an onyx cuff link with the monogram *CTB* etched in swirling platinum. Interesting. My family was full of *CTB*s. Collin Theodore Brinsley and Clarke Thomas Brinsley. I was Christina Violet Tempest Brinsley. I had a good idea which *CTB* this cuff link belonged to. I extracted it and the corkscrew. Uncorking a new bottle of Chardonnay, I topped off my glass.

"I think the real question here, Ms. Jaymes, is what is going on with you and Clarke Thomas Brinsley?" I held up the cuff link with a smirk. Carey shot me the evil eye. I stuck my tongue out. Two could play this game.

"Hold up, let me sit my pregnant ass down." Jackie maneuvered over to a side chair and plunked down. "When do you heffas have time to get all this freaky-sneaky in? Carey has been here less than ten days and has got her entire house unpacked and a Brinsley man in her bed. Christina been all up and through YouTube and television, but somehow landed a new man. I ain't been nothing but fat, bored, pregnant, and hungry. Lynne, what you got going on?"

Lynne's face twisted into a grimace. "None of the fun stuff. Eric and I just started marriage counseling."

Now it was my turn to steal Carey's phase. "The *hell?* You and Eric have always been the most stable couple I know!" Eric and Lynne met just after college and had been together ever since. They complimented each other. Where Lynne was flamboyant and outgoing, Eric was quiet and steady. Lynne was all bright colors, bold opinions, and big picture. Eric was neutrals, no comment, and the-devil-is-in-the-details. In my outside-looking-in opinion, they were a couple to be emulated and envied.

"Yeah, well—that's the problem. Do you realize that this year will mark fifteen years that Eric and I have been together? *Fifteen years.* And the last five have been exactly the same. Day in, day out—same song."

Carey asked the question that I was thinking. "Did you expect it to be all rainbows and fairy tales fifteen years in?"

"We'll get to you in a second, Carey Cufflinks." Jackie put a pillow behind her back and shifted. "I know what Lynne is talking about. Sometimes the everyday grind blurs the good stuff and it's just getting from one day to the next."

I thought that was what marriage was: getting from one day to the next but with somebody who was down in the trenches with you. Then again, what did I know? I had three failed engagements on my relationship record.

Lynne added some chips and salsa to her plate. "Well, neither of us remembers the good stuff. We have nothing to say to each other. The sparks are missing in action; we haven't had sex in months."

"Months?" I squeaked out. First Celia and Collin, now Lynne and Eric. What was with folks going for months without acknowledging the problem? Here I was wondering how I was going to wait another three weeks for Steven.

"We don't all have hot-n-cold running dick on delivery, Christina." Lynne's voice was waspish.

"You know what? I'm not going to be too many more slut references up in here. Let's just all be clear about that. Okay?" Girls or not, some lines just didn't need to be crossed. A short silence fell over the group. With a nod to indicate that I was positive I had been understood, I turned to Carey. "What is the story with you and Middle Brother Brinsley?"

She shrugged. "We're just hanging out."

"What kind of hanging out involves the taking off of cuff links, sister girl?" If anything, Jackie's pregnancy had made her less subtle . . . as if the world needed a less subtle Jackie.

Carey reached for the guacamole before answering. "Not that I need to explain myself to you nosy heffas . . . but it was raining the other night when he brought me home. I put his shirt in the dryer."

Reaching over to dip a chip, I wondered how much of this story I really wanted to hear. Not a whole lot. "Upon further thought, I don't believe we need to hear any more of this story."

"There were no naked aerobics. We're taking our time."

I threw my hands up. "Again, that's plenty. I haven't thought about Clarke naked since he was twelve. I prefer to keep it that way. Please and thank you." Before they started in on me next, I looked over at Jackie. "How's Sam Jr. doing in there?"

Jackie rubbed her belly. "Don't even put it out there. Sam wants to go with Samuel Alvin Hubbert II in the worst way. I see no need to pass all of that along. But to answer your question, Baby Boy Hubbert is restless. He never sleeps, so neither do I. He has taken to showing his displeasure by turning and kicking whatever vital organ he feels like abusing. This child is a bruiser. Future athlete, I'm positive."

Lynne piped in, "And speaking of athletes, Ms. Brinsley . . . have you heard from Dante?" She sent back the smirk I'd sent her way earlier.

"He left a message, but I'm trying to get sleeping dogs to lie."

"So if you're not seeing him, who *are* you seeing?" Carey asked.

Internally, I debated the merits of telling the whole story, part of the story, or as little as possible. I opted for as little as possible. Hell, I didn't really understand exactly what Steven or I were up to. There was no way I could explain it to them. I answered simply, "Steven."

"Steven who?" From Lynne.

"Young delivery Steven from back in the day?" From Jackie.

"Professor Williams?" Carey shrieked. "Seems as though you left a little sumthin' sumthin' out of your interview notes." She turned to the other ladies. "Steven was the delivery dude who was there the day of the Jay / David implosion. He and Christina had a week-long fling in New York City. Christina walked away. Young Steven went on to get a master's and a PhD. He now runs a big deal foundation and is a professor on the tenure track at Bayside. Christina went to interview him for her story on high-speed rail and apparently . . . the old vibe was still there."

Pursing my lips, I set the wineglass down on a coaster to reach for the bottled water. "And now that we have the post-game color commentary all caught up . . . yes, that Steven."

Jackie could be counted on to ask the basic questions. "How old is he?"

"Thirty-two."

Carey would always ask the trivial questions. "Is he still fine?"

"Only improved with time." That might have been the understatement of the night. Steven looked damn good.

And Lynne always brought it back to her. "When can I meet him?"

"There's a reception in a few weeks. Let me see about the

tickets." The minute I said it, I wondered if it was a good idea. Steven and his twin sister, Carey and my older brother, Lynne with her feuding husband. Did I just invite drama where none was needed?

Jackie sighed. "Hopefully in a few weeks I will be spitting out this bambino. I would tell you to take pictures but knowing Christina, there will be a film crew or mobile video at the ready. It'll be high-def on someone's blog before she even gets home. You're such a celebrity chick now."

Carey grinned. "She's big-time."

"Oh, I see you got jokes." I walked over to the media center to pick out a movie.

Lynne piped up, "But it does beg the question—did you throw that man out of bed naked? In the rain? I mean, Dante Esteban is a man I couldn't imagine tossing out of bed for any reason."

"Lynne, you only say that 'cause you're not getting any right now. Without getting too deep into the details, the man was all steak, no salad. All pump, no polish. And every time he hit the track, it was a marathon. Never a sprint. All finish line, no prelim. It was exhausting and somewhat painful. Are you getting my drift?"

Jackie wrinkled her nose. "Eww. What happened to the legend of the Latin lover?"

"Maybe he missed those lessons because his bed game was *no bueno.*" Not good. I held up *Die Hard* and *Lethal Weapon.* "But to answer your question, Lynne: Yeah, I did. One night, a rainy night it just so happened, I was tired and he was not finishing fast enough, and I couldn't do it anymore. I asked him in the nicest way to speed it along. I even attempted to help speed things along. He wasn't hearing me, so I hit the EJECT button. End of story."

Lynne asked, "You literally ejected him?"

I nodded. "Yep, out of me and out of the house."

"You couldn't let Mr. Dante get dressed first?" Jackie asked.

"To put it delicately, he was getting persistent about want-ing to stay, so I chucked his clothes and keys into the street. He was forced to follow them. I gave him a towel. Which he never returned, by the way."

"Wow, I think you've seen the last of that towel. What will it take for him to let it go?" Carey wondered aloud.

"I have no idea. But I wish he would. On to the important stuff: It's action movie nostalgia night, ladies. Which one is it gonna be?"

"*Die Hard*—and we're gonna get the rest of the Steven story before this night is through!"

I smiled at Jackie, but there was a greater chance of Jesus ice-skating in hell than me sharing all the scoop.

23

Meet Stefani

Steven—Saturday, November 20, 11:56 p.m.

My bad. My bad. My bad. I completely underestimated the potential for dramatic foolery that could pop off at the Chi-Wind banquet. I stood sipping a scotch in the presence of two of Christina's former flames. It was an uncomfortable place to be. In hindsight, neither Christina nor I gave people enough credit for their ability to show their natural asses in public. Not literal asses, attitudinal asses.

The night began wrapped in deceptive perfection. I was holding down my cocoa-sexy vibe in a midnight blue tuxedo jacket, crisp white shirt, and black tuxedo pants. Not everybody could pull it off...I managed.

My business partner insisted on ordering a limousine for me. Knowing that I still didn't have a good handle on how the finances were operating, I declined. He insisted it had already been paid for and the money would be wasted if I didn't take it.

Well, I wouldn't want to be wasteful—I was a huge believer in conservation. Grabbing my coat and a wishful-thinking duffel bag, I climbed into the back of the sleek black Lincoln. After chatting briefly, I gave the driver Christina's address. The ride from my loft in the SoMa district of San Francisco to Christina's house was blessedly drama-free. The traffic on the Bay Bridge was relatively light for a weekend evening. I could get used to someone else navigating the crazy traffic.

The moment Christina swung open her front door, I should have known what sort of evening we were in for. You just don't have a woman who looks like that on your arm without inviting some drama. Christina was in a strapless, skin-tight long tube dress in a fabric I'd guess was silk. If I was forced to name the color, I'd call it copper. That chocolate skin and ebony curling hair against that copper dress was stunning. There was a slit up the side of the dress that showed more than a hint of thigh. Her feet were in sky-high green shoes with criss-crossing straps. She looked classy and beautiful. I was con-flicted. A part of me wanted to show her off and another part of me wanted to scoop her up and stay in for the night and the next day and the next night after that... until I'd had my fill. I was suddenly hungry, and not for the seafood bar awaiting us at the banquet.

"Look at you, Ms. Brinsley. You brought out the secret weapons in the arsenal tonight."

Inclining her head, she gestured me inside. "Good evening, Dr. Williams. You are looking rather tasty yourself this evening."

I stepped inside the door and watched while she put on a matching ruffly jacket that wrapped around her, showing off the gym body. "You don't have to cover up on my account."

She reached for a long wool coat in a pumpkin color and a little green purse that looked like an envelope. "I'm not about to freeze so you can get an eyeful, S. Dub." She added her house key and cell phone to the purse. "Ready?"

I was more than ready. Sliding over to her, I moved a long, curly lock of hair to rest on the front of her shoulder. "You know, we could skip this thing. Order in some Italian food, eat in bed..."

The look she gave me was classic disgusted Christina. "Oh,

now you offer up a little bump-n-grind? It took me hours to get ready and you know I have work to do tonight."

"First of all, I was going to make sure you put in the work. Secondly, it wasn't going to be a 'little bump-n-grind.' I was bringing my A-game smash to the table."

"Your A-game smash? Is that a Gen Y euphemism for sex?"

I took her coat off her arm and held it open so she could step in. "You know what I meant. You always do. And reminding yourself of our age difference isn't going to keep you from thinking about me, even when you don't want to."

She looked up at me over her shoulder and I could see the minute she considered my offer to ditch the party and stay home. I could also see the moment she discarded the idea. "You're still a cocky thing."

"You doubt I can back it up?" If nothing else, we had the verbal sparring down to an art.

"I don't doubt you can do anything you put your mind to. Are you ready to go?"

I nodded. "If you're ready, I'm ready."

"Then let's go." She turned back toward the door.

"Oh, and Ti-Ti?"

"Yes?"

"If I don't get a chance to say it later, you look incredible this evening." Her face softened into a smile. I loved the moments when she let her guard down and just allowed herself to feel.

"Thanks, Steven."

Little did we know that the smooth forty-five minute ride down to The Grande Palo Alto Resort and Spa was the last peaceful moment either of us would have for hours.

We had just stepped into the lobby and stowed our coats when a tall, gorgeous woman in a slim-cut halter dress launched herself at me. Catching her, I gave her a hug and winked at Christina over her shoulder. Setting her down, I made introductions. "Christina, meet Stefani."

My twin sister's face, which only moments ago was wreathed in smiles, shifted into almost haughty lines. Her voice was nothing less than icy when she spoke. "So you're Christina." Oh great, she was in protective-sister mode. I forgot she had never really forgiven Christina for the New York walkaway. I may have over-shared some of my anger about that.

And of course Christina picked up on that ice and matched it with considerable frost of her own. "So you're Stefani."

"The one and only."

"A pleasure."

Any second now and I was going to toss some Meow Mix and break for the door. My two favorite ladies did not get along. That could be a problem. And just as I thought it, another problem entered my peripheral vision. Stefani saw it too, and her fake smile turned even more brittle.

"Christina, looks like your boyfriend's here."

Christina looked up at me in confusion. I shook my head and pointed in the other direction. "Sorry, sweetheart, she's not referring to me." I pointed.

Christina turned to see Dante Esteban stepping out of an elevator at the far end of the lobby, complete with fawning entourage and much fanfare.

With a deep sigh, she linked her arm through mine. "Is it too late to take you up on that Italian-food-in-bed offer?"

Two congressmen, a senator, and a governor's aide stepped out of the banquet room. Lance spotted me and called my name. "Steven, a few people I want you to meet."

I squeezed Christina's hand. "Did you ever see the movie *All About Eve,* where Bette Davis has that great line?"

She flung her head back in delighted laughter. "Yes. 'Fasten your seat belts, it's gonna be a bumpy night.'"

"Definitely too late for the bedside Italian." With a final squeeze of our joined hands, we turned toward the drama.

24

Is There *Anyone...*

Christina—Saturday, November 20, 10:17 p.m.

"Senator, may I have a word?" For the record, it was no easy task to pull off professional journalism when you are shrink-wrapped in metallic silk and balancing a flute of champagne in one hand. But for all the hell I was in that evening, I was determined to get something productive out of it.

Not only did one half of the Williams twins hate my guts, I had an ex FwB, two brothers, a girlfriend on the verge of a breakdown, my professional rival, and the senior vice president of Valiant all in one spot. The words "hot seat" took on a whole new meeting.

After Stefani went all bitch-back-off-my-brother mode, Steven and I worked the room. It was exhausting keeping half a room-length between me and Dante and me and Stefani at all times. But that was our clear, unspoken but agreed-upon goal.

Steven impressed me at every turn. During dinner, he gave a brief but powerful speech about the future of transportation and the opportunity to be a part of history that could positively impact lives for generations. It was brilliant. He had the entire room in his thrall.

Our table of twelve held me and Steven; Carey and Clarke; Steven's partner, Lance, with his date; an engineer from China with his plus one; a shipping magnate with a woman who was so obviously not his wife; a former child star who now spent his time backing worthy causes; and a California state representative.

One table over sat my senior vice president, Julie, with her husband; Stefani and her husband, Marcus, (who was far more pleasant than his wife); Collin and Celia; the mayor of San Jose and his wife; two football players and their wives. This was the event to see and be seen in the Bay Area this evening.

Steven handled politicians, millionaires, and my brothers with equal parts grace, charm, and intelligence. We were in the midst of chatting with Julie and the secretary of transportation when I noticed Lynne walk in alone. Nor did she appear to be entirely sober. I gestured to Carey to go check that out.

After the secretary was called away, Julie clasped my hand and squeezed it. "Our presence at this function is a huge win, Christina. Being the only station allowed to film inside the event puts us head and shoulders above the competition."

"Yeah, who'd you have to sleep with to pull that off?" The snarky, slightly nasal voice came from Lisa. Though I had no idea she would be there (I knew I didn't authorize her travel), I wasn't totally surprised to see her. With the number of entertainers and sports celebrities in attendance, it made sense for her to cover the event. Though I had the distinct feeling she was just there to stir up some drama while trying to steal my shine.

Before I could fashion a retort, Steven stepped closer and slung an arm around my shoulder. "I believe I'll be the lucky recipient of those favors whenever Christina is ready to share. Good to see you again, Lisa."

I had completely forgotten that Lisa met Steven way back during our New York Fling Week. From her face, I could tell she had, too. "This is *that* Steven?"

Turning to face him, I looked up and smiled. His eyes were green tonight, and the dark blue of his suit made his skin look absolutely lickable. He grinned down at me with an I-know-what-you're-thinking-and-you-better-stop glint in his eye. A cameraman chose that moment to click and capture. "This is that Steven. All grown-up."

"So I see." Lisa looked from him to me and back again. It was clear she had a million questions. "Are you interviewing him for your story?"

"Yes."

"Isn't this a little pay-for-play, even for you?" Lisa's tone went from silky to downright snarky.

You know, you would think I'd been walking the stroll turning tricks for Pretty Tony in my spare time, the way people kept alluding to my so-called trampishess. Steven made to answer and I shot him a just-let-it-go look.

Julie jumped into the breach. "Lisa, have you interviewed Terry Rex yet? He just walked in with his supermodel girl-friend." Julie referred to the latest action movie superstar.

Lisa spun away and headed off, knowing better than to take it any further.

"Christina, it's gotten worse between you and Lisa."

"Admittedly." I couldn't deny it.

"That's unacceptable," Julie snapped.

"Completely."

"Either fix it or make it go away." Julie swirled away and headed back to her table.

Deep cleansing breath, deep sigh. I turned back to Steven. "I'm going to go corner the senator, grab an interview, and make it look like I deserve my job title. Is Congressman Walker here yet?"

Steven nodded. "At three o'clock, clutching a martini and smiling a little too brightly. How about I approach him while you handle the senator?"

"Deal," I agreed.

"Christina"—Steven paused and gave me his best Professor Williams lecturing look—"please try to stay out of conflict for five minutes, can you?"

"It's not my fault," I hissed under my breath.

"That's the troublemaker's anthem." He handed me a fresh glass of champagne. "Sip slowly."

That's how I found myself huddled up with the senator, chatting "strictly off the record" about how government dollars are allocated, spent, and tracked, while sipping champagne. It was one of those conversations that would be quoted later, citing "high-ranking Washington officials."

It was from this vantage point that I watched with morbid fascination as my ex-fiancé Perry strolled into the room. Perry was the fiancé who had been confused about his sexuality. He certainly was not anymore. He was flamboyant with it now, in a way that made me wonder how I'd missed the signs before. He walked over to Lynne and they headed toward the dance floor. I quickly envisioned a few hundred ways this could go badly.

I wrapped up my conversation. "Senator, can I get you to promise an on-camera interview with me soon?"

"Next time you're in DC, sweetheart. Call my office and set it up. It's not all graft and skimming—some of us are trying to do the right thing by the American people." He sent a flinty side-eye over to Congressman Walker, who was still huddled up with Steven.

I filed that away for future reference. "Yes, sir. Thank you, sir. I appreciate your time."

He patted me on the shoulder. "Ms. Brinsley, you tell that man of yours to keep up the good work."

That man of mine? How I hated the labels. But I smiled

extra pretty; he was a United States senator, after all. "I will do it, sir. You enjoy the rest of your evening."

I was headed back toward the table when Collin pulled me to the side. "You can stand down your investigation for me."

It took me a second to remember that he was talking about Celia and her supposed infidelity. I had been so busy, I hadn't done much more than pull up some basic information on Dax. "Oh really?"

"Yes, we are back on schedule. In fact, we are making up for lost time. It's as if someone relit the pilot light."

Trying to block the mental images his words conjured, I thought about his words instead. Hmm, that could be good or bad. As long as Collin was putting out the flame, did it matter who ignited the spark? I didn't think Celia was cheating. I thought she was flirting with the young cutie and funneling that energy into her time with Collin. Was that emotional cheating? I had no idea.

Collin sensed my hesitation. "You have doubts."

"I have a theory, but I don't want to make waves over a theory."

Collin frowned. "A bad, get-a-lawyer theory or a good, don't-even-think-about-it theory?"

"Closer to the good than the bad."

"Can you check it out for me?"

"Of course, not a problem."

"By the way, we like Steven."

"Who exactly is we?" I raised a brow.

"Me, Celia, Clarke, Carey."

I rolled my eyes and said drily, "So glad to have your approval."

"Don't be snide; it doesn't suit the Brinsley name. What do you think of that, by the way?"

"The Brinsley name?"

"No, Ti-Ti—Clarke and Carey."

"Between you and me, I think it's a fit. But I'm wondering

if you two only pair up with women whose names start with *C* so you don't have to alter your monograms or stationery."

"Come on, now. Even we're not that shallow and bougie."

"I hear ya talking, but evidence points to the contrary," I teased.

Something over my shoulder caught his attention. "Oh, you know what—you might want to break that up."

I turned to see what he was referring to. Next to the martini bar stood Perry, Dante, and Steven deep in conversation. Not far from them stood Lynne, Lisa, and Stefani blatantly eavesdropping. Nothing good could come of this. I downed the champagne in my hand. "Thanks for the heads-up."

Heaven help me, I had spent all evening averting disaster. I crossed the room as fast as my heels and tight dress would get me there. Halfway across the floor, Carey fell into step with me. "Riddle me this, girlfriend. Is there *anyone* here you don't have some drama going on with?"

"Don't bring it here, Carey. I'm so not in the mood. I mean, I'm good people, aren't I?" I paused and lowered my voice to speak my peace.

"The best."

"And I've been gracious in the face of ridiculous odds to the contrary, have I not?"

"For the most part, you have, indeed."

"Carey, I've been kicked in the ass by love three times and I'm still out here trying. Don't I get some credit for that?"

"Sort of," she hedged.

"Sort of?"

"Well, before Young Steven showed back up, you weren't so much trying again at love as rotating temporary bed buddies."

"Temporary bed buddies is a harsh turn of phrase but okay, I'll own that."

"Some of those bed buddies wanted more. You know that, right?"

"Like who?"

"Dante, for one. Brandon, two. Steven, for three."

"You knew about me and Brandon? It was just a week-end." That was not one of my prouder moments. Brandon had come out to the West Coast office to help out about eighteen months ago and I gave in to a the-hell-with-it, it's-only-the-weekend moment.

"Everybody knew about you and Brandon. Why do you think Rita refused to move out here?" We had offered Rita a promotion with relocation and she had turned us down.

"I just thought she was a dyed-in-the-wool New Yorker who didn't want to come out West."

"She is a woman who has loved Brandon forever, and you used him, turned him inside out, and didn't look back. She kinda hates your guts."

"Stefani hates my guts, too."

"You used her brother, turned him inside out, and didn't look back. Do you see a pattern?"

"I just didn't want to get hurt again. And I was completely up front with people all the way around."

"I know, sweetie, but you hurt a few people along the way. You got cold and superambitious and didn't raise your head up enough to see the damage you were causing as you sped by. You kinda went all succubus for a while. And this cluster right here"—she gestured toward the group by the bar—"this is a case of your man-eating chickens coming home to roost."

I grabbed a glass of champagne from a passing waiter. "How do I fix it?"

She snatched the glass out of my hand. "Not by getting so blitzed you can blame your behavior on the tipsiness. You're damn near forty, girl. Woman up and be accountable." She put a hand on my shoulder and shoved me forward. "I love you though."

"If this is the love, I'd hate to get on your bad side." But I kept moving forward.

25

Last Man Standing

Steven—Sunday, November 21, 12:16 a.m.

I was so ready to end this evening, and from the look on Christina's face as she marched in my direction, so was she. I was curious to see how she'd handle this situation. If three women I had slept with were all in the same place at the same time, talking to each other, I'm not sure I'd look as serene as she did.

Her first stop was Lynne. I know that was her girl, but Lynne was mad jealous of Christina. The fact that she hit on both me and Dante in the span of thirty minutes told me all I needed to know about her. I didn't catch what Christina whispered in her ear, but Lynne nodded and headed toward the door, escorted by Carey and Clarke. I took a step closer.

Next, Christina stepped over to Lisa and slid a hand under her elbow. "Lisa, you've done a great job covering this event tonight. Why don't you make sure to send me your travel expenses for the weekend and I'll make sure Valiant covers them."

Lisa stood with her mouth open, shocked at the offer. "Uh, thanks. Okay."

"As a matter of fact, why don't you stay over through

Monday so we can toss around a few of your ideas on how to broaden your show?"

"Are you drunk?"

"I'm seriously sober. Now if you'll excuse me, I want to talk to Stefani for a minute. Thanks." With that, she sent Lisa packing.

She stood and faced my twin straight on. "I know I haven't always done the right thing by your brother, but I genuinely care about him and I hope you'll give me a chance."

I almost choked on my scotch. She just said words to my sister that I didn't think she would have said to me for months yet. Definitely good words and words I wanted to hear, but was I okay with her declaring feelings to my sister before me?

"He's my only sibling," Stefani announced with a skeptical eye on Christina.

"I know. You must be so proud of him. He's actually doing what he set out to do. How great is that?"

Got her. Stefani's face softened and they both turned to look at me. "He is pretty great, isn't he?"

Christina smiled. "One of the good ones. I think I see Marcus gesturing to you."

Stefani gave me a hug. I leaned down. "You're gonna like her, sis." She didn't hug Christina, but she touched the back of her hand as she went past.

"I'll see you both soon." Stefani strolled toward her husband.

Having dispatched the women, Christina turned her attention to us. "It's such a small world. Dante, can I talk to you for a second?"

"Of course, *querida*, whenever wherever."

She pulled him to the side and spoke into his ear, quickly using her hands to emphasize her points. When she finished talking she took a step back and extended her hand. "Apology accepted?"

He flipped it and kissed the back. "How can I not?" He

held her hand a second longer. "But if you should change your mind..."

She extracted her fingers one at a time. "I know where to find you, Dante, I really do."

Dante motioned to some people and headed for the door.

I had to hand it to Ms. Brinsley. In less than ten minutes, she had defused a potentially explosive situation. She took three steps and leaned into my side. Automatically, I raised my arm and put it across her shoulders, bundling her close. We fit together as if we'd done this a million times before. We simply fit.

"Why, Perry Marsh, as I live and breathe. How is life over the rainbow?"

"Ooo, shots fired! You look good, baby girl. You must be getting your protein."

Perry Marsh was tall, whisper-thin, and manscaped. I'd never seen a man with waxed brows before. He was dressed in a winter white wool suit, tan lace-up patent leather shoes, and a suede cape. Yep, a tan suede cape. How did she not know that this ninja was gay? I had no issues with my gay brethren as long as they are on the up-and-up with it. The fact that he strung Christina along until just before their wedding and then came out of the closet didn't endear Perry to me. And he was just a little too extra for me.

"Perry, seriously. What do you want?"

"Don't fret, love. It will give you premature wrinkles on that beautiful face. I was in the neighborhood; I just wanted to say hello. I heard on the news that you were going to be here and the guest list intrigued me, darling. I wanted to meet your men. I also wanted to donate some money to this fabulous foundation."

"We only accept cashier's items." Christina's voice was tart and I recalled her telling me that Perry had not only skipped out on the wedding but the wedding costs as well.

"I brought a cashier's item." He took a folded piece of paper out of his jacket pocket and handed it to Christina.

She looked down at the check, blinked, and back at Perry. "I don't understand—$78,192.64?"

"That, my darling girl, is the exact amount plus ten years' interest that you spent on our canceled nuptials." Okay, I had to give him points for that. That was a class move.

Tears welled up in Christina's eyes and she blinked them away rapidly.

He leaned forward to kiss her check and whispered, "I never really apologized. I hope this will do."

She kissed him back. "You're forgiven. This means a lot. Thank you, Perry."

"You two be good to each other—Perry out."

We watched him exit and stood silently for a minute. "And then there was one." I set my glass down.

"Last man standing is the only one that counts. You ready to get out of here?"

"Would it be ungentlemanly of me to point out that I wanted to skip this shindig in the first place?"

"Quite."

"Then yes, let's get out of here."

"Dr. Williams?" she said in a soft voice that boded well for the rest of the night.

"Yes, Ms. Brinsley?"

"You were brilliant tonight. You made me so proud."

You really can't hear that enough from someone you admire. There's no feeling as great as validation. Those words coming from her lips actually brought a swell of emotions I wasn't prepared to own yet to the surface. I shoved them back down and took her hand. "Just trying to be worthy of your time and attention."

She tugged my hand. "S. Dub."

"Hmm?"

"Take a compliment, will you?"

"Thank you, Christina. Sincerely, thank you. Now, can we be about the business of leaving?"

"Oh, I need to know how your talk with the congressman went and what Lance said and what Dante said and what Lynne said."

I took my thumb and stroked it across the inside of her wrist. "Do you need to know all of that right this instant?"

She stilled. "Um, no, actually."

I ran my thumb across the back of her knuckles. "Do you need to hear about that tonight, even?"

She swallowed and resumed walking toward the door. "Not really."

"I didn't think so." We strode toward the exit with determined haste. The banquet was over, but the party was just getting started.

26

Just Ask Me to Stay

Christina—Sunday, November 21, 1:47 a.m.

A cold blast of wind hit my face and I awoke with a start. I was secure in Steven's arms, being carried to my front door. Blinking twice, I realized that to the limo driver we made an unlikely picture. He was a huge bear of a man, carrying a green clutch purse and green strappy sandals in his large hands. He dug out my key, swung the door open, and took a step back.

I let my head fall back on Steven's shoulder as he carried me into my home. He turned right and went down the short hallway to my room. He placed me like precious cargo atop the queen-size sleigh bed and kissed my forehead. "Get some sleep, Christina. I'll talk to you tomorrow."

I tightened my grip on his shoulders. "Tomorrow?"

"Technically, I guess it's later today."

"You're not going to stay?" I wasn't *that* sleepy.

"Do you want me to stay?"

"Do you have to go?"

"Christina," he said slowly, standing with his hands in his pockets, "do you want me to stay?"

"Do you have somewhere else you want to be?"

"Why can't you just ask me to stay?" Grown Man Steven again. We locked eyes for a heartbeat. How important was it that I keep any sort of upper hand right now? I stared back into those expressive eyes and officially put myself in check.

"Stay," I asked with a sigh. "Please."

His eyes heated with promises of things to come. "Excellent choice. One second." He tried to straighten up and I gripped him tighter.

It seemed imperative that he know I was serious. I sat up and took his face in my hands to make sure he heard me and understood. "Steven, I want you to stay with me."

"Then it's good that I'm staying." He dropped a kiss on the inside of my palm.

I stroked my hand down his cheek. "Good."

"Babe, I gotta let the driver go. Unless you want witnesses?"

"No, thank you. I'm trying to live life off of YouTube. Come right back."

He gave me a lopsided grin that made him look about twelve years old as he took a step toward the door. "I'm coming right back."

As I was reaching around to unzip my dress on the side, his voice interrupted me. "Don't do that."

I froze. "Don't do what?"

"Don't get undressed."

"I'm not sleeping in this formal gown."

"You're not sleeping for a while. I want to unwrap you."

Well, damn. That was undeniably sexy.

"Just lie there and wait for me."

Grown Man Steven was no joke. I lay back down and waited. Even a month ago, I would have bristled over Steven's dominant, assumptive approach. But on this night, in this moment, I had to admit that it was nice to let someone else take the wheel and steer. Someone I instinctively knew would not run us off the road, who was headed in the same direction that

I was. I seriously pondered, for the first time years, letting down my guard and just trusting a man with more than the most superficial parts of me. He prowled back into the room and let his jacket slide down his arms.

"I take it I can count on you for a ride home tomorrow?"

"Why would you even ask?"

"It's starting to drizzle outside," he said with a slight smile. I watched as he loosened his bow tie and started on his cuff links.

"And?" I prompted him to explain.

He opened his shirt by releasing a stud at a time. "I don't want to get Dante'd."

Before I could think to be offended, I was already cracking up. "Did you just say Dante'd—like a verb?"

"Yes, ma'am." He toed off his shoes, unfastened his pants and let them drop to the ground. "You tossin' out ninjas buck naked in da streets. All out in da harsh elements and whatnot. I ain't trying to go out like dat." He set the cuff links and studs on the bedside table and peeled off his socks.

I reminded myself to breathe as he went about folding his clothes, wearing nothing but extremely tight black boxer briefs that left nothing to the imagination. "Oh, am I getting South side S. Dub or San Fran Steven tonight?"

"That depends." He walked into the closet and selected a hanger. Aligning the shoulders on his jacket, he hung it on the robe hook attached to the door. Just as calmly, he strolled over to my nightstand, opened the top drawer, and rummaged around before pulling out a square packet. He tossed it on top of the table.

I frowned at him. There was confidence and then there was just making your damn self at home. He raised a brow. I sighed. Not worth the battle. "Depends on what?"

"Am I getting Ti-Ti or Christina tonight?" He literally lifted me bodily from the middle of the bed and set me down on the edge. "Lift up."

I raised my arms. "What difference does it make?"

He opened the hook and eye closure on the side of my dress and slid the zipper down. He peeled the dress down slowly. I had on a strapless bustier and boy shorts in a chocolate satin. "This is nice, by the way. It depends on whether you are just looking to get done or looking to make love tonight."

That stunned me silent. I didn't believe anyone had ever given me the option before. If really pressed, I wasn't 100 percent sure I knew the difference. "Umm..."

He paused in his unhooking of the closures on my bustier. "What's it gonna be?"

I shrugged and looked down at his hands, feeling a little exposed and very vulnerable all of a sudden. "You decide."

He finished with the bustier and set it to the side. Sliding a finger under my chin, he tilted my face up. "Okay, baby. I got you." Wrapping me up in his arms, he rolled onto the bed, taking me with him so I was underneath him.

He placed a kiss on my left temple, my left ear, to the right of my lips, along my jaw, and down my neck. Lifting his weight off me, he rolled onto his side and traced his fingertips along the same path that his lips had just taken. "Like the finest chocolate: rich, sweet, beautiful, and addictive," he muttered before capturing my lips with his. He threaded his hand through mine, raising one of my arms to the side of my head. For long moments, he held my hand and kissed me. I lost track of time and place and thought.

When he kissed me, it was like no other kiss I'd received before. How could I describe it? He kissed like poetry, infused with thoughts and feelings and insights and promises. He stole my breath away. I felt he spoke to me through his kisses, accepting me, asking me to accept him. "Enjoy me and let me enjoy you" were the unspoken words in his every motion. I strained toward him, seeking more of the magic. And he gave it willingly. Keeping his lips and tongue engaged with mine, he deployed his hands to roam softly.

He explored my body like he was discovering a brave new world, leaving no plain, no valley, no crevice unattended. His hands sent me the same message as his mouth, and I found myself trembling at the slightest touches.

When he rolled me onto my stomach, I marveled in the revelations his hands wrought. Had I known that the center of my spine was an erotic zone? Had I realized that angel kisses at the small of my waist made me shiver? A finger teased across the curve of my shoulder, a tongue touched the point of my elbow. I was irrevocably seduced.

"Steven." I whispered the single word in a shuttering breath.

"Just let me, baby. Just let me." He slid farther down on the bed. I jumped when his hand wrapped around one ankle to lift and explore. He alternately stroked, massaged, and tasted my toes, the ball of my foot, the side of my calf, the dip behind my knee, nudging my inner thighs. He slid a hand under the fabric of my panties and squeezed my cheek. I shifted impatiently. He leaned down and placed a light bite on the side of my hip. "God, you smell incredible."

"I smell ready."

"That too." He rolled me back over and straddled me. I arched up to him. He placed his palm on my breastbone and pressed down gently. I settled back down. He palmed my breasts in his hand and rotated lightly. The touch was subtle, the effect wasn't. It was as though I had been jolted with electricity and sparks reached every nerve ending.

He leaned down and began to suckle on my nipples in earnest, moving from one to the other and following up with sliding touches from his fingertips. He was relentless, drawing the tight, sensitive buds into diamond-hard points. I was helpless to do anything but ride the waves of pleasure. My breathing grew choppy, sweat formed on my brow, and I undulated my hips in supplication. He pushed both breasts together and sucked both points into his mouth at once. I shrieked and erupted in a powerful orgasm.

He stroked my face and kissed me softly. "Now you're ready."

I was a puddle and simply couldn't fathom what more he thought he'd get out of me this evening. That climax had been too powerful and fulfilling. I was done.

He shed his boxers and sheathed himself in the condom. Rolling back to lie beside me, he rested his hand on top of my panties. I'd forgotten I was still wearing them. With the heel of his hand, he pressed down once and circled hard. My hips bucked, my thighs parted, and I was instantly ready again.

He smiled a knowing little grin and slid the soaked panties off. He flung them to the side and rolled on top of me. He clasped my hands in his and raised them high. I parted my thighs wider and strained upward. He slid through a river of moisture to land deep inside. We groaned in unison.

Canting his hips back, he slid in, slow and deep, again. "You are so tight and juicy, it's unbelievable."

"Yes." My head thrashed on the pillow.

"You're like hot honey, sucking me in."

"Yes." My eyes fell closed.

He stroked hard again and again and again. "Do you feel me?"

"Yes, baby."

"Open your eyes, Christina. Open your eyes." He paused.

I forced my eyes open.

"I want you to see me." He looked down at our joined bodies. I watched as he slid in and settled. "I want you to taste me." He leaned down and matched the stroke of his tongue with the rhythm of his hips. He lifted his head. "This is me making love to you, Christina." He ground his hips in tight circles and stroked deep again. "This is making love." He stroked again. "This. This. And this."

Tears leaked out of the corners of my eyes as I understood what he was showing me. This was more than sex. I lifted my head and licked the line from his neck, up his chin, and landing on his lips. "Thank you."

He rolled over so I was on top. "Just take what you need, baby. Whatever you want."

I brought my thighs up and sank down, taking as much of him in as possible. Still holding his hands, I tossed my head back and growled, "Thank you, Steven. Thank you for showing me."

He arched up, making sure to hit just the right spot. He lightly slapped my thigh. "Go ahead and take it."

I dropped his hands, braced my hands on his chest, and rode him hard and fast. "Thank you, thank you, thank you," I chanted as I pumped and gyrated, using my inner muscles to milk him as I rode.

"Yessss!" he hissed between gritted teeth, matching my strokes by arching up to meet my down stroke.

I couldn't get enough. I was burning and needed something more. "I need..."

"I got you, baby. Lean back."

I leaned back and reached behind me at the same time that he slid a finger past my navel and between my pouty lips. He zeroed in on my aching button and I found that spot at the base of his manhood. Looking into his now dark brown eyes, I smiled. We circled and pressed in symphony.

"Christ!" he barked, and pulled my convulsing body tight. He pumped and emptied into me as I writhed atop him. We finally stilled against each other. I was inexplicably crying again. I made to lift off of him. "Wait a second," he whispered.

I lifted my head to meet his gaze. He slid his hands down to my thighs and opened me wide, then put his hands on my rear and pressed down while bucking up sharply. "Ah! Steven!" I moaned as another explosion ripped through me. My convulsions rippled against his shaft and he flung his head back to ride out the aftershocks.

We lay, sweaty, jumbled, tangled and tired, in a squishy mess, straining for breath. He ran his hand down my back, stroking softly. I felt sated. I felt complete. I felt loved. And I had no idea what to do with that.

"You freaking out yet?" he said with a laugh in his voice.

I smiled. "Should I be?"

"You remember." It was the exact same thing he had asked me after our first night together in New York.

"I remember everything, Steven. Every single thing."

His hand stilled on my back. He recognized that for me, that was a major thing to reveal. "You know what you told my sister earlier?"

"Yes," I answered quietly, raising my lashes to meet his eyes.

"Did you mean it?"

"Yes."

"Why tell her before me?"

I gave a half shrug with my left shoulder. "It was easier and I knew you were listening."

"It's not always gonna be easy."

"I know."

"Are you willing to try this time?"

"You don't need to worry about getting kicked out in the rain." I smiled.

"I'm serious." He certainly looked serious.

"I know. I am, too. What we just did..."

"Yeah?"

"It was more than I expected. I've never had that kind of connection before. There's a lot of complexity here. It meant something." No one had taken the time to show me it could be about the care and the attention.

"I know."

"It scares me a little," I admitted.

"That's a good thing." He was sounding supremely confident.

"I might get more scared."

"I have a plan for that."

"Do you now?"

"I do." He nodded.

"What is it?"

"I can't tell you. You'll find weapons to fight me."

I sighed. "I know I'm difficult."

"Definitely not easy."

"Why do you even bother?"

"I know what I want."

"Me?"

"So far, yeah."

"I'm so scared to believe you, to want you, to need you. If you walk away like the others, I don't think I have it in me to bounce back."

"Don't borrow trouble. Let's revel in the win."

"The win?"

"Christina, today was a win. We made lots of money for the foundation. We got a ton of information for your story. We won over our siblings. You made up with an ex. You got rid of Dante, you put Lisa in neutral, you wowed your VP. I impressed my dean. I was on TV, you weren't on YouTube. And we just had the best sex ever."

"Oh my God, it really was. You're like the vagina whisperer."

He opened his mouth, shut it, and then burst out laughing. "You just called me . . ."

"Yeah, I did. It's your new nickname. . . . VW—oh! V. Dub."

"You're a fool."

"I kinda am. Now I'm hungry and dirty. Food first? Shower first?"

"I need food to replenish myself before the shower. I recall exactly how you like your back scrubbed."

Just like that a flash of heat ran through my body. I remembered that shower as well. "In that case, let me feed you first." I sat up and looked around for my robe. "I might have a pair of Collin's or Clarke's sweats around here for you."

"Oh, I have a bag in the living room."

I paused in the middle of tying my robe around my waist. "You have a bag in the living room?"

"I had a wishful-thinking bag in the car. The driver brought it in for me."

"Wishful thinking, huh?"

"Boy Scout motto—be prepared."

"You were a Boy Scout?"

"Okay, no. Hood motto—stay ready."

"I don't see a lot of Hood Steven left in you."

"He's still there. He lurks under the polished, tuxedo-wearing surface. You feed me properly and I might break him out for that shower."

"Hood Steven doesn't make love?"

"Hood Steven smashes. He's a little rough and raw. Hood Steven doesn't whisper, he screams."

"Oh. My." Whichever Steven showed up in the kitchen was about to get the best middle-of-the-night meal I could put together.

27

Who Is Grown Man Steven?

Steven—Sunday, December 5, 4:24 p.m.

"Steven, I can't tell you what a joy it's been to meet you, spend time with you, get to know you." Joanna Brinsley hugged me like I was a long lost child, rocking me back and forth in a warm hold. Never mind that her three children were looking on with varied expressions of amusement and resignation.

I hugged her right back. "The joy is mine, Mama Brinsley. All mine." My grin widened as Christina put a hand on her hip and rolled her eyes.

"Suck-up!" she mouthed behind her mother's back.

"Hater!" I mouthed back with a wink.

Joanna squeezed once more and stepped back. "You know you remind me so much of my late husband."

I wasn't sure I wanted to know, but I took it in the spirit it was given. "I'm sure that's a compliment of the highest order. A man smart enough to marry you is a man worth emulating for sure."

Joanna Brinsley had a whole timeless beauty, Lena Horne, upper-crust look about herself. In her late sixties, she had meticulously flawless skin, thick chestnut hair cut above her ears, and a petite frame. At hearing my words, she blushed like a schoolgirl. "Now isn't that sweet?!" She turned to Christina. "Isn't he sweet?"

"The sweetest." Her tone was dry.

"Oh, Christina. Wry doesn't suit the Brinsley face. You know your father was from the hood, too."

I stifled a chuckle, but the word "hood" should never come out of that woman's mouth. "Was he now?"

"Yes, he was, but just like you he pulled himself up and made something of himself."

If the size of her Pacific Heights Victorian was any indication, he'd done more than just "something."

"Well, I won't keep you young people from the rest of your afternoon. Steven, the next time you come, you bring that twin of yours."

"Yes, ma'am."

Joanna tilted her head and looked from one couple to the next. "Everybody looking so happy, you'd think one of you could give me some grandbabies."

Dead silence. I knew I wasn't touching that one.

"Fine. Act like you don't hear me. Don't forget to get your leftovers from Odessa on the way out."

Odessa was the live-in housekeeper. She was apparently something like a permanent fixture in the Brinsley household. She had been with "Miss Joanna" for close to twenty-five years. When we all filed into the kitchen she was stretched out in the window seat with a glass of wine and the remote control, watching football. Odessa was a stick-thin woman with olive-brown skin and wavy, long gray hair pulled back into a ponytail. She wore a Forty Niners sweatshirt, faded jeans, and sneakers. If I had to guess, I'd put her age somewhere between sixty and seventy-five.

She gestured toward the counter. "I made up one bag per couple. I ain't getting all up in your business as to who sleeps where. But, Christina, that's a good-looking piece o' man you brought round this time. You sho'nuff betta not let him sleep alone. Fine young thang like that. Carey, you come over here and give Miss Odessa a kiss. Finally get some babies running around this house." Carey complied. "You know I like to watch my games in peace. 'Bye, children." Now that's a rare skill to both welcome and dismiss people in the same breath.

We had grabbed the bags and stepped outside when Collin spoke. "You know, I believe I've heard enough about Christina's sex life to last me a lifetime."

Celia sighed. "Did you think she was a virgin?"

Carey laughed. "*No* one thought that."

"Hey! Not my fault," Christina said, stamping a foot.

"Troublemaker's anthem," I reminded her.

Clarke broke out laughing. "Yes! That's it exactly."

Christina sent him a side-eye. "Where are your cuff links resting these days?"

"Direct hit," Collin said.

"So with all the baby talk—who's trying to get pregnant?" I asked out of curiosity.

"A sister needs a ring first," Carey said.

"It better not be you!" Clarke dodged Carey's statement and hooked an arm around Christina's neck.

"Get off me!" she squealed, and ran over to Collin.

"Seriously?" Celia said, tapping her foot. "Sometimes you three act like you're back in kindergarten."

"And on that note..." Carey looked at Clarke and then at the car.

A round of hugs and good-byes rolled before Christina and I were finally settled in the car. Waving to the others, I pulled out into the street and pointed the car south toward my place in the SoMa district. "Sounds like you sho'nuff betta not let me sleep alone!"

"Apparently not, fine young thang that you are."

"By the way, you need to put your girl Lynne in check."

"What? What did she do?"

"I told you about her hitting on me at the party, right?"

"Yeah, but she was drunk and acting out. Her marriage is on the rocks and she's sex-deprived."

"No doubt. She's taken to texting me on the regular. To be precise, it's more like sexting."

"The *hell*? When?"

"It started a week ago. I asked her to stop. She hasn't. I'm about to block her."

"You're just now telling me? All casual-like, with a 'by the way'?"

"Like I said, it started a week ago. We've both been crazy busy. I'm telling you now." Really, when is the best time to tell your girl her friend is trifling?

"How did she get your number?"

"It was on my card from the foundation."

"I *cannot* believe this . . . I know you kept those messages to show me."

"You know I did." I handed her my phone.

She started scrolling and reading. "Oh, that's not too bad. That's an unfortunate turn of phrase. That's downright inappropriate. Is this fourth one even legal?"

"In the City and County of San Francisco it is." I was so glad she saw the humorous side of the situation.

"I'm embarrassed for her. And for me. And for you."

I braked to a stop at the light and looked over at her. "Thank you."

She kept reading and, by her body language, I could tell she had gotten to the more troubling messages. "I am so gonna *Kick. Her. Ass.*"

"Hold up, Ti-Ti. How about you start with a conversation?"

"Eff a conversation! This is wild! Did she have an attachment on this last one?"

"I deleted it."

"Was it a picture?"

"A short video." The light turned green and I made the left turn toward my condo.

"Ain't this a bitch! I'm calling her ass right now!"

"Christina!" I wondered if this whole thing could turn ugly. She put up her hand. "Dialing!" She switched to speaker-phone.

Lynne picked up. "Hey, sexy, I was hoping that video would get you to call. When can we hook up?"

Christina pursed her lips. "Hey, Lynne, what's going on?"

As Christina would say, you could hear crickets chirping in the background. I pulled into my parking structure and headed up the ramp.

"Lynne? I take it you expected someone else."

"Girl, I thought you were this young man I've been flirting with." Lynne giggled nervously.

"Young man as in my Steven?"

"What are you talking about?"

"Don't play dumb, Lynne. You're one of the smartest women I know. As you have no doubt deduced, I'm sitting here with Steven's phone in my hand, having just read the messages you sent him. Now what is going on?"

"I'm sorry to tell you this, but your boy hit on me at that party. I assumed that meant he was available."

I backed into my space and watched Christina's eyes narrow into slits. Uh-oh.

"He absolutely did not, and you assumed no such damn thing, Lynne."

"Oh, you just gonna take his word over mine? Is he putting it down like that?"

"Lynne, what the hell are you thinking? I know you are going through some things but don't bring it here. Whatever mess you were trying to start...stop it now."

"You know your track record with men is not that great. How can you be one hundred percent sure that he didn't roll up?"

"Wow, friend, is it like that? I'm one hundred percent sure that you are lying. Grown Man Steven doesn't roll up. I don't fight over men, especially when it wouldn't be a fair fight. So what say we chalk this up to a lapse in judgment and forget it ever happened?"

"I still can't believe that you—"

"Lynne, I'm giving you an out. Please take it. We've been friends for too long to let your hormones and momentary crazy get in the way."

"Momentary crazy?!"

"Or we can swing by and the four of us—you, me, Steven, and Eric—can talk it over. Why don't you take the out and we'll leave it here?"

"Fine. Whatever."

"Okay, then. Talk to you later." She tossed me the phone and climbed down from the car.

Walking to the elevator, I took her hand. "You handled that nicely, I thought."

She shook her head. "Trying to do the mature thing all the time wears me out."

"That's your family, though."

"She's not family. We just left my family."

"Point taken." I stepped into the elevator and pushed the button for floor 16.

"All right then."

"Speaking of fam…" I decided to go ahead and broach the subject.

"What now?"

"Calm down. I'm going to Chicago for Christmas."

"Okay."

"Want to come?"

"Really, with you?"

I rolled my eyes. "As opposed to?"

"No one. It just surprised me, that's all."

"Why?"

"Meeting your family at Christmas. That's a step." She looked nervous.

"I've met all your family and your close friends, Christina."

"Yes, I know. It just seems soon for meeting the parents."

"I'm confused. Didn't we just eat with your entire fam?"

"Well, yeah."

"So what's the difference?"

"These are your people."

"And?"

"What if they don't like me?"

"What's not to like?"

"Hmph. Ask Stefani. She's still iffy about me."

"She's overprotective."

"And your mother isn't?"

"She doesn't know about New York."

She sent me a side-eye. "I see."

"You pick the strangest things to get insecure about. Next topic, then? I was thinking we'd go meet some people at Candlestick for the game tonight."

She looked at me in horror. "Are you a Forty Niners fan?"

The way she said it made it seem a completely implausible thing. "I take it you are not."

"No way."

"Is that a deal breaker?" This chick had more rules.

"It's pause worthy, I'll tell you that."

"I'm a Bears fan. They play the Niners tonight. What are you—a Raiders fan?"

"Repping for the East Bay, yo!"

"Um—don't do that tonight. Promise me."

"I'll try not to embarrass you. So tonight, I finally get to meet some of the boys?"

We stepped out of the elevator on my floor. "It's Jimmy and Rob. You met both of them back in the day. They were two of my roommates in New York."

"Oh, Jimmy was the funny guy from St. Louis?"

She really did remember everything. "That's the one."

"Rob was in software or something—what's he doing?"

"He owns a software company. They make gaming software."

"Anything I might have heard of?"

"Mix-a-lot Dance Jams is one of his company's games."

"Oh, that game that lets people DJ?"

"That's the one."

"What is Jimmy doing now? Stand-up comedy?"

I laughed because that was what he was truly suited for. "No, believe it or not, he's a motivational speaker."

She nodded. "I could see that."

"So, you down?"

"Let's do it. But I cannot stay up too late tonight. We start filming the special series on the high-speed rail in the morning."

"When's it going to air?"

"The end of January. We're doing a five-night special. Are you still good to do the interview next week?"

"Sure." I unlocked the door and ushered her in. I set the leftovers in the refrigerator and joined her on the couch. She turned on the NFL Network. I loved how much she was into football.

"Is it going to be weird, me interviewing you on camera?"

"Are you going to be naked?"

"Of course not."

"Then it's not going to be weird."

"Okay then."

Sometimes I really wondered what was going on in that head of hers. Then I remembered something she had said earlier. "But since you brought up weird...who is Grown Man Steven?"

"Oh...ah." Ms. Brinsley actually blushed.

"I'm waiting." I sat back and folded my arms.

"That's what I call you in my head."

Huh, that was an interesting admission. "Because?"

"I do it to remind myself that Grown Man Steven is not to be played with or taken lightly."

"Or is it to remind yourself to keep your guard up?"

Her eyes widened slightly, letting me know I'd touched on some of the truth. "Maybe a little of both."

"Hmm. By the way, thank you for never even considering that Lynne might be telling the truth."

"Never crossed my mind."

"Why do you think that is?"

"I trust you, Steven."

I reached over, grabbed her, and swung her onto my lap. "I'm sorry, could you repeat that?"

"I said I trust you, Steven." She buried her face in the side of my neck. And just like that it was over for me. I accepted the reality. I was in love with this beautiful, talented, complicated woman. I closed my eyes and said a quick prayer: *God give me strength for whatever may lie ahead.*

"Enough to let that guard all the way down?"

"You've already got me pretty open."

I glanced at the clock. "Grown Man Steven has just enough time to see how open he can get you." I stood up, flung her over my shoulder and headed toward the bed.

She shrieked and slid her hand down to my ass. She smacked once. "You've got to quit flinging me around."

"You love it, lightweight." I swung her around and set her on her feet. She pushed me backwards and I fell onto the bed. In no time she had my pants and underwear pulled down. She held me in both hands and guided me to her mouth. "You know, on the other hand, there's no need to rush. We can be a little late . . . a lot late, in fact. These games never get good until after half-time." She could call me whatever she wanted as long as she kept doing that right there, just like that.

28

I Am Not Without Options

Christina—Thursday, December 17, 12:13 p.m.

Steven's loft was located in SoMa (South of Market) near downtown San Francisco in a beautiful new high-rise. The space was a reflection of him—a little urban, a little uptown, cultured but quirky, and very easy on the eyes. He favored shades of gray and green with silver and red mixed in as accents. The floors and countertops where poured concrete and there was an entire wall of windows with incredible views of the Bay Bridge and AT&T Park.

He came toward the door, rolling a small suitcase with his laptop case on his arm. We were on our way to the Napa Valley region for a miniature vacation. We had rented an estate between St. Helena and Calistoga for four days.

"The laptop, really? I thought this was a no-work weekend?"

"I won't work. I may just surf the Net. Update my Facebook, tweet something."

"Do you tweet?" I asked, wondering why I just now knew this.

"Sporadically. Do you?" he answered as he ushered me out to the hallway and into the elevator.

"Someone at the station opened an account for me, but I haven't done anything with it. Do you have followers?"

"Of course, I'm a popular guy." He opened the trunk of his Land Rover. "Need to do anything before we hit the road?"

"I don't think so."

He helped me into the passenger seat, shut the door behind me, and slid behind the steering wheel. "All right then, you ready to go?"

"I guess."

"You guess?"

"I'm good. Let's go."

"Uh—huh." He flipped on the radio and we rode in silence through the city, over the Golden Gate Bridge and down the 101 for a few miles.

"I seriously doubt that this is a good idea," I finally said as Steven slowed to get on the exchange to Highway 37 toward Vallejo.

"When was the last time you took a long weekend? Just got away?" Steven asked patiently.

I thought about it. And thought some more. I couldn't recall the last time I'd even taken a day off, to be honest.

"I'm waiting," he said.

"Okay, so maybe I could use a little downtime, but the story is just heating up and this whole couples thing isn't setting well with me."

Steven was wearing dark sunglasses, but I could sense the eye-roll behind them. "Clarke and Carey, that's your brother and one of your best friends. Stefani and Marcus, my sister and her husband. What's the problem?"

"Your sister hates me."

"Hate is such a strong word."

"What would you call it?"

"You're not her favorite person, but she's warming up. She was nicer to you when we swung by the other day."

"She kept a permanent, laser-beam side-eye on me all day long. Not relaxing. That could make for a long weekend."

"I'm sure she'll be on her best behavior. Who could stay stressed in Wine Country for the weekend? C'mon now. Let's not anticipate drama. We're here to chill. Drink a little wine. Relax, relate, release."

"If you say 'woo-sah,' I swear to God you can take me home now."

"Woman, what is your general problem now?"

"I don't know, I don't know. This is a whole lot of serious relationship-type vibe."

"I get that you don't trust men, they've let you down, yada yada, but what does that have to do with me wanting to have a decent weekend?"

"I just don't want us getting too comfortable." In other words, I didn't want to get used to having him around since he was going to walk sooner or later.

"Fine. We're just two people who happen to hang out together and see each other naked regularly, changing locales for the next few days. How's that?"

"Don't mock me. I know it sounds crazy, but I have to look out for me for the long run."

"Is that why all your interactions for the past few years have been hit-n-quit? You're looking out for you?"

I wouldn't have put it that way. "Let's just say I keep things light."

"Well, who asked for heavy? You're the one putting a label on things."

"You don't think going away together with this group is setting expectations?"

"For who?"

"For you, for me? I just don't want us to get ahead of ourselves."

Steven shot me a look and at the next exit got off the highway. He pulled into a parking lot and turned off the engine. He took off his sunglasses and tossed them on the dashboard. "Why did you agree to come if you don't want to be here?"

"Who said I don't want to be here?"

"You've been half-assed salty and borderline pissy since we got up this morning."

"No, I haven't!"

"You kind of have been. It's rude."

"Rude?"

He set his jaw. "Could you pretend that this will be fun? Must I talk you into everything?"

"You don't have to talk me into everything. I just want us to level-set our goals for the weekend."

He started the car and pulled out in the lane to go back towards San Francisco.

"Where are you going?"

"Not to Napa. Not with you. Not like this. No, thank you." Steven was mad. Like angrier than I'd ever seen him. It was something to see, and tough to be on the receiving end of. He looked like he wished he could kick me out on the side of the road.

I sighed. Of the two of us, I wasn't sure who was more dramatic. "What are you talking about?"

"I'm not up for whatever phobic bullshit you're on today. I just want to have a nice weekend with a nice lady. Spend time with some friends and family. Go out to eat, make conversation, drink too much, have a little sex, tour a few wineries. No drama. I have no energy to coax somebody into having a good time with me. I don't want to freaking 'level-set' goals. If you're not feeling it, I can drop you off and find someone not scared shitless to enjoy a simple weekend."

"Well, damn, am I that replaceable?" Did he seriously just say he was going to drop me off and pick up someone else?

"C'mon now, I'm into you. You know you're my first choice, but please believe I am not without options."

"Uh, wow." I was stunned. Looking over at him, I realized he was dead serious. "What if I prefer to stay?"

"I guess that depends on you."

"I see. So either I get with the program or I'm out?"

"There's not a program, there's no grand conspiracy theory . . . it's a weekend away. I'm already weary of propping you up today. What's it gonna be? You in or out?"

"Grown Man Steven, damn! I would like to go with you, thank you very much." Sheesh, he was not playing. All line in the sand, putting down of the foot—it was a little harsh.

He got off at the next exit and made the U-turn to head back north. He didn't say a word.

"So, dramatic much?"

"High-maintenance much?" he shot back.

"Do you even wonder why we're together?"

"Are we together? I thought that was a scary word never to be applied to the two of us," he said with considerable snark in his tone.

I threw up my hands. "Okay, you've made your point. I'm all supercautious and it's making you nuts. I get it. I'm working on it. But can you answer the question?"

"Why are we together?" He shrugged. "One word. Chemistry."

"Is that all?"

"Isn't that enough for now? You're the one not wanting to define things, putting too fine of a point on the pencil."

He was really not feeling me today. "Ya mad, huh?"

"Christina, you wear a brother out. I was looking forward to a nice little time and you just had to make it into a thing. It shouldn't have to be this hard."

He was right. "I'm sorry. I'll make it up to you."

He raised a brow. "Will you now? How are you planning to do that?"

"I might not have been sure about this getaway, but I came prepared. I brought a little sumthin' sumthin' to model later on tonight, if you're up to it."

"Oh, I can rise to the occasion if you're gonna make it worth my while."

"But Steven?"

"Um-hmm?"

"Don't ever mention picking up some random chick as a substitute to me again. I'm a handful, not a doormat."

"Two handfuls."

"Still..."

"Understood."

"Are we going to stop at Domaine Chandon on the way to the house?"

"We can. Why?"

"My making it up to you involves two bottles of their rosé sparkling wine."

"Two?"

"One to sip out of glasses, the other to sip off of body parts."

"Oh, you *do* plan on making it up to me. Let's get there, then."

I slid my sunglasses on and smiled. "I may be two handfuls but they're full of good stuff, no?"

"For the most part, Ti-Ti. For the most part."

29

Bring It On, Berkeley

Steven—Thursday, December 17, 3:28 p.m.

Christina, in one of her mercurial personality flip-flops, was back to being happy and pleasant by the time we pulled up to the vacation cottage. Our detour to the Chandon winery had put us behind schedule, but it was worth it to have her mood as bubbly as the liquid we just picked up.

The house was beautiful. It rested on four acres of premium land; the house was Tuscan in style with a stone archway to the front drive. I saw that Marcus's and Clarke's cars were already there, which meant Christina and I were the last to arrive.

I pulled in behind Clarke's Mercedes SUV and Christina hopped out of the car. Flashing me a smile, she grabbed the box of sparkling wine and dashed for the door. I guessed that left me to bring in the bags. Grumbling under my breath about finding an easier woman to have around, I popped open the trunk.

"Plotting to off my sister somewhere in the vineyard?" Clarke asked as he walked out to join me.

"Man, I almost left her by the side of the road in Marin. It was a near thing."

Clarke snickered. "I can't even say I would blame you. She's not for the faint of heart. But she's worth it."

Whatever, I thought to myself, deciding not to share that portion of my thoughts. Instead I said, "The harder to attain, the more worth it in the end, right?"

"That's what they say," he agreed. "Then again, there's something to be said for it all being so easy, you know it's right."

I wouldn't know anything about that, so I just nodded as he grabbed Christina's bag. We headed into the house. It was as advertised, lushly decorated with amazing views of the vineyard out back and hills beyond. State-of-the-art kitchen, huge living room with a pass-through fireplace—the house gave a warm and homey impression. Downstairs was a huge great room with one wall dedicated to a built-in wine rack. The opposite wall contained a massive flat-screen television, game console, DVD, and stereo system. I set my bag down inside the door.

"We have a problem," Christina said from the kitchen.

"Oh?"

Stefani came over and gave me a big hug. "Three bedrooms, two with king-size beds and one with twins. You single folk need to figure out who gets the twin."

I looked over at Marcus. "Why you married folks claiming the grown and sexy bed?"

Marcus and I exchanged the fist bump as he answered, "We are the only couple sanctioned by God to sleep together, heathen."

Carey whistled. "Oh, ouch, the brother-in-law played the morality card. That stings."

Christina said, "Since you're all wounded, you and Clarke can take the twin beds."

Clarke piped up, "I don't think so, sis. You and Pretty Boy over here just as sinful as Carey and I."

"Hold up." I asked, "Did you just call me Pretty Boy?"

Stefani laughed. "He is easy on the eyes, isn't he?"

Marcus shook his head. "Modest much? You look just like him!"

"So then the pretty people get the big beds, is that what we're saying?" Christina added.

Carey was pulling deli containers out of the fridge, "Okay, now I'm personally offended and the answer would be no."

Clarke walked over to her and kissed her on the forehead. "Aw, baby, you're pretty, too."

I put my hands up. "Enough! Everybody's pretty, but there's only one way to solve this."

"Hand-to-hand combat?" Marcus asked.

"Arm wrestling?" Christina offered.

"Short straw loses?" Clarke added.

I reached in my laptop case and drew out a disk. "Trivial Pursuit 90's Edition. Who wants some?"

"Yes!" Carey called out. "Prepare to go down, people. Winner picks their room, next highest score gets next pick, losers rock the twin beds. Let's eat and then let's rumble."

"Bring it on, Berkeley," Stefani said, pulling plates out of the cabinet.

"Did your sister just knock my alma mater?" Christina asked, looking around in drawers and cabinets until she found the silverware and place mats.

"She might have, a little bit. She's a Northwestern girl." I teased my sister.

"You know how those Chicago girls are," Marcus said as he helped to set the table.

"Who ordered the food?" Clarke asked, selecting a bottle of wine and grabbing some glasses.

I raised a hand, picked up a bowl of fruit salad, and headed over to set it on the table. "You might want to pull out a second bottle. I thought we'd appreciate a little ready-made something when we got here."

"Speaking of which," Carey said, bringing a platter of rotisserie chicken and roasted veggies to the table, "what took you two so long to get here? I thought you left the city before Clarke and me."

Christina and I exchanged a glance and didn't answer. I shrugged.

Stefani looked from me to Christina and back again. "Please tell me you two did not pull over for some side-of-the-road slap 'n' tickle?"

"Ugh, I don't need the mental imagery—thank you!" Clarke protested and opened the first bottle of wine.

Marcus said, "Seriously though, we can wait if you two want to shower."

"We're good," I said and held out a chair for Christina. Everyone started taking seats around the table.

Carey scooped some salad onto her plate. "Are you two seriously not going to tell us what happened?"

"Steven tried to boot me out the car," Christina said with a pout.

I shot her a look. "Technically, I never tried to put you out the car. I invited you to take your moody ass home."

"You told me to get right or you would replace me with some random chick who kisses your ass!"

"Steven for the win!" Clarke said.

Christina stuck her tongue out. "Hey, brother—thanks for the backup."

"Damn, Grown Man Steven does not play," Carey said.

"Who is Grown Man Steven?" Stefani asked.

"Long story," I supplied before addressing Christina. "I said it was up to you. We could either kick off this weekend the right way or not at all."

"I agreed, didn't I? I said I was sorry and everything."

"You brought it up, woman. I was content to let them think we were getting freaky in the backseat."

"Ooo-kay," Clarke said with a laugh. "You two win, you get the bed. I think you need it."

Marcus said, "Jeez, put them in the room all the way at the back. I have no desire to hear the angry make-up sex."

"Ugh, my brother we're discussing!" Stefani frowned.

"Still beating y'all down in Trivial Pursuit, though...recognize that," Carey said.

Christina and I exchanged another loaded look. "Can you pass the chicken, please?" I asked her.

"Certainly. Leg or breast?" She smirked at me.

I smirked right back. "Both, if you don't mind."

"I do not mind at all."

"Dear God, pass me the wine," Stefani said. "This weekend is going to be TMI all the way around."

"I don't know," Christina said with a twinkle in her eye. "This weekend might be just what we needed."

I sent her a smile. Finally! She was seeing things my way. Let's see how long this lasted.

30

Does That Answer Your Question?

Christina—Friday, January 6, 5:25 p.m.

There was something patently unfair about the fact that I was huffing and puffing as though in need of oxygen while Steven ran on the treadmill across from mine twice as fast, not looking the least bit winded. It had been forty minutes already. We were at the University Health Club, a nice perk of Steven's job, and he was kind enough to get memberships for just about everybody we knew.

Steven worked out with Jimmy, Rob, and Lance about four times a week. I was happy if I made it twice, and I only did twenty-five minutes of cardio. I watched him and his boys jogging along on the treadmills, talking as if they were on a Sunday stroll. Steven had added a 30 percent incline to his run. The boy was an anatomical freak.

Across the gym was Celia, dressed in matching pink Nike gear from head to toe. She was in the advanced step class and looking for all the world like she was enjoying herself. Just outside the room on the free weights was Dax. I didn't know what the whole story was on them, but I still didn't like it. I was on campus quite a bit and whenever I saw him, I saw her.

I relayed the information to Collin and told him to do with it what he felt comfortable with.

A stitch developed in my side and I decided enough was enough. My only consolation was Carey, looking like she could pass out at any second on the StairMaster. I decided to put both of us out of our misery. I pointed to the café and raised a brow. Carey nodded gratefully. I pressed the stop button.

"Giving up?" Steven called out.

I slapped my thigh and wiggled my hips. "I think I'm fine enough."

"Tell him," "Go, girl," and "You looking good" were the choruses that met my declaration.

He sent a smile my way. "I cannot argue with that."

"How much longer?"

"Oh, you know, a brother gotta keep a bedroom physique. Make sure my stamina is all it can be."

"Keep talking that talk." I sent him a look and walked off with Carey.

We flopped into chairs in the café. We both ordered smoothies and sat in comfortable silence until they arrived.

Carey took a deep draw on her straw. "Who is the puma with Celia?"

"What's a puma?"

"Cougar bait."

"Ah. Believe it or not, his name is Dax Fredericks. He is pursuing a dual master's in business administration and finance."

"So he's more than just beefcake with a porn name."

I picked up my cup and clinked it to Carey's. "That's why you're my ace. Those were my thoughts exactly."

"You think she's doing him?"

"I don't know. But I do know she has supercharged her schedule with Collin."

"Schedule?"

"They schedule the nookie."

"They do *not*."

"I'm so sad to report that they do."

"That's more than I ever wanted to know about Collin and Celia."

"Ya know?"

"But as long as we're talking about your brothers."

"Carey, do *not* start sharing kinky sex stories about Clarke. I will make Valiant put you back on a plane to New York *soo* fast!"

She patted my shoulder. "I wouldn't share. I don't wanna make you jealous."

I snorted. I most assuredly did not need a better sex life than the one I had right now. I could barely keep up as it was.

"Ooo-kay. That look that just crossed your face. That was TMI. Let's move on, shall we?"

"Let's."

"Your brother asked me to marry him last night."

"*What!* Oh my God! Oh, Carey." I hopped up and hugged her, then waved my hands in the air and started a happy dance, until I noticed she didn't look so gleeful. "What's that look about? You turned down my brother? Are you kidding me?"

"Don't make it a family thing. Put the sister hat to the side for a minute. Now let's think about the relationships you and I have endured since college. What are our thoughts about marriage?"

I sat down, sobered at the thoughts. "Okay, we've been through some hot mess. Steaming piles of hot mess, to be truthful. You've been through it, but Clarke is *so* not Bryan. You cannot think it's anything close to that."

A gym agent walked up right at that moment. "Would you two be interested in meeting with our personal trainer?"

"Sure, sure—whatever." I waved her away. "Come on, Carey. This is Clarke. Even if he wasn't my brother, I would tell you he's one of the best guys in the world. It's clear to me that you two have had a thing for each other for over fifteen years. You need to hop on that and enjoy the whole ride. Do not let that get away."

A wry smile crossed her face. "I won't if you won't."

"Huh?"

"Christina, look at that man."

I followed her gaze. Steven was standing next to the Nautilus machines, talking to Dax and Celia. He said something to Dax that had him grabbing his towel and walking away. Then he whispered something to Celia, who flashed him a brilliant smile and nodded before walking away. He sat down on the crunch machine and looked around for me. When he caught me watching, his entire face broke out in a smile and he winked. I caught my breath—the eye-twinkle was back! I hadn't seen the S. Dub eye-twinkle in over five years.

Something about him stirred me up and drew me to him. The fact that a simple smile from across a crowded room had my heart fluttering told me I was already in deep. The smiled ebbed from his face as we continued staring at each other. The air between us grew charged. His friend Jimmy nudged him teasingly and he threw back his head to laugh. He pointed at me and they laughed some more. "Later." He mouthed the promise before beginning his reps.

"Wow," I said, feeling the impact of that promise all the way to my toes.

"Wow is right. What is stopping you from falling head over heels in love with that lovely, sexy man?"

From behind us, another club employee spoke. "Ladies, my name is David. I understand you are interested in signing up for some personal training sessions?"

We both spun around slowly at the voice. The smiles fell off all three of our faces. I pointed at him and looked at Carey. "Does that answer your question?"

The personal trainer was none other than Jay / David himself.

31

I Remember You Too

Steven—Friday, January 6, 5:38 p.m.

I wanted to finish my workout, get Christina home, and find out what that look was about. It was the first time I'd seen that look on her face outside of the bedroom. It was a look that gave me infinite hope.

"Brah, you are so far gone over this woman." Jimmy nudged me and we laughed.

"I know, man, but just look at her." I pointed across the room and mouthed "Later" before starting my reps. Midway through the first set, I glanced back over. She and Carey were looking at a gym employee who looked somewhat familiar. By their body language I could tell they were not feeling whatever he had to say. Confident in their ability to handle it, I was about to turn away when he reached his hand toward Christina's face. She ducked away violently and her face showed shock and pain. It suddenly became crystal clear where I had seen that fool before.

It took me less than thirty seconds to get off the machine and get across the room. "You put one finger on her and I swear to God I'll give you the ass-kicking you deserved years ago, you lying son of a bitch."

Okay, that was a little dramatic and loud. Half the club went silent. I didn't give a damn. This man hurt my baby and put that look back on her face. I wasn't having it. Not today. Not even.

Jay / David took a step backwards and sized me up. "I remember you."

"I remember you, too." I nodded slowly. Yeah, I remember Jay / David's punk ass. And the memories were not fond ones. Christina got up and stood beside me.

Now you would think this ninja would have the good damn sense to recognize the waves of hostility headed his way, and leave gracefully. The tension in the place was thick as hell. I suddenly felt like I was back in an alley off Western Ave. in the Chi, fighting knuckleheads before curfew. I hadn't had to swing on a fool in a minute, but I had no doubt of my ability to break off a much-needed beat-down on this clown. I really hoped he would keep it classy.

But instead of the classy way, Jay / David had to go grimy. "Christina, you couldn't do no better than the deliveryman after me? Did I ruin you like that?"

I flexed my fist and was actually relishing an opportunity to connect it with his nose when I felt Lance, Jimmy, and Rob lining up behind me.

"Are we having a problem with the help?" Lance said in a deceptively silky voice.

"This is Christina's last fiancé," I announced.

Rob looked around. "Is this a new NSA hot spot or does this ninja lift weights for a living?" He nodded at Christina. "You dodged a bullet here, CB—definitely come up the food chain a ways."

"Way to upgrade, girl," Jimmy chimed in. He not only defused the situation but made all of us laugh, which we absolutely needed.

The gym manager came out of his office. "Is something wrong, David?"

"No, Jerry, I was just offering the ladies my services...in case it's something either of them is interested in or feels that they need."

Carey piped up. "David tried to inappropriately touch my friend, and her man came from across the room to protect her."

Jerry started looking very concerned. "David, is this true?"

Jay/David had not yet learned not to answer a question with a question. "Her man? I was engaged to her! Where's your ring now, Chris?"

Christina folded her arms across her chest and tapped her foot. "Let me ask you a couple of good questions. How the heck are Dina and Daisy? Are you undercover here, too? Are we blowing your cover?"

"Ouch, shots fired!" Rob said.

We were all aligned, waiting to hear what Jay/David had to say for himself next, when an announcement came over the loudspeaker. "Dr. Williams to the front desk for a phone call. Dr. Steven Williams." We all turned to look at Steven.

"Doctor?" Jay/David asked.

"You getting pages in the gym now? They do know you're an engineer, right?" Jimmy said.

Christina and I exchanged glances and I shrugged. I had no idea what I was being paged for. I linked my fingers with hers. "You come with me." I pointed at Jay/David. "You might want to think about transferring to another location. You don't want to see me again. You really don't."

We walked to the front desk. I leaned forward and announced, "I'm Dr. Williams."

The perennially chirpy brunette behind the counter handed me the phone. "It sounds urgent."

I took the receiver. "Hello?"

"Steven?" Heavy panting and a bunch of other weird noises came across the line. "It's Jackie. Is Christina with you?"

"Yeah, hold on." I passed her the phone.

She held it so that I could hear. "Oh, thank God. I called all y'all damn cell phones and no one answered! I called the station, your houses—this was my last resort."

"What's wrong?"

"Ti-Ti, I'm in labor and Sam is driving me crazy. Can you get here?"

"Where are you?"

"University Hospital. And hurry. If Sam tells me to breathe one more time he may be dead when you get here."

"I'm on the way. Don't kill him—it's hard to scare up bail on a Friday night."

I took the phone from her and handed it back across the counter. "What a day we're having. You want me to drop you off?"

"Are you kidding? I want you to come with me. Let me spin twice in the shower and we'll head over."

She wanted me to come with her. I smiled. "Okay, I'll meet you by the elevators."

She smiled back, turned toward the women's locker room and then turned back. "By the way..."

"Yes?"

"Major points for riding to the Jay/David rescue there, V. Dub."

I was way on her good side when she called me V. Dub. "Are you okay?"

"I wasn't and then I was. Thanks to you." She stretched up and gave me a kiss. I pulled her in closer. She sighed before pulling away. "Don't start or we'll miss Jackie's delivery."

"Right. Baby on the way. Stay focused. Don't forget to grab Carey. Are you going to call Lynne?"

"We've had enough drama for one day."

"Agreed."

32

What's Holding You Back?

Christina—Saturday, January 7, 1:13 a.m.

I walked over to the sofa and sat down gingerly in Steven's lap. He woke up and blinked, then blinked again. "Meet Christopher Samuel Hubbert. My godson." I was holding this beautiful, tiny, sleeping newborn in my arms. I looked from his scrunchy brown face to Steven's. He was looking at the baby with the same sense of awe and wonder that I had.

"Look at that," he said in his sleepy voice, which I loved. "Welcome to the world, baby Christopher. You're already a step ahead, with great parents and a doting godmother."

"Speaking of great parents, his are knocked out in the private room they moved Jackie into." Jackie's labor was relatively short at seven hours, but I felt every minute of it now. It had been a long day.

Steven's arms circled my waist and he rested his chin on my shoulder. "You know...we could just take this one and make a break for it."

I giggled until I thought about what he said. "You want one?"

"More than one."

"Oh." I was on the tail end of my thirty-seventh year—I didn't know how much time I had left, from a biological standpoint, in the baby-making business.

"Christina, we have all the time in the world."

He always knew what I was thinking. "You want one of these with me?"

"At some point, sure. Who else?"

I shrugged one shoulder. The brother was talking kids, too? It was one thing to let a man in and have him walk away. It was a whole other thing when kids were involved. And in my world, eventually the men always left. One way or the other.

"You wear me out. You go from supremely confident to completely insecure in the span of minutes. I know words hold no weight with you, so I try to show you how I feel in every way possible. When's it gonna be enough?"

Sam stepped out into the hall. "Who's got my boy?"

"I'll go look in on Jackie right quick. Let you fellas have a moment." I got up slowly and Steven took baby Christopher from me. Watching him holding that child in his arms shifted something inside that I didn't even realize was there. I swallowed and fled inside Jackie's room.

She was propped up in the bed with a smile on her face. "Girl, I know I'm not going to have another good night of sleep for twenty-five years, but I'm so glad to get that child out of me."

"Yes, you screamed something to that effect at the top of your lungs about two hours ago."

"Did I cut a complete fool?"

"Please, I told you that shiggity that Lynne pulled. Now *that* is cutting a complete fool."

"Look up 'hot mess' in the dictionary and she's posted up. I thought about calling her today, but I didn't need the drama. I'm a little selfish today."

"You're allowed to be. You were bringing an entirely new human being into the world." How cool was that?

"I was, wasn't I?" She smiled. "He's a handsome little thing, isn't he?"

"Charmer, just like his mama. Already got Steven talking about he wants one."

She pressed the button to raise herself up a little in the bed. "Aw, sookie sookie now! Did he really? I like that young man. What did you say?"

"I fled in here, girl. You know I'm the definition of gun-shy."

"Still? Come on now. All that mess was years ago. Move on already."

"Speaking of mess, we ran into Jay / David at the gym today."

Jackie's mouth fell open. "Dammit, I'm missing all the good scoop, spitting out babies. Tell me everything!" She yawned.

"Later, little mama. Save your strength for baby Chris. He's gonna wake up hungry and mad as hell."

She reached out and touched my arm. "Ti—I want this for you, too. I want you to feel just like this. Minus the aches and pains." Tears welled up in her eyes and spilled over. "You're the best person I know. You deserve to be happy."

I deflected by spilling some news. "Clarke asked Carey to marry him last night."

"Girl, stop—all this in the last twenty-four hours, and none of you bitches texted me to keep me in the loop?"

"We were told not to stress you out. You recall the crying jag you broke off at your shower? Sweetie, no one wanted to risk a repeat. You were already past the due date, and more than a little testy."

"But look at me now: new mommy, propped up on good painkillers, no cake to throw at you. So stop changing the subject. Listen to me. You're the only one standing in your way. Everyone can see you holding that man at arm's length. What's holding you back?"

Now she had me tearing up. I reached over to the night-stand and grabbed some Kleenex. "I'm just so scared, Jax. You know I completely trusted Cedric and Perry and Jay / David, and they turned out to be complete strangers to me. In the end, I had *no* idea who they truly were. I'm so scared the same thing is going to happen with Steven. If I go all in and this falls apart, I don't think I can put myself back together again. He means too much. So much more than the others. He gets me, you know. He gets me. What if it's just another illusion? What happens if he's not what he seems to be?"

"What happens if he's exactly what he seems to be?" Steven said from the doorway. He was leaning against the jamb in such a way that I knew he'd been standing there for a while. Sam was standing behind him, holding his son.

"Oh." I looked back at Jackie and leaned down to give her a hug. "You set me up," I whispered in her ear. She knew Steven was standing there when she asked the question.

"For your own good. Don't let him get away," she whispered back.

I nodded once and kissed her cheek. "All right, Hubbert family—we're going to leave you to it." I walked over to Sam. "You done good, Daddy."

"He ain't do nothing but plant a seed and bark some or-ders!" Jackie snapped from the bed.

Sam rolled his eyes. "Now, woman, we are not beefing on the first day of our son's life." Sam and Jackie loved to bicker; they had always done it.

"That was yesterday."

"Good Lord, has the postpartum kicked in already?"

Steven and I exchanged a look. "We're out." I kissed the baby on the forehead and exited into the hallway with Steven.

He took my hand as we wound through the corridors to get back to the wing where we parked the car. He sighed deeply.

I glanced over at him. He looked tired. "You look exhausted."

"I am exhausted, Christina. And I'm wondering if I'm just wasting my time here."

I looked around. "Where?"

"With you. Am I just wasting my time with you?"

"Wait. What?" I stopped dead in the middle of the corridor. He was scaring me.

"Are we gonna talk about this or are we just gonna go home, have amazing sex, and assume that's all this is?"

A nurse walking past faltered in her step as she sized us up. She shot me a look that clearly said "you might want to handle that."

"Okay, okay. Let's go to your place and talk about it."

33

Just You and Me

Steven—Saturday, January 7, 1:41 a.m.

I hadn't said a word on the short ride from the hospital back to my place. Truthfully, I was more than a little angry to find myself back here. And by here, I meant feeling like that twenty-six-year-old at the airport in New York, asking for something I wasn't sure I was going to get. This was not what Grown Man Steven was all about.

What a day. I contemplated just letting this go until morning because if Christina did not say some of what I wanted to hear, my entire mood was going to be shot. Then again, let's just get into it already. I set down the gym bag and turned around to look at her. She looked terrified—like a tiny, frightened bird hovering near the exit and dying to fly away. *Toughen up, Steven.* I steeled myself against sympathizing.

I clapped my hands together. "Okay, let's peel this back a little bit. What's up, Christina? What's the master plan?"

"Is this the 'let's define what we are to each other' conversation?"

I tightened my jaw. "No, this is one where we decide if it's even worth moving forward. Maybe we've gone as far as we can go at this level."

"Well, what do you think?" she asked quietly.

"Oh no, ma'am. It's not that type of party. That is classic Christina avoidance, and I'm not taking the bait. This is on you. The floor is literally and figuratively yours. Ball's in your court."

"All righty then, Grown Man Steven on deck, I see. Fine. You heard what I told Jackie. I don't trust myself to believe what I feel. To believe what I see. I just am terrified that you're going to rip my heart into a million pieces and I'll never get them back together. I won't recover. Not from this. Not from you."

"Why is that?" I pressed. "What makes me different?"

She took a deep breath and then let out a long sigh. "You're important to me. I care a lot for you. You make me feel things. Not just sexual things. You stimulate my brain. You make me happy. Does that make you happy to hear that you do all that to me? Does it make you happy to know that I think about you when I shouldn't? That I want to be around you all the time? Does it make you happy to make me admit that?"

I allowed a small smile to cross my face. "You know what? It does. It really does. I'm sorry you're so scared, but why don't you be honest with yourself for a minute."

"What do you mean?"

I explained. "Your problem, at least with Perry and Jay/ David, is that you only saw what you wanted to see. I don't let you do that with me. I make you see all of me. This is who I am, this is what you get."

"They fooled me, Steven—maybe you are, too!" Her tone was accusing.

Okay, if she really believed that, she was fooling herself.

Apparently it was time to take the gloves off. "That is one of the sweet little lies you tell yourself to make it all their fault. So you're always the victim."

"I beg your pardon?" She was clearly insulted, but I was speaking the truth and damning the consequences.

"I beg yours back. You can't stand there and tell me you had *no* signs that Perry might be batting for the other team? None? His sexual technique or sex drive or mannerisms or expressions? No clues, not one?"

She opened her mouth and closed it again.

"You background-checked Jay/David, but did you use your common sense? All those times he was 'traveling'?" Yes, I broke off the air quotes on her. "All those times you couldn't get him on the phone or didn't know where he was. Every time he couldn't spend a holiday with you and had last-minute excuses for not being where he was supposed to be, and you had not a twinge?"

Tears started slowly trickling down her face, but I had to make this point.

"Christina, you're too smart. I'm sorry. I've watched you work and interact with your coworkers and families and the people you interview, and no one can hold a candle to your intellect. Your brain is always working. There's no way you will ever convince me that you didn't suspect something."

"What is your point?!" she snapped.

So my voice got softer. "My point is that you can't hide behind the failed engagements anymore without acknowledging your own role in that crap. You really can't. And if you can't use that as an excuse for never trusting yourself or anybody else again, then you're fresh out of excuses, aren't you?"

"Steven. Stop it."

"No. I won't. You have nothing else to hide behind. There's just you and me. Now, I'm willing to put Grown Man Steven away tonight. I don't need to hang on to what happened in an airport lounge five years ago to protect myself from caring too much about you. I want you to do the same. I want you to put all the bad stuff that happened to you before in the back of the closet and board it up. Can you do it?"

She shook her head back and forth. "I don't know. I don't know. I have to think about it."

I nodded slowly. "Well, baby, you're out of time. You are thirty-seven years old. I'm thirty-two. This is it. You and me. Right here, right now. I'm willing to stand here with nothing but this moment and say I want this. I want you. I want us to take it as far as it can go. And if you don't, if you can't do the same—just walk away now. Just turn around and walk out the door. I'll bear no grudges. I'll accept that you gave all you have in you to give, and we'll call it a day."

She frowned. "You're giving me no shades of gray."

"None at all, sweetheart."

"So, is this an ultimatum?"

"It is."

"Seriously? Either I agree to be all in now, or I have to walk."

"I'll call you a cab."

My gut was churning. This was the poker equivalent of bluffing with nothing but a pair of deuces in your hand. But outwardly, I looked calm. Resigned. Resolute.

So quietly I could barely hear her, she answered, "I guess that's that, then." She turned and walked out the door.

I stood for a second in complete shock. Christina Brinsley walked away from me without a backward glance. Again. I gambled and lost. Something inside me felt like it was tearing, and my knees gave out. I sank to the floor, staring at the door, willing it to open. "Open, open, open, open," I chanted and prayed. "Dear God, let that door open. Open, dammit!"

It opened. She stepped inside, shut it, and locked it behind her. She leaned back against it and looked at me on my knees on the floor. With a running start she flung herself at me. I caught her as she started talking and crying at the same time. "I'm so sorry. I'm so stupid, I almost completely jacked this up. Why did you let me walk out? I was walking down the hallway asking myself *Christina, what are you doing, what are you doing?*" She pressed kisses over my face. "How could you let me walk out?"

I swallowed and sent up a prayer of thanks. I wrapped her up in my arms and held on tight. "You had to decide on your own. You had to come back on your own. I can't believe you walked out. What were you thinking? Don't you know I'm the best damn thing to ever happen to your bougie ass? What were you thinking?"

She threw back her head and laughed. "I wanted to have the last word, I wanted to be right."

"So why did you come back?"

"I wanted you more. I want you more. More than anything. I'm in. I'm all in." She rolled so I was on top of her. With both hands, she pulled down my sweatpants. Because we rushed to the hospital straight from the gym, I was naked underneath. She pulled her own sweats down. "Now I want you all in me. Now."

"Here?" There was only an area rug on top of the hardwoods.

"Here, now. Steven, please. I need you."

"Okay, baby." I made to move away. "Let me just get…"

"No. Nothing between us. All in. I'm safe."

"I'm safe."

"I know. I trust you."

I stroked my hand along the side of her body and she grabbed my hand. "No, nothing fancy. Just you and me. Come inside."

It was by far the sexiest invitation I had ever received. I slammed inside and gasped. I had never been unsheathed inside a woman before. It was indescribable ecstasy and snug warmth.

"Yes." Christina dug her nails into my arms and arched. "Mine. More."

"This is gonna be hard and fast," I warned as I surged forward again.

"I'm so far ahead of you, it's not even funny." She started shivering under me. "You just worry about keeping up."

True to her word, she met my first flurry of thrusts and then let out a high-pitched wail I had never heard from her before. I yanked her hips upward with each of my downward strokes to make sure I was hitting exactly the spots she loved. Her entire body stiffened and her internal muscles milked me in rippling waves that went on and on. I was toast—I grit my teeth and let go, shooting deep inside of her.

After a few minutes trying to catch my breath, I rolled off her and lay next to her, staring up at the ceiling. "Was that what you had in mind?"

A smile spread across her face. "That was perfection."

"When you go all in, you mean it."

Her face turned serious. "I've never done it like that before. With no protection, no pill, no nothing."

"Me either. Wait—did you say no pill, no nothing?"

She raised a brow. "Mr. I-Want-One-of-These-and-I'm-All-In is nervous now?"

"Not necessarily. I just thought you were on the pill."

"I am. I just haven't taken it since yesterday morning." She looked at my face and laughed. "Don't worry about it. The chances are *very* slim that this one time will result in anything."

The more I thought about it, the more okay I was with it. "If it does, I'm good. Are you good?"

"If you're with me, I'm good."

"Then we're good. Anything you want to talk about before we get off this hard floor?"

"Just one thing," she said in a small voice.

"What's up?"

"Are you at all concerned that we're deliberately avoiding usage of the L-word?"

I wondered if she'd noticed that. "No, I think it's a great sign. I think it means we're saving it. Giving the word the respect it's due."

She sighed. "You're so smart, Dr. V. Dub."

"Smart enough to get to that leftover Chinese food before you do."

She snorted. "I was smart enough to order some more and have it delivered earlier."

"A smart woman is a good one to have."

"You're a lucky man, then."

"Don't I know it."

34

No YouTube! No YouTube!

Christina—Saturday, January 28, 11:02 p.m.

"I'm happy for you, Lynne. I really am." I hugged Lynne and Eric and kissed both their cheeks while holding a bottle of champagne in one hand. Somehow, according to them, they had worked out their differences. They were together and happy. I was willing to let bygones be bygones. Though you could bet the very next time she and Eric had a falling out, I'd be eyeing her like an eagle. Lesson learned.

It was like Steven had told me: I couldn't keep turning a blind eye to people's faults and flaws. I had to own them and get ahead of them before they bit me in the ass. But there was time to worry about that on another day. We had almost finished filming all of our segments for the final installment on the foundation story. And today was Steven's birthday. We were throwing a party at his loft and it was a night for celebration.

Lynne hugged me back. "You're happy for everybody tonight, girlie. What time did you start on the champagne?"

"I'm high on life, sweetie. Haven't had a sip all day." I laughed.

"How was Christmas?"

"Brilliant. His parents loved me and I loved them right back. We're going to go back in the spring when the cold doesn't freeze all coherent thought out of your head."

"Well, we're heading over to Jackie's."

"Send her my love and tell her I'll be by next week." I waved and I moved on to the next cluster of people.

Jimmy was in deep conversation with my CEO, Jennifer. That was an interesting pairing. The laid-back comedian with the type A executive. I floated past to a group of Steven's students, including Jeffrey and Susan, whom I'd seen the first day outside of his office. A couple of the kids looked pretty young. "Do I need to card any of you?" I asked, only half joking.

"Dr. Williams already did," one of the kids said.

"Of course he did. Who wants a refill?" I topped off their glasses, exchanged some chitchat, and moved on.

A cluster of VNN employees including Vic, Tracey, Diane, and Brandon were huddled near the television. "Guys, are you seriously watching the station on your night off?" I emptied the bottle into their glasses and set it down.

Tracey laughed. "I like to see if the New York crew is better than us."

"They aren't," I stated. "And if they are, we'll just recruit them to come out West."

"That's the same speech she used to sucker me into it." Carey's voice drifted closer as she joined the group.

"Hey!" I gave her a hug. "Where have you been?" I looked over her shoulder to where Clarke was high-fiving Steven like he had just won the lottery. "Or do I not want to know?"

"I don't know," she said, waving her left hand around dramatically. "How do you feel about gaining another sister?"

"Woo!" I grabbed her and we bounced around in a circle. I ran across the room and launched myself at Clarke. He caught me in a bear hug and swung me around, laughing. "You finally did something brilliant. Took you long enough." I kissed his cheek and ran back across the room. "Let me see the rock, let me see." That solitaire had to be at least four carats, set in platinum. "Good Lord, you've spent the entire Brinsley fortune!" I teased.

"I didn't know there was a Brinsley fortune," Steven called out from across the room.

"Exactly my point." I laughed as Celia and Collin came over to take a look.

Collin took his glasses out of his pocket and put them on. "Christ Almighty, I'm going to have to upgrade Celia's ring. We cannot be outdone."

Celia and Carey exchanged a high five. "Score!" Celia shouted, and my mouth fell open. That was the hippest thing to fall out of Celia's mouth in . . . well, ever. I don't know what happened with the whole Dax thing, but he and Celia appeared to have gone their separate ways. Whatever the thing had been seemed to be a thing of the past.

"Well, let me come see this rock," Steven said as he sidled up. He lifted Carey's hand and whistled. "Damn, son, why don't you just strap an anchor around her hand and be done with it?" He turned to me. "Don't get any ideas—I'm not putting the Hope Diamond on your finger. You'll have to make do with dignified."

My mouth fell open.

"Twin, was that a proposal?" Stefani called out.

I shook my head back and forth violently. No more engagements, no thank you. Lesson learned . . . three times over.

Steven laughed. "Eventually, all in good time. There's no rushing Ms. Scared Straight over here. My baby takes her time."

"Speaking of babies . . ." Collin announced dramatically.

"What?!" I shrieked and turned to Celia. She was holding a large glass of wine. My eyes narrowed.

"We have a surrogate—the baby will be here in eight months," she explained.

"Wow! So much to celebrate," I murmured amidst another round of hugs and high fives. It was all a little overwhelming.

Everything was changing so fast. It made me a little nervous. But now wasn't the time. I looked at my watch. Steven's present was due to arrive any second. Right on cue the doorbell rang.

"Steven, can you get that?" I said as I moved to the kitchen to start clearing off space on the countertops.

He sent me a "what is this?" look and I shrugged and smiled. He opened the door and a line of wait staff walked in carrying covered trays. Delicious fragrances wafted in the air. After the tenth waiter filed in, Chef David walked in with a birthday hat tilted jauntily to the side. "Happy birthday, bro."

"My boy!" Steven's face lit up as he embraced Dave. Stefani flew across the room to get a hug in as well. As the three of them embraced, Steven looked at me and pointed. "Did you do this?"

I shrugged again with a big smile on my face. The waiters were lining up some of Dave's best dishes. People were already circling.

Dave shook his head. "Did she *do* this? Man, she harassed, begged, pleaded, and bribed to get me out here during a busy season. Promised me all sorts of sexual favors."

Heads swiveled in my direction. "Not from me! Diane, introduce yourself to Chef David." Everyone laughed.

"I don't think that's part of my job description, boss!" She laughed, but there was a gleam in her eye as she went over to shake his hand.

Dave gave me a thumbs-up. "You ready for the other thing?"

"Yep. Stefani first."

Over the past months I had discovered that Stefani had a weakness for sweets, particularly cannoli and truffles. Chef Dave had a cart wheeled in. On it was a three-tiered cake with pink and green flowers, Stefani's sorority colors. HAPPY BIRTHDAY, STEFANI was written down the three tiers. Stefani clapped. "It's too pretty to cut!"

Dave handed her a knife. "Girl, you better cut that creation."

She sliced into it. "Oh my God, it's cheesecake with truffles and cannoli. That's just evil." She pointed the knife at me. "Did you do this?"

"I had a little help from Marcus."

"We'll be needing to keep you two separated," she teased. "I'm going to wait to taste it until Steven gets his."

Another cart was rolled in. I stepped out of the kitchen; I wanted to see if Dave had pulled off my idea. He lifted a huge box and flipped a switch. On the table was a replica of a high-speed train on tracks. The train started moving.

"Wait, did you make me an actual train of cake?" Steven said.

"Yes, I did," Dave answered. "But wait until it comes around the track."

Everyone watched as the train came around the circle slowly. On the side of each car a word was written in frosting. Everyone read aloud as each car passed. "Steven. Happy. Birthday. I. Love. You. Christina."

A group "Awwww!" swelled up.

I looked over at Steven. His eyes looked a little glassy. He put his hand out; I stepped forward into his embrace. He wrapped me up, closed his eyes, and whispered in my ear, "I love you, too. So much."

"I swear before God, I will pull your player card right here if you cry over this cake!" Dave announced, and everybody laughed.

I pressed my lips against his once, and then again, and one more time because I loved his lips, too.

"Hose 'em down!" Carey called out.

I stepped back and wiped a little moisture out of the side of his eye. He did the same for me. I noticed a few others dabbing with napkins. "Okay, sorry y'all had to witness the sap.

Dave, that is officially the coolest damn cake ever. Let's top off the glasses. Steven, Stefani—you want happy birthday or something else?"

"Just a plain old happy birthday will do."

I lifted my glass and started singing "Happy birthday" to Stefani and Steven. As others started gravitating toward the food and cakes, Steven wrapped his arm around my waist.

"Best birthday ever, baby."

"You like the cake?"

"The cake is cool, but I like what it says more than anything."

I turned in his arms and tilted my head up. "I meant it. I mean it. I love you, Steven."

"Well, you can't take it back now; it's on the cake and everything."

"I'll never take it back."

"You promise?"

"I promise."

"I'm going to hold you to that."

"As long as you hold me."

We were in our own little world. I wanted to take that moment and bottle it. Everything was absolutely perfect. So of course I started wondering and worrying about what would go wrong...because something always, always did. There was that little part of me that was constantly waiting for the other shoe to drop.

"Whatever it is, think about it tomorrow," Steven said.

I kissed him again. "You know me so well."

"Believe dat. Kiss me like it's my birthday, girl." He twirled me into a dip and laid those lips on me. By the time I caught my breath, I was back upright.

"Clarke, hit the birthday mix!"

Clarke pressed some buttons and the room filled with the booming bass of 50 Cent's "In Da Club."

I took my first drink of champagne for the night, raised my glass, and started shaking my hips from side to side. "Go shorty, it's your birthday."

Steven threw back his champagne and stepped behind me. "You don't want none of this, you don't want it. You know I will dance you out of those sexy-ass shoes."

"Bring it on, birthday boy." I dropped down to the ground and came back up.

"Aw shit," Carey said as she and Clarke starting dancing. "It's about to be on. Brinsley dance-off. If somebody scared, they should go home right now."

I saw one of the students reaching for his cell phone and I pointed at him and started chanting, "No YouTube! No YouTube!" Everybody joined in.

When out of the corner of my eye I caught sight of my very proper CEO, Jennifer, chanting and grinding on Rob, I knew we were in for an epic evening.

35

And We're Back in Four...
Three...Two...

Christina—Friday, February 4, 7:02 p.m.

The reason I knew it was done deliberately was that I had planned how every single segment of this series should flow. I wrote, directed, produced, and edited, so I knew down to the second what was on that film. What I did not script was the follow-up panel, which, for some reason, we decided to film live.

The series on high-speed rail research and funding was called *Project Mercury—Fact, Fiction, or Fraud*. It had run for the past five days with our highest ratings ever. Tonight we aired the final segment. Then we planned a live postshow panel that included myself, Congressman Walker, Lance, and Becky Fine, an independent accountant and auditor. Standing around the newsroom watching were Steven, Tracey, Carey, the three Js, Brandon, and various members of the congressman's staff.

Taking a deep breath off camera, I caught Brandon's eye for a second. There was a look of anticipation on his face that threw me for the slightest second. Then the red light went on and I began.

"Welcome back. I'm Christina Brinsley and I hope you enjoyed our in-depth look at Project Mercury. I'm joined by a number of esteemed guests this evening: Congressman Walker of California, Lance Porter—chief operating officer of the Chi-Wind Foundation, and Becky Fine—a forensic accountant who specializes in auditing government-funded entities. Welcome."

After the choruses of "good evening" and "glad to be here," I dove straight into the issue of the day.

"I think this documentary has shown what a great thing high-speed rail could be for this nation. The prevailing concern from our viewers is what is it going to cost, and who is going to pay for it. Mr. Porter, your thoughts?"

"China invested in the neighborhood of 300 billion dollars to get their so-called bullet train from idea to inception. And they are still expanding. Here in the U.S. it's going to take that same level of financial commitment. The plan is to build a long-term funding effort from both public and private sources."

"And are you prepared for the level of scrutiny that organizations such as Chi-Wind will be under from all the watchdog groups?"

"After this series, you bet we will."

Smiles all the way around. I waited a beat and then continued.

"Congressman Walker, when we hear the term 'public funding'—is that just code for more tax dollars out of citizens' pockets?"

"Absolutely not. Let me talk a little bit about how the government earns money...." He launched into a preapproved, rehearsed two-minute speech where even his strategic pauses and my thoughtful "Is that so?" were planned.

When he wrapped, my face turned serious. "Now, sir, you have been under a lot of scrutiny lately."

"Can't take a leak without a witness these days."

Oh, he was rolling out the good-ole-boy charm. I flashed a smile. "I know a little about that myself."

"Indeed."

"But, sir, according to our records there appears to be an amount of money missing from this project, totaling over 500,000 dollars. How do you account for that?"

"Well, I don't. I believe somebody took it."

We all chuckled.

"I'm assuming you do not mean you."

"Correct. Somebody who is not me took it."

"How do you respond to the questions about your lifestyle versus your income?"

"Budgeting and a wealthy wife."

More laughter. Carey held up her hand in the sign that meant "break for commercial, it's time to pay the bills."

I turned to camera two. "When we get back, we'll go a little deeper to find out where the money went and who is spending it. You may be surprised at the answers. Come back after the break. This is VNN, where your news is what counts."

"And we're clear."

I turned sideways while the makeup guy patted and dabbed. Carey came up to the desk. "It's going well, don't you think?" I asked her.

Carey nodded. "The Js are in ecstasy. Ratings through the roof, advertising dollars pouring in, journalistic integrity... yada blah—it's all win / win."

"I'll take it."

"Maybe you can put a little more stock in the reality of a happily-ever-after?"

I glanced over to where Steven was standing deep in conversation with two of the Js. I loved that he could talk to anybody, anywhere, about anything. "Maybe so. Just maybe."

"See you after."

"And we're back in four... three... two... go!"

"This is Christina Brinsley. You have joined VNN in the

middle of a discussion panel following a five-part series on Project Mercury—a dream to build high-speed rail from sea to shining sea. Ms. Fine, you've been poring over the income and expense books from several foundations and state-run entities to align them with the allocated funds from the U.S. Government Accountability Office. Can you start by explaining how an audit like that works?"

She launched into her preapproved, rehearsed two-minute speech, but when she came to the ending, it was different from what she'd shared earlier. "In this case, however, a second set of books was found at one of the foundations."

My eyebrows raised and my pulse sped up. This was new to me. "Intriguing. Which foundation?"

"Chi-Wind."

And this is where the term "dramatic pause" came from. There was everything but the ominous "da–dum–dum" pounded out on the organ. I recovered quickly and asked the next logical question. "When did you receive those?"

"Just this afternoon."

"And what did you find out?" I saw Steven's face; he looked as stunned as I felt.

"A lot of inconsistencies, unfortunately. There is income where we cannot locate the sources. There are a lot of cash withdrawals which always send up a red flag."

I felt a little sick. "Why is that, exactly?"

"Well, as you may imagine, once money is converted into cash, it gets harder to trace and easier to make disappear."

I did not want to ask the next question. In fact, I wanted to pull the plug on this whole thing until I could figure out what was going on. But this was live television, so I plowed forward. "And exactly how much cash are we talking about that has disappeared?"

"At my last count, 1.3 million dollars."

"Did you say 1.3 million?"

She nodded. "Yes."

"I am *vindicated!*" Congressman Walker announced. "My name is cleared! I would like to take this opportunity—"

I cut him off. "Congressman!" I turned blindly to camera one. "When we return, we'll continue with these shocking revelations. You're watching VNN, the people's news channel."

"And we're clear."

"What the *hell* is going on, guys?!" I said to the room at large. "Who knew about this? Have we verified the books? Why am I on TV with my drawers showing? Someone? Anyone?" As I looked, a smile spread across Brandon's face and he turned to walk away. I yanked off the microphone and hopped off the stage to catch up to him. "What do you know about this?"

He shrugged. "I just do the research. I found out new information this afternoon, but as usual you were too wrapped up with your man to talk to me. I took it straight to Becky. That's my job and my role as a law-abiding, tax-paying American citizen."

"You sent me a text at two o'clock asking if I had time to chat. That's what you call giving me a heads-up?"

"Maybe you need to reassess your priorities. Don't get mad at me because your boyfriend isn't squeaky-clean. You always seem to pick the wrong guy, don't you?" He headed down the hallway.

I spun back toward the newsroom and shot Steven a look as I passed.

He put his hands up. "I don't know anything about this."

"You better not," I hissed, and slid back into the anchor chair. I closed my eyes. *Deep, cleansing breath. Deep, cleansing breath.*

"We're back in three . . . two . . . one . . ."

"This is Christina Brinsley and you're watching VNN. Before the break we heard allegations that over one million dollars is missing from the Chi-Wind Foundation books. Congressman Walker, do you know where the money is?"

"Once the money goes to the foundation, to Mr. Porter and Dr. Williams, I have no access to it. If anything, I believe this clears my name."

"Well, that remains to be seen, sir. Mr. Porter, what if any light can you shed on this for us?"

For someone supposedly thrown for a loop, he looked surprisingly calm and serene. "I can tell you that I have no idea where this second set of books came from."

"Well, who else has access to your financial reporting systems?"

"It's just myself and Dr. Williams, of course."

"So you are alleging what, exactly?"

"Well unfortunately, Christina, I'm looking over some documents that Betsy just handed me. It appears that several weeks ago, Dr. Williams opened up a personal account offshore with a starting balance of $78,192.64. Money that you and I both know was given to the foundation. Since then, there have been several cash deposits totaling over a quarter of a million dollars."

I swayed a little in my seat before turning to the camera. "In light of these recent revelations, I find I have a significant conflict of interest and cannot objectively report on this story any further. When we return, this panel will be hosted by Tracey Tulum, who will continue to hunt for the truth."

"And we're clear."

"Lance, what the hell are you talking about?" Steven yelled. "You know I don't have any offshore accounts."

"I'm sorry, buddy. I'm just looking at this documentation. It's pretty damning."

The set was deathly quiet as I unplugged my mic and motioned to Tracey. She was very pale. "Christina, oh my God."

"Don't worry about it. Focus. Here are my notes. These questions in red were the next up. My closing segment is here and here. You can totally do this."

"Christina." One of the Js called out, and I just put my hand out. There was only one person I wanted to hear from right now. He was arguing heatedly with Lance and looking as shell-shocked as I felt.

"Steven, can I speak to you in my office, please?"

"We're going to want him on camera."

"*No!*" we both said in unison.

"We're back on in ten, people. Make the call."

"My office...now."

As we walked down the hallway, I heard Tracey speaking. "You are watching VNN, the place where your voices are heard and your questions are answered. In light of the information brought to light implicating noted professor and engineering wunderkind Steven Williams, I have taken over the panel discussion on Project Mercury."

36

I Was Set Up

Steven—Friday, February 4, 7:36 p.m.

My BlackBerry was buzzing like crazy in my pocket as I followed Christina back to her office. What the hell had just happened? Was it my imagination, or had my whole life just imploded on nationwide television?

I couldn't think and I had to think. I needed to think. I just needed a minute to sit down with Christina, sort out what just happened and decide what to do next.

"Maybe I should go back on air."

She pulled me into her office, slamming the door and locking it behind her. "To say what, Steven? To what end? To deny it?"

"Of course to deny it! What else?"

"Do you know how many people go on TV to deny scandals like this?" she asked. Her arms were crossed tightly in front of her and she looked as irritated as I felt.

It suddenly occurred to me what was going on. "I was set up. Duped. Somehow made the scapegoated patsy in the whole thing."

"Seriously, Steven—by who, for what reason? Generally,

people who say they've been set up look guilty as hell." Her tone was accusing.

I took a step backwards as I absorbed that. "You think I'm guilty? Is that what you think?"

"I don't *know* what to think, Steven. I just got blindsided on my own damn TV show. What the hell? What the *hell?*"

"What the hell what? I don't know about any of this." I looked at her face closely for the first time. "Wait a damn minute. You can't possibly think I knew about any of this?"

"What is Perry's money doing in an offshore account in your name?"

I couldn't believe that I had to defend myself to her. Of all people! Wasn't she supposed to be on *my* side? "How the hell should I know? You were right there when I got it. You've been with me every day since. Did you see me leave these shores?"

"Well, what did you do with the check after that night?"

"I stuck it in my top drawer at the foundation and forgot about it."

"You put a check for nearly eighty grand in a desk drawer and forgot about it?"

"Yes! What's the implication here? And I assume we're talking reporter to subject? Do you seriously think I stole money? From you? From my own foundation? From the government? Are you kidding me?"

She shook her head slowly. "Thirty minutes ago, I would have said no. But all of a sudden I'm remembering you and Congressman Walker all buddy-buddy at the banquet. I'm thinking about your clothes and your loft and your car. You live well."

"I'm a thirty-two-year-old man with very little debt and two six-figure incomes. Are you kidding me about this? Are you really making me justify my lifestyle to you? Because if that's what's going on here, that's a huge problem for me. That's bigger than the pile of crap I just had dumped on my good name in public. This is about you and me now. Either you trust me or you don't. Christina? You either believe me or you don't."

She remained silent. The look on her face was one I'd seen before. It was the accusing, disbelieving, wounded look she'd given Jay / David when he was standing naked in her foyer. She had now lumped me in with the Jay / Davids of the world. And that was unforgivable.

"Wow, Christina. Between the two of us, only one revealed a huge flaw tonight. It wasn't me. One test of faith and you failed. Just know that. You failed me miserably this evening. For the record, *love*"—I emphasized love—"the proper response is 'Steven, I know you didn't do any of the terrible things they're accusing you of. We'll get through this together.'"

She shook her head and tears started streaming down her cheeks. The sight of those made me even more angry than I already was.

"What are you crying about? Your whole world didn't just get blown to hell. You are exactly where you thought you'd end up, right? The victim? Lied to by another man you should have known better than to trust?"

"I just don't know what to think, what to believe."

"And that's the problem. You should believe in me." I turned away. "This is sabotage. This is sabotage! Oh my God. This day sucks in ways I could've never anticipated. But maybe I should have." Maybe I should've known she was not a girl for the long haul or the tough road.

"Who would sabotage you, Steven?"

"You are, right now. You're killing us. Right now. All those years you picked the wrong men on purpose, and now that you have the right one, you're looking for an excuse to bail. Well, guess what?"

"What?"

"I don't want a woman who doesn't trust me. I don't want a woman who's constantly looking for reasons to leave. I don't want a woman so damaged that I have to prove myself over and over again."

"What do you want?"

"I want to clear my name. And I'll find a way to do it because I believe truth prevails in the end. And I want out of this relationship because I believe it's not supposed to be this hard. I don't want to put the rest of my life on hold, waiting for you not to freak out when someone mentions marriage. I want someone who wants to be with me so badly that she's willing to risk everything for it. Through good times and bad. Like tonight...these would be considered very bad times. But instead of being a comfort to me, you stand in accusation. I am actually having to defend myself to you. To *you!* You are supposed to be on Team Williams. 'All in'—do you remember that? I want a woman who would look squarely in the eye of that camera and say 'there is no way that *my* man is involved in that.' That's what I want." And clearly not what I had.

"I want to trust you. I want to believe you but..."

"Yeah, save it. I already know. It looks like neither of us are getting what we want here. I have no more time to waste on this. On us. On you. I have to look out for me. Good-bye, Christina."

I opened the door. Clarke was standing outside. He looked from his sister to me and then put his hand on my shoulder. "I want to represent you. I have a theory. Do you have time to talk?"

I looked back at Christina, who was still standing in the middle of the room. "I've got all the time in the world." I shut the door and walked away without a backward glance.

37

Was It All Just a Hustle?

Christina—Monday, February 14, 2:51 p.m.

I waited until I could not put it off anymore. It had been almost two weeks since the "drama." I had to go to Steven's apartment and get my stuff. I wouldn't have minded leaving the clothes and shoes there, but my mini laptop was there and I had notes I needed to give Carey.

I had taken a leave of absence from Valiant and, in fact, from the world. Steven's face was everywhere. I was all cried out and sick of it. I was just done with the whole thing. I was holed up in my house with the phone and the television off. I quit checking e-mail and I only answered the door to close friends and family.

Since the story broke, Steven's entire life was open for scrutiny. Seemed he hadn't shared the full extent of his street life in Chicago. He had run with some really unsavory characters back in the day. Does a leopard change his spots? I didn't think so.

Clarke was working with him to clear his name and told me (on a daily basis) that there was more to this than met the eye, and I was making a huge mistake. As a matter of fact, everyone seemed to be taking Steven's side on this thing. My own mother called to tell me I was being a damn fool. Was I wrong? Maybe so, maybe not. I had decided it was easier to just be alone.

On the upside, if you could call it that, I was a hero at the office. The VNN ratings had never been higher. Snippets of my series and the panel-to-end-all-panels were on every major news outlet. There was talk of a Peabody Award nomination in my future.

Did I want an award for exposing my lover as a fraud and grand larcenist? I thought not. But again, the Js had never been happier.

I let myself into the apartment quietly, though I didn't expect anybody to be home. Steven had a two-hour class on Mondays plus office hours, so I felt sure I could get in and get out without seeing him. We hadn't spoken a single word to each other since that night. I was looking to keep it that way. Really, what was left to be said?

The apartment was pretty dark, but when I looked over, I saw my red crocodile suitcase sitting by the bar. Lifting it up, I set it on a stool and unzipped it. Everything I had ever left here was in the bag, including clothes, toiletries, some snacks, and a book I had been reading. Even though I had come to get my stuff, I was more than a little insulted that he had packed it all up for me. Like he was the wronged party here? It was as if he was erasing my very existence from his space, his life.

Tucked in the front zipper was my notebook and charger. Behind that was a framed 10" x 12" picture of me and Steven from his birthday. We were kissing beside the "I love you" train cake.

"Well, we know that was a damn lie," his voice said from the shadows.

I jumped and almost dropped the picture.

He was sitting on the edge of the bed at the far end of the loft, which was usually cordoned off with a floor-to-ceiling room separator.

"Steven, what are you doing here?"

"Happy freakin' Valentine's Day to you, sweetheart."

I had been so much in my own head these last few weeks, I didn't even realize it was Valentine's Day. It was maybe not the best choice of a day to come by and pick up the leftovers of our tumultuous relationship. "Sorry, I didn't realize."

"What difference does it make? It's a day like any other."

"Steven." He sounded so harsh. "Let's just be mature about this, shall we?"

"By all means."

"So why are you home?" I asked again.

"I live here."

"Yes, why are you home alone in the dark in the middle of the day?"

"I'm on a leave of absence."

I hadn't known that. "So am I."

"Good for you. Hope you're enjoying yours more than I'm enjoying mine."

I sighed deeply. "I hope things work out for you, Steven. I really do."

"I'm sure they will. I'm just a street hustler from Chicago, right? I always land on my feet."

"Was it?" I asked. "Was it all just a hustle?"

"Funny you should ask. I'm wondering the exact same thing."

"You're wondering if I hustled *you?*" I was incredulous. He could not be serious.

"Yes, Christina, I am."

"Me? For what possible gain?"

"Oh, I think you came out ahead on this one. From where I'm standing, you got a great story, a career boost, and an enthusiastic bed buddy for a while. It's all wins across the board for you, sweetheart. I got shafted."

"So Grown Man Steven is back." And nastier than ever.

"Whose fault is that?"

"There's no winner or loser here, Steven. What would you have me do?"

He stood and marched forward. He was in a pair of navy sweatpants with a Columbia T-shirt. He looked tired and really angry. His eyes were almost forest green. He yanked the picture out of my hand. "What would *I* have *you* do? What would I have you *do?* I would have you honor this!" He pointed at the words on the cake. "I would have you believe in me, believe in us, stand *by me.* I would have you just once put me above those fears you can't seem to let go of." He threw the picture across the room and it shattered against the wall.

I cringed in the face of his anger; I'd never really seen him like this. He had been irritated with me before, but this was the first time he really seemed to have no positive feelings for me at all. Whatever he had felt for me seemed to be gone. It gave me pause, but at the heart of it I just didn't believe him. In a small voice I said, "You lied to me."

His entire body went visibly tense. "You have some damn nerve saying that to me. Out of every man you have ever lain under and pretended to care about, I am the *only* one to be upfront and true. I never lied to you. Not once. Not ever. In the entire time I've known you. Not even those sweet little lies you seem to like so much. I have always dealt straight with you. Can you say the same to me?"

That took me aback. "Wait—you think I set you up? For what?" What kind of conspiracy theory had he created to assuage his guilt and culpability?

"What else? For your career, the only thing you really love," he said bitterly.

Curious, I probed deeper. "And I put this master plan in place when?"

He shrugged. "I have to wonder if you didn't walk into my classroom last October with a plan."

"Wow. So this is where we are."

"Pretty much. This is where we are."

"Do you ever think about that red-eye flight?"

"What about it?"

"Do you ever think what would have happened if I'd just watched my movie and you'd just read your book?" I thought about that all the time. All the what-ifs and should-haves and could-haves...they drove me crazy.

"What difference does it make now? Here we are. Unlike you, I don't second-guess fate and destiny. I take life as it comes. Come what may." He turned around and walked back toward the bed. "You can leave the key on the bar when you go."

Guessing there was nothing left to be said, I zipped up the suitcase, took the key off the ring, and set it on the counter. Without looking back, I let myself out and walked away.

What Comes After

38

I'm Not Twenty-six Anymore

Steven—Friday, March 5, 6:11 p.m.

"I am not feeling it, Jimmy," I said as another group of tight-skirted girls teetered by in sky-high heels. Seemed like every ten minutes or so, a new set walked by with the same coy glances, giggles, and outfits. They all started looking the same to me. Jimmy and Rob talked me into coming out to a happy hour at whatever the latest hot bar in SoMa was. Hadn't been to one of these in years, and I was quickly reminded why. I know the guys wanted to cheer me up and get me back in the game, but like I said...I wasn't feeling it.

"I know, bro, but you're going to sit out here and have a couple of drinks and pretend like there are more women in the world than Christina Brinsley, okay?"

I sighed. This was one more thing to be really pissed off at Christina for. Because of her nonbelieving behind, I was back on the market. Dammit. There comes a point where a man does not feel like dating. He thinks his dating days are behind him, and you know what? He's happy about it. I didn't want to play the games, ask the questions, learn all the little things you have to learn about someone new. I thought I was done with all of that. If not forever, for a long, long time. I was extraordinarily pissed off to find myself in this situation.

"Professor Dub—are you listening?" Rob asked, waving a hand in front of my face.

"Yeah, I got it."

I saw him and Jimmy exchange glances as the waitress dropped off a round of beers with an appetizer platter. I picked up a beer and took a sip.

"Enough is enough," Jimmy said. "Please pick out one of these tasty treats eyeballing your pretty ass, have some rebound revenge sex, and let's get on with living, shall we?"

"Seriously, Jimmy. I'm fine. What does my sex life have to do with you anyway?"

"Listen, son—if you're not with Christina, you've cut off my access to the fancy and fine sisters in this fair city. I'm left to collect your castoffs from these types of places. So please, my brother, dial up that thousand-watt smile and make it rain."

I had to laugh. Jimmy was perfectly capable of pulling women on his own, and he knew it. "Aren't you seeing somebody?"

"Didn't work out."

I looked at Rob. "Aren't you seeing someone from VNN?"

"It's just a physical thing."

"Yeah, that's how they start," I said with a sigh. I felt old all of a sudden. "Anyway, sorry to cut your supply line to the fine and fancy."

"I'll survive," Jimmy said soberly. "Will you?"

Rob piped up, "Remember, we were there the first time you two went your separate ways. If we need to line up the tequila shots and the ladies of questionable virtue to get you through it, we will do it."

"Ha!" I laughed shortly. "I'm not twenty-six anymore. Ladies and liquor aren't the cure, but I appreciate the gesture."

"Dr. Williams?" a young female voice said from behind me.

I swung around to see Sarah, one of my students—former students—standing there. She was in her little black dress with heels and more makeup than any one woman should wear.

"Hey, Sarah," I said kindly. This right here was the reason I quit coming to places like this.

"Um, we really miss you in class. When will you be back?"

"I don't know. Hopefully soon."

"Can I buy you a drink?" she asked nervously.

Can a nineteen-year-old baby buy me a drink? Oh hell, no. "Thank you, Sarah, that really wouldn't be appropriate."

She turned bright red. "Oh, okay. Have a great night. Hope to see you back in class soon."

As she walked away, I turned back to Jimmy and Rob. "Can we go now?"

"That was painful to watch," Rob said.

"Tell me about it," Jimmy added. "Listen, when are you going back to work? The university said they had no grounds to suspend you."

"I know, but I'm working with Clarke and Collin. It looks like this whole thing was an inside-job setup."

"Well, we knew that." Rob put his hands up in an "of course" gesture.

I set my beer down with a thud and stared at it. That was the reaction I'd wanted from Christina. Unconditional, unwavering trust in me. Hadn't quite turned out that way, now had it?

Jimmy clapped his hands together to get my attention. "Damn, son! What did he say?"

"Sorry, it's nothing. Just a bad thought." I shook it off.

"So who's the inside guy—Lance?" Rob asked.

"Probably. Why do you say that?"

"Never liked him. He was always just a little too slick. You remember that girl both of you had a date with way back when?" Jimmy asked.

I frowned and thought about it. "Vaguely. I know she dou-ble booked us and we both left, but I don't remember her name or what happened to her."

"Well, your boy Lance went back a week later to have that date and a little something more. Then he went around cam-pus telling everybody she chose him over you."

"What? Why?"

" 'Cause you're the golden boy and he wanted some of that shine. Looks like he's still trying to steal it," Rob added.

"Why is this the first I'm hearing about this?" I was as-tounded. Was I just as blind as Christina when it came to peo-ple? She only saw the bad, I only saw the good? Had I been telling myself the same kind of lies I had accused her of hiding behind? The thought was sobering.

"It never seemed important. I thought you knew he was jock-riding, waiting for his opening for the number one spot. He wanted to be you, son."

I shook my head. "I never saw it."

"That, my friend, is because you suffer from nice-man-itis," Jimmy teased.

"Damn, I thought I'd really grown. How did I misjudge people so close to me?"

"Don't beat yourself up. You kept Lance around for his fi-nancial genius, and that he is. You wanted Christina because she's an amazing, beautiful woman, and that she is. Both of them just have a few issues to work through. But there's noth-ing you can do about either. Some folks just got to find their own way," Rob said.

Jimmy shook his head. "Isn't this fine table talk to attract the women? You two are killing my game."

"Then my job here is done. Can we please get the hell outta here?" I asked.

Rob signaled for the bill. "We'll back off for now, but you need to either get your girl back or get back out there. You're a testy brother when you're by yourself."

"Amen," Jimmy agreed.

"Get my girl back? Are you crazy? You want me to take back a girl who believes I stole money, hustled for a living, and lied to everyone I know? Really?"

"She didn't mean it," Rob said. "She's just confused."

That was an understatement.

"C'mon, man, you know she loves you," Jimmy said.

"Wel, she has a hellified way of showing it. That's all I know!" I raised my voice a little at the end.

They exchanged glances again. Rob took some bills from his pocket and tossed them on the table. "Okay, brother, we can go."

I was more than ready to leave.

39

You Will Fix This

Christina—Saturday, March 13, 6:28 p.m.

Girls' night in had taken on a different flavor. We were at Carey's house again. Jax brought the baby, Lynne brought a new (humbler) attitude, Carey brought bridal magazines, and Celia joined us. The last six months had forced all of us to reprioritize.

"So how was your first week back at work?" Celia asked me while she rocked baby Christopher back to sleep.

"Difficult." That was an understatement. Though the Chi-Wind story had moved to the back burner, the fallout from the story still reverberated around the station. Brandon was on a forced leave of absence. Primarily because you don't deliberately, with malicious glee, setup your on-air personalities for humiliation.

The Js forced an all-hands meeting on us, where they laid down the law. Things were going to change. There would be no more office vendettas played out on the air or on the Internet. Those who couldn't play nice were invited to find alternate employment.

The heightened profile of the network meant more pressure on us to continue to deliver the kind of insightful but personal news stories that the advertisers loved. I was starting a new series on the billion-dollar business of weddings. Ironic, but I had planned three, and could consider myself an expert on everything from Ecuadoran roses to seating charts. Let's just say my heart wasn't in it.

I had turned a corner on my failed relationship with Steven. I was no longer angry, I was sad. Carey said I had my stages of grief all mashed up. I skipped past denial, bounced around angry, ignored bargaining, and settled into sad depression. Apparently I was only one step away from acceptance and moving on. I was ready to get there already. I was tired of feeling like warmed-over crap every day.

The newsroom itself was a reminder of the latest episode of *Watch Christina's Life Go Up in Flames*. I couldn't even sit in the same chair when I was on air. I shifted to take the right-hand chair on the anchor desk.

And then there was the whole "Are you okay?" sympathy gauntlet to get through. You could almost fool yourself into thinking that you're okay until someone asks you about it for the third time in an hour. Work was exhausting, but it was all I had left.

With a sigh, I looked up to see four sets of eyes on me.

"What?"

"You're gonna get mad," Lynne said.

"Tell me anyway. I can't take y'all giving me the eye all night."

They looked at Carey. So I did, too. Clearly, she'd been chosen as spokesman. She put down her magazine and came over to sit across from me on the sofa. "There's a very good, very real chance that Steven was set up."

"What are you talking about?" My heart started beating rapidly.

"Clarke and Collin hired an independent investigator," Celia said.

"When? What did they find out?"

"What does it matter?" Jackie said. "The point is—that man is innocent."

"How can you be sure? Who set him up? Are they sure?"

Lynne piped up. "They're sure. It looks to be a combination of the congressman, Lance, and Brandon."

"Lance and Brandon? Are you kidding?"

"Now why would we lie about it?" Carey sucked her teeth. "Christina, this is big business. That 1.3 million dollars is just the tip of the iceberg of what can really be pocketed if this project gets off the ground. We're talking millions and millions of dollars that will be lost forever if someone doesn't do something to stop it. Steven hasn't seen the report yet. You have an opportunity to clear his name and do the right thing."

"Someone like who? Me? Oh hell, no—I'm not touching this story again. No way." I think I sacrificed enough, chasing this story.

A woman's voice came down the hallway. "You little chicken-shit bitch. You will, too!" Stefani appeared in Carey's living room looking very, very ill.

I looked around at the other ladies, who were suddenly looking everywhere but at me. "Um, hey, Stefani."

"Hey my ass. You broke my brother again." She paused strategically. "But this time you will fix this. You hear me?"

"Um." What to say to that?

"Christina, I'm pregnant."

"Oh, congrats—"

"Bump that." She cut me off. "I'm pregnant. My twin is miserable, so I am miserable, which means my baby is miserable. I spend a third of my life sleeping, a third of my life clasping the toilet, and the other third propping up my brother. My husband throws chocolate, ginger ale, and stale crackers at me and flees my presence. This sucks. Now you have the power to fix this, and by God, you will do it."

"Well, actually...um...." I had no intention of getting back into it. Any of it.

"Stop saying um! Now I like you, Christina. It's taken me a while to warm up to your heart-breaking ass, but now that I have...I feel comfortable in saying this. You are a wuss."

I looked around and noticed that no one, not a one of my friends, was jumping to my defense. "Did she just call me a wuss?"

Jackie cackled. "Stop her when she's lying!"

"You all think I'm a wuss?" Again, no dissent from the crew.

Amongst the nods, Carey added, "I like 'chicken-shit bitch' myself."

"You like 'spoiled, entitled princess' better?" Stefani suggested.

I frowned in confusion. "Seems a little harsh, doesn't it?"

Lynne yelled, "Girl, quit acting brand-new! You trusted him enough to know that he wasn't the least bit interested in me, but you all of a sudden decided he was capable of jacking funds from his own foundation? C'mon, now."

Celia said, "What do the kids say—GTFOH?"

"Translation?" I asked.

"Get The Eff Outta Here with that," Carey supplied. "You cut and run on that boy at the very first sign of trouble. Unsubstantiated trouble, at that. You need to be shamed."

Stefani stomped her foot. "Bitch, you wanted to bail, so you bailed."

Okay now, it was getting a little hostile for me. "Stef, I know you're with child and all, but I'm not gonna be too many more bitches up here, okay?"

"Hmph. You're lucky that's all I call you. I'm from South Side Chicago. Don't let the new bouge fool you. You fix this or I am coming for that ass."

I couldn't help it. I dissolved into laughter. Stefani was

plenty siddity, so to hear "coming for that ass" flying out of her mouth amused the rest of us greatly.

She rolled her eyes. "Before this setup..."

"Alleged setup," I interjected.

"Whatev. Before this, did you love my brother, or were you just using him?"

I closed my eyes. I could see him, right before I walked on set that night. "Knock 'em dead, Ti-Ti. I'll be right here when you're done," he'd said in my ear. When I opened my eyes, I smiled sadly. "I loved him. I mean, I love him. But—"

"No buts," Jackie said.

"I really hurt him. He'll never forgive me."

"Yes, you did and yes, he will." Stefani said.

"No, Stef, you don't know—he's really mad at me."

"Uh-huh. The picture he broke?"

"You mean the one he smashed against the wall before telling me to drop the key and get the hell out? That one? Yes, I recall it."

"Get over yourself. He got another one. Bigger. It's hanging in his office."

My breath caught in my throat. "Seriously?"

Stefani rolled her eyes. "Yes, seriously. Me? Personally, I would've written you off after New York, but that brother of mine is all about some Christina Brinsley. He's proud as hell. You're gonna have to work to get him back, but he's yours. You betta be worth it."

"Christina, really—who else is gonna put up with your difficult ass?" Jackie said.

"Have you seen what he does to a pair of running shorts?" Lynne said.

"Hey!" Stefani grimaced.

"Watch it!" I scolded with a grin. He did do something magical to stretchy cotton.

"He's in the wedding. He's one of Clarke's attendants. Your

foolishness is not about to ruin my ascension into Brinsley-hood," Carey snapped. "You better get that boy back."

"Beg if you have to."

I winced. I might have to. "Okay, here's what I need. All the evidence from the investigator Collin and Clarke hired, I need Rita on the next plane out here from New York, five minutes with Congressman Walker, a half hour of airtime, a prayer, and a hug."

They all stared at me as if I'd gone off the deep end. "Not necessarily in that order, people—huddle up! Group hug!"

"She's back."

"Crazier than ever."

"Her crazy ass better fix my brother."

I was going to do my damnedest.

40

Pride Goeth Before a Fall

Steven—Friday, March 18, 8:30 a.m.

W hat I wouldn't give for a moment's peace and quiet. Introspection, reflection, and review. What do they call it now? Some "me" time. That's what I longed for. Just a little bit of Steven time. There's thoughtful concern and then there was helicopter hovering. Friends and family had moved firmly into the helicopter side of the scale.

Stefani was wearing me out. She hadn't given a brother a moment to breathe. I had been reinstated at the university pending further review, but my class load was still light. That gave me lots of time that was supposed to be to myself. But I couldn't kick my pregnant twin out on her ass without appearing rude.

She was currently fiddling with the TV. Flipping channels, checking the time, and acting very fidgety and nervous. It was making me a little crazy.

"What are you looking for?" Anything to stop the rapid-fire rifling through the channels again and again.

"Here it is. Come sit down and watch with me." She patted the sofa beside her.

I shuffled over and saw the VNN logo come up on the screen. "You're kidding me with this, right?" I tried to reach for the remote.

"Shut up and sit down. For once in your life, just listen to me for a change. Please?" She sounded stressed. I did not want to stress out a woman carrying my niece or nephew.

But this was the *last* thing I needed. There in 52-inch high-definition was Christina, smiling into the camera. I guess she was back at work. "We're back. This morning, we're going to take time away from our normal news recap to do a follow-up on a story I covered about a month ago concerning Project Mercury."

"Oh hell, no! Give me a break, Stef." I jumped up and Stefani pulled me back down.

"I asked nicely the first time. Don't make me get nasty."

With a resolved sigh, I crossed my arms and sat back.

"Here with me now is Lance Porter, chief operating officer of Chi-Wind foundation. Lance, how are things at the foundation?"

I leaned forward to listen.

"A little different. We've placed Dr. Williams on an indefinite, unpaid leave of absence, so I'm wearing quite a few hats right now." He launched into a short soliloquy on how he was doing his best to hold down the fort in the midst of this storm because the work was so important. I rolled my eyes.

Christina nodded, put her elbow on the desk, her chin in her hand, and blinked at him.

"Oh shit, she's got something!" I said, slowly standing up and moving closer to the screen.

"How can you tell?" Stefani asked, a small smile lifting the corners of her mouth.

I pointed. "The chin, eye-blinky thing. It's one of her tells. It means she's about to break her foot off in somebody's hind parts. Shhh, I want to listen."

I didn't see Stefani's smile get wide; I was too busy watching Christina's face.

"Mr. Porter, speaking of hats...I have some video here of you walking into a bank in Costa Rica. Roll tape, please."

A short video played showing a man in a large beach hat and sunglasses walking into a bank. He spoke to someone who directed him to a desk. He shook the banker's hand and then took off the hat and sunglasses. It was Lance. He took a check out of his pocket, signed the back, and handed it over along with a passport.

"Mr. Porter, while I admired your style of hats, why were you in a Costa Rican bank with a falsified passport, claiming that you were Steven Williams? And why did you forge his name on the back of this check?" She held up the check to the camera. "A check that was clearly from a Mr. Perry Marsh and made out to Chi-Wind Foundation in the amount of $78,192.64?"

"Er, uh—" Lance's eyes shifted to the left.

"Isn't this the money that you and others accused Dr. Williams of embezzling from the foundation?"

"Well now..." Lance was starting to sweat a little bit.

"And can we conclude by your inability to articulate any plausible response that you were involved in some sort of cover-up to frame Dr. Williams?" Her tone was silky and her eyes were wide.

"Yes!" I said, lifting my arms over my head.

Lance looked around. "I think I need to invoke my right to counsel."

"This isn't a courtroom, sir. You have no such rights. Now, do you know the significance of this amount? This $78,192.64?"

"No, no I do not." No, he did not.

"That's right. Only three people in the world do, sir. Me, Perry Marsh, and Dr. Steven Williams. Can you tell us why you tried to frame Dr. Williams?"

"I'm going to have to decline to answer any more questions at this time."

"Oh, that's fine by me, but I believe there are some authorities waiting offstage to have a little chat with you." She turned back to the camera. "When we return, the origin of these second set of books, and Congressman Walker's response. You're watching VNN, where truth matters to us because it matters to you."

I looked at Stefani. "What just happened?" Before I could finish asking, my cell phone started ringing and buzzing with new text message notifications. I glanced at the screen.

It was Clarke calling. "That sister of mine has her uses, huh?"

"You could say that again."

"I'll call you back. I want to watch the rest. Congratulations, my friend. Looks like the monkey's off your back."

"Thanks, Clarke. And thank your sister for me, too."

"Hmm, you may want to do that personally."

I didn't know about that. "I am doubting the necessity of that, but we'll see."

"Pride goeth before a fall, Dr. Williams."

"So they say." I wasn't going to argue with the man about his sister.

I hung up as Christina came back on the screen. Over the course of the next thirty minutes, she brought out Rita, who admitted that, with Brandon, she had made up a set of fake ledgers and fake bank statements because they wanted Christina to be humiliated. They didn't seem to mind if I got trashed along the way. Christina called Brandon live on the air and he cracked under pressure and admitted that he had been approached and paid by Congressman Walker to set up the entire thing. She then cut away to an interview she'd done earlier in the week where Congressman Walker said he was just a concerned citizen trying to make sure the crooks of the world didn't rob Americans blind.

As icing on the cake, she brought back Betsy Fine, the forensic accountant.

"So, Ms. Fine, in light of the information I brought you earlier in the week, what are your conclusions?"

"First of all, Ms. Brinsley, I want to thank you for your tireless effort to bring the truth to light like this. Secondly, let me say that I had your information independently validated by a former member of the FBI. Something I should have done when I received the second set of books in the first place. Your information holds up; these second books do not. And finally, upon further investigation we were able to locate a shell company that traced back to Congressman Walker. The bank accounts tied to those companies held close to a million dollars."

"So that would be the balance of the missing $1.3 million?"

"Give or take a few thousand dollars, which we suspect was used for cash bribes, yes."

"One last thing, Ms. Fine."

"Yes?"

"What are your final conclusions as far as Dr. Steven Williams's involvement in this entire enterprise?"

"Wholly innocent bystander caught in the crossfire. From what I can tell, he is a brilliant engineer and I sincerely hope he will continue his research. We need more men of intelligence and integrity in the world today."

Christina turned back to the camera with a brilliant smile. "Amen to that. And on a personal note, as a woman and a journalist, allow me a moment here. In America today, with the 24 / 7 / 365 availability of information, it's easy to not trust what you know to be true. It's easy to get jaded and only see the worst in people. If I could take anything from this experience to leave with all of our viewers, it's that the concept of innocent-before-proven-guilty was put into place for a reason. Trust your instincts and take a chance. I know that's a lesson I've had to learn the hard way. After the break, Tracey Tulum takes over with the top stories in today's news. Again: Dr. Steven Williams—absolved of all wrongdoing. Lance Porter, Congressman Walker, and a host of others—in hot water. More after the break."

"That's my girl." I smiled and nodded as her picture faded away to commercial.

"Your girl, huh? Are you gonna go get her?" Stefani asked.

"Oh hell, no." I shook my head empathically.

"Steven. You know you love that woman. She obviously loves you. Look what she just did for you!"

I appreciated the grand gesture, I really did. But how many times was I supposed to put my hand in the lion's mouth? "Funny, twin. Weren't you the one who told me to stay away from her in the first place? Weren't you the one who warned me that this could happen?"

She shrugged. "Maybe she's growing on me. You should give her a second chance."

"You mean a third chance, don't you? This being the second time she let me down," I pointed out. Yeah, I was still a little bitter about it. Christina seemed to make a habit of walking away from me a little too easily. Call it ego or pride, a man can only put so much on the line for one woman.

"I'll tell you what I told her: Get over it already."

"You've talked to her? What happened to her being all kinds of bitches and you were gonna kick her ass?"

"I got some licks in, and then I looked closely enough to see that she's wearing the same sorry expression as you. You're both miserable. Your trifling, high-maintenance butts deserve each other."

"Interesting. But it won't be me begging for a chance this time, sis. She's gotta work for it if she really wants it. I honestly don't even know if she has it in her to be what I need her to be, and I don't want to settle for anything less. I deserve more."

Stefani gave him a hug. "You deserve the best; you deserve the world."

Damn straight. "Well then. That's what I'm waiting for. If I can't get it from her, I'll get it from someone else."

Stefani rolled her eyes. "Something tells me either now or five years from now, it's going to be Christina Brinsley."

I shrugged. "She'll have to really show me something. Something I haven't seen from her as yet." Christina didn't stick when the going got tough and she didn't seem to admit when she was wrong.

"I think she's going to surprise you. I'm just going to sit back and watch her work, then."

"You're so sure she will?" I had my doubts that Christina even wanted to fight for me, for us.

Stefani gave me another little smile. "You just wait."

That's exactly what I planned to do. After all, I had all the time in the world now.

41

A Woman Like Me

Christina—Tuesday, April 22, noon

Admitting you were a damn fool and dead wrong was a long, arduous process. Figuring out why you are the way you are and wondering how to repair it...equally difficult. Having to face up to your own flaws and let go of the past was grueling. The past few weeks, I had been working on the rehabilitation of Christina. I knew that I had to fix me before I could face Steven. Even admitting to myself that I wanted Steven in a white-dress-and-forever kind of way was a huge step.

Why it took so long for me to figure out that I kept punishing the next man for what the ex-man did, was puzzling. Overall I was an intelligent, capable woman. But for some reason when it came to my relationships with men, I was a little slow on the uptake.

So I came up with a plan. There were four things I wanted to do before showing up naked on Steven's doorstep and begging him to take me back. One was to clear his name—done.

The second was to spend some time alone getting my head right—working on it.

The third was to let him know what I was thinking. So every day at some point, I wrote him a letter. Technically, I typed him an e-mail. Sometimes they were two lines, sometimes they were pages and pages. Some days I just apologized, others I just shared a moment of my day with him. Some days they were sweet and filled with lighthearted memories. Some nights they were steamy and full of detailed longings. I told him he didn't have to write back. It was enough to get the read receipt and know that he opened them.

The first letter I sent he didn't open for three whole days. I was so terrified of getting that delivery failure notification showing that he deleted it without opening. That was a rough three days. When that read receipt finally came back, I danced. I mean I boogied. Because at least he was listening (reading—you know what I mean). By the sixth letter he was opening them immediately. Sometimes from his BlackBerry, when I knew him to be in class. I imagined him pausing in midlecture to read my words, and I smiled.

This past week he had begun to send back short answers. *Thanks for this. I remember.* And my favorite: *Wow.*

The fourth thing I wanted to do was to bury the past for once and for all. I felt I had closure with Perry; he had to go live his truth. I even felt I had closure with Jay / David; he didn't know how to live in truth. Today I was meeting with Cedric for lunch. He was the fiancé who had married his college sweetheart in the middle of our engagement and didn't tell me until three weeks before our wedding date. He was the last piece of the Christina doomed-engagement puzzle I had to solve so I could relax, relate, release, and get on with my life.

Cedric walked into the restaurant looking nervous as hell. You know how you see one of your exes and suddenly remember all the good things about him? Yeah, this wasn't that. I sat and watched Cedric weave his way toward me and thought to myself, *What was I thinking?* Not that Cedric wasn't okay to look at. He was. He was your garden-variety, middle-class boy next door. No sparks or tingles, just your basic nice-guy vibe. But now, I honestly could not remember why I agreed to marry him in the first place. I could not remember what the spark was between us. Had there ever been one?

When I stood up to give him a hug, he was visibly startled before he returned the squeeze lightly. Then I remembered that the last time I saw him, I chucked a crystal vase at his head. He hadn't ducked fast enough. I touched the scar on the right side of his forehead with my finger. With a slightly rueful grin, I apologized. "Sorry about that, Ced."

"Ah, Christina." He sighed. "I can't say I didn't deserve it."

"True. Have a seat." Poor thing, he had the look of a man who expected a vase to be chucked at him at any moment. "You look well, Ced."

"You look amazing, Christina, and you're still the only person in the world who calls me Ced." He smiled for the first time.

"I'm sorry, do you only go by Cedric now?"

"Yeah, but it's okay. It's a good memory."

"We did have one or two," I agreed.

"Maybe a few more than that."

I nodded. "How's Vanessa?"

"She's great. Nervous about me coming here today."

"Why?"

He shrugged. "She thinks you want me back."

"Ha!" I threw back my head and had a good long chuckle at that. Picture that! "I'm sorry, no offense. But that's absolutely the last thing on my mind. Did you have kids?"

"Four."

He had been busy. "Four! Wow, okay then."

The waiter came around and inquired if we were ready to order. I considered before replying, "Just an iced tea for now, please."

"I'll have the same."

"So Ced, I'll get straight to the point. I don't want you

back, but I'm kind of trying to get closure on a few things. So I'm hoping you can help me out."

"Sure, whatever I can do."

"Well, I do want you to explain. Why her and not me?" That was the one question I probably should have asked years ago but never did.

He leaned back heavily in his chair and let out a puff of air. "Wow. I did not see that one coming. That's it? That's what you want to know? After all this time?"

"Yes. That's it."

"Can I be really honest with you here?"

"Of course."

"I mean honest and not get something lethal thrown at me?"

I laughed. "I've grown a little bit. I tend not to assault people physically these days. I do my damage with words. But please feel free to speak your mind. That's why I came."

He took a deep breath. "You were my ideal, Christina. When I approached you on campus, I never thought I could get a woman like you. I was swinging for the fences."

"A woman like me?"

"Classy, beautiful, ambitious, sophisticated, sexy, smart."

"I was all that, huh?" So far, so good.

"You were, still are. But, Christina, you are like a force of nature."

"Uh . . ." That did not sound good.

"Like a tornado. It was go, go, go. Full steam ahead. You knew what you wanted, you put the pieces where you wanted and rolled forward. I was just a piece in his place. I mean, I would have died if you left me—but I knew if I left, you'd replace me with someone else and keep rolling."

"Oh." I kinda had done exactly that.

"I wanted someone who thought I was *that* guy. That irreplaceable force of nature in her life. I wanted to be the guy you couldn't live without, couldn't imagine not being in your world.

Not just that guy who fit neatly there. When I ran into Vanessa that weekend, I saw it in her eyes. I was that guy for her."

"Aw, she got you with the you're-the-only-one-for-me look," I teased.

He smiled. "She really did. As sexy and hot as you were, you never looked at me like that, and I knew you never would."

"So it was more important for you to feel wanted than to want."

"Exactly. Eventually, I felt the same for Vanessa as she felt for me, but yes. Having someone tell you they knew they'd never be as happy with anyone else as they were just thinking about you . . . that's some seductive stuff there."

"Mmm, pretty irresistible, actually." I nodded.

It made perfect sense. And yet again, I had to realize my own culpability in a relationship collapse. The waiter brought the tea and we made small talk for a few minutes, but I had what I needed.

As we hugged good-bye, I told him, "You tell Vanessa she got a good one. One of the very best."

"Forgiven?"

"Nothing to forgive."

He sighed as if a great weight had been lifted off his shoulders. "You were one of the great regrets of my life."

I patted his shoulder. "Regret no more. You absolutely did the right thing."

"Thank you for saying that."

"Thank you for dumping me."

We snickered. "Take care, Ced."

I walked away feeling a bit lighter myself. Climbing into the car, I had one last order of business.

I scrolled through my contact list and hit DIAL.

"Hello?"

"Brandon?"

"Christina?!" He was shocked to hear from me.

"I worked out a little deal. The charges against you and

Rita are being dropped." I had spoken to the Js. They were ready to put the whole thing behind us and get on with the business of news. Without them, the authorities decided to not pursue the case. They elected to let me handle it as I saw fit. I was ready to put it to rest myself.

Brandon was stunned. "Why would you do that?"

"I owed you...sort of."

He was silent.

"It's okay. We really don't have to go into a whole lot of who did what to who. I was a little wrapped up in me and you suffered for it and I never saw it. So while you were real shady, I get it. I apologize. I sincerely do."

"And I apologize."

"Do you think we can call it even?"

"I would say we're more than that," he said quietly.

"Okay. Go live your life and, Brandon, for the love of God—either commit to Rita or cut her loose."

He laughed. "I hear you. You gonna take your own advice?"

I sighed. "I'm going to try. I'm really going to try. Brandon, good luck to you." I hung up. Neither Brandon nor Rita would work at VNN anymore, but I felt it only fair to clean the slate.

I felt like Michael Corleone in *The Godfather* on the day of his nephew's christening: "Today I settled all family business."

It took me a little while, but I finally got it. No more little lies, no more evasion. It was time I grew up and took responsibility for what happened before and whatever was coming next.

I realized now that I had seen what I wanted to see in Cedric, in Perry, in Jay/David, and not much more. I saw them as a means to an end that I had planned out in my head. Chances were, they didn't show me much because I wasn't really looking for it. I wanted someone to fill a particular role, and they filled it for as long as they could. I never really took the time to see who they were.

Steven, on the other hand, had been the same person since the day I met him. I don't know why I couldn't see it before. He was the one who stayed true to himself and true to me through thick and thin. He didn't waver, he didn't change, just steadfastly stood beside me. I wasn't sure what he saw in me. I had ducked, dodged, waffled, and whiffed ever since the airplane to New York.

He asked me to believe in him, but I hadn't believed in anything. He was right—I played the victim and acted like my whole life had happened to me instead of owning my role. Well, I was ready to own it. What the hell was I thinking? Men like that don't come around too often, and he had come my way twice. And men like that don't wait around forever.

Long story short, if I couldn't make it work with someone who was as good and true as Steven, I couldn't make it work with anybody. I was ready to try. I was ready to grovel if need be. Now I was truly ready to move forward, and I knew exactly what I was putting in today's letter to Steven.

42

Be Ready

Steven—Thursday, April 24, 10:29 p.m.

Okay, she got me. I had to admit. She was smart. She knew that showing up at my doorstep or calling would have gotten her a door slammed in her face or a dial tone. So instead, she snuck in on my weak side. She appealed to the literary romantic, the professor in me. She wrote me letters. A single letter every day. The very first letter was an apology. An apology for not being what I needed her to be. She vowed to do better in the future. She used the phrase "plan to be worthy of the love you gave unselfishly."

After that, I was hooked. I was addicted to these letters from Christina. I knew what she was doing. She was wooing me. This was a good old-fashioned (albeit gender-reversed) woo. It was flattering. Some of the letters were sweet, some sad, some sexy, but on the whole seductive. She always did know how to draw me in. Mentally and physically.

Each word was a balm to my bruised little ego and restored some of my spirit. Before receiving the first letter, I truly wondered if she was capable of the depth of emotion and steadfastness I needed. And I really didn't think I was asking for much. But her inability to believe in me and stand beside me hurt more than I would have believed possible. But I was also tired of being angry and feeling betrayed. That kind of emotional outrage is exhausting. Battling that sense of loss was harder to deal with than the threat of losing my profession and reputation. Those were things I always knew I could rebuild. Christina, for all her faults, was one of a kind and not easily replaced.

She caught me with the first letter and drew me in closer with every one since. With each letter, I felt renewed and almost as if I was falling in love with a brand-new person. I wanted to believe; I really did. There was always that thing between Christina and me that was undeniable.

But it wasn't until her letter this past Tuesday that I knew. I knew it wasn't a matter of "if" but "when." Our time was coming. I was perfectly comfortable letting her set the pace. My days of pushing Christina to take the next step were over. I had, at the very least, learned that lesson.

The past weeks had been one teachable moment after another. After Christina's piece clearing me aired on VNN, things moved very quickly. I dissolved Chi-Wind Foundation and reopened it as The Williams Research Foundation. Now that my name was golden again, might as well maximize the brand. I hired Stefani's husband, Marcus, as the chief operating officer and brought on Betsy Fine herself as the government liaison. There would be no more getting over on Professor Williams.

We would be kicking off a study testing existing railroad beds (foundation under the tracks) for their capacity to carry high-speed trains and move them quickly. I was excited and couldn't wait to share the news with Christina. I missed talking to her, I missed being around her, I missed her cooking, I missed her touch. But I was willing to move at her pace.

I popped open my laptop to reread Tuesday's letter, which

was my personal favorite so far. It had a tone that was so authentically Christina, I could hear her as if she were in the room reading the words aloud to me.

Dear Steven,

It's finally come clear to me now. You are an irreplaceable force of nature to me. You are THE man I cannot imagine the rest of my life without. I am happier just thinking about you than being in the presence of anybody else. You are that which brings me peace and strength and hope. You are sun when it's raining and refuge in a storm. And I want to be that for you, too. You used to look at me in a way that I called the "eye-twinkle," but I knew it was really your way of telling me that I pleased you. That you found delight in me. I delighted in you, as well. Not just physically, though I don't have words enough to express our connection there. I think you know that we are once-in-a-lifetime for each other.

I know I'm not easy, I'm not for everybody. But I am for you. Just as you are for me. You see, I'm your force of nature as well, but you know how to control me and tame me without lessening my force.

If we are never together again, know that I love you. But I hope we will be. That's the other thing I have now. I have hope in tomorrow. I can come to you now. Unchained from the past, unchained from childish fears. A woman. Your woman. Your match and mate in every way.

My only fear now is that I haven't grown enough, shown you enough, said enough, done enough, to earn back the trust and love I threw away. But that fear won't stop me. I'm coming for you. Be ready.
Yours. Forever.
Christina Violet Tempest Brinsley.

It was the first time she'd told me what the *T* stood for. I took it as a sign that she was ready to let me in. Tempest was an apt name for her. Christina was a storm unto herself. I was curious to see what her next move would be. Hitting the REPLY button, I typed quickly and hit SEND. I sent back two words. "I'm ready."

43

You Call This Easy?

Christina—Saturday, April 26, 8:44 p.m.

I pulled up outside the restaurant and unclenched my hands from the steering wheel. I was so nervous, I wanted to throw up. Sorry for the graphic detail, but I really did. Though I had given up my self-medicating bouts of drinking to excess, I had tossed back a small glass of Merlot to settle my nerves before leaving the house. That damn wine felt like vinegar in my clenching stomach. Other people got nervous and had cute little butterflies fluttering in their stomachs; I had the whole damn militia from *Apocalypse Now* battling it out in there.

Handing my keys to the valet driver, I took a deep breath. *Inhale in, exhale out.* I tried to remember the calming exercises I had learned at yoga, but none of that Zen crap was working for me right now. There was nothing else to do but march myself into this party and face the man and the music. Technically, this was Carey and Clarke's engagement party. But I was the one trying to kickstart the rest of my life tonight.

Lord, what if it was too late? What if he had met another woman? What if he was in there with some other woman? What if he ignored me? What if he didn't feel the same? What if, what if, what if? I was making myself crazy in an attempt to stall for time.

"Grown Woman Christina, move your ass," I whispered to myself.

I took two steps forward and stopped to steady myself on my admittedly ridiculous shoes. In Steven-speak, I had all the weapons of the arsenal out tonight. He once said he loved seeing me in green. So tonight I had on a floaty dress in sheer chiffon layers of forest and lime green. Inch-wide straps crisscrossed my shoulders and molded into cups that raised and separated the girls in a very cleavage-flattering way. Then the dress floated away, swaying around my body to fall a good two inches above my knees. My legs were lotioned to a healthy glow and my freshly pedicured feet were looking super sexy in emerald snakeskin gladiator sandals with a wicked heel. My hair was styled in a curly updo and a few long curls kissed my shoulders. I went all chocolate and bronze with the makeup.

I just thanked God that I looked better than I felt. *Okay, Christina.* I was starting to freak out the valet dudes. I had been standing there by the CLOSED FOR A PRIVATE PARTY sign talking to myself for more than a minute or two. Dear God, I *was* a chicken-shit wuss. "I'm okay," I told them when it was clear they were growing concerned.

I tucked my little silver clutch purse under my arm and clapped my hands together like I was psyching myself up for the big game. I did a little shimmy to shake off the rest of the nerves (no, it didn't work). "Let me go get this man."

Two more steps forward when I heard his voice. "You gonna come for me, woman? Or are you going to stand out here talking to yourself all night?"

Looking up, I had to brace myself to keep from falling down. My knees literally went weak. He stood farther up the walkway near the entrance to the restaurant and looked amazing. Slate gray suit, purple striped tie, crisp white shirt. Dreads held back, eyes fully green and loaded with twinkle. But it wasn't all of that, it was him. I drank him in. He was right here, he was alone, he was smiling, and he was waiting on me. When I didn't take a step forward, he raised a brow. "Well, Tempest?"

My nerves fell away in that instant and I smiled. "Oh, I'm coming for you." I closed the distance in a hurry. As I neared, he held out his hand. I reached for it and linked my fingers with his. I was home. "Just like that?"

"Just like that." He smiled gently.

"Could it be this easy?" I wondered aloud.

He snorted. "You call these past months easy?"

"But I had a speech and a whole down-on-my-knees thing prepared."

"Hmm, that on-your-knees thing sounds promising. Why don't you save that for a little later on?"

I flushed. "Oh! But really, I wanted to..."

"For the record, Ti-Ti, all I wanted was for you to stand beside me. Aren't you doing that?"

"I am."

"I mean beyond the literal sense, are you ready to stand beside me?"

"I'm ready to be what you need me to be. What you deserve."

"All of that, huh?"

"Whatever you want."

"I like the sound of that."

"I like the sound of you." Just hearing his voice again made me giddy.

He kissed my forehead. "Then let's go in and celebrate for now."

"One thing though." I paused.

"Conditions, right now, really?"

"Just one," I said. "I hope you'll agree to it."

"You won't know unless you ask."

"I want to walk in there with you to celebrate their engagement only if we got next." I held my breath.

"Whoa. Where did that come from?"

"Grown Woman Christina."

"I think I like her. Ti-Ti, is that a proposal?"

"Is that a yes?"

Instead of answering, he leaned down and kissed me. Slowly and sweetly. Dear God, I had missed that. Stepping back, he strode through the door, pulling me behind him, and a cheer rose up from our family and friends. I hadn't realized they were watching the entire exchange from the window. Walking to the middle of the room, Steven held up our clasped hands. "Guess what?"

"What!"

"We got next!"

The party was only going to get better from here.

SWEET LITTLE LIES

Michele Grant

ABOUT THIS GUIDE

The suggested questions that follow
are included to enhance your group's
reading of this book.

DISCUSSION QUESTIONS

1. What did you think of Christina walking away from Steven in chapter 12? Should she have given them a shot, or was it a case of right person, wrong timing?

2. How would you feel if one of your best friends started dating your brother?

3. How would you feel if one of your best friends hit on your significant other?

4. Discuss how past relationships (especially those that went wrong) influence your current and future relationships.

5. Do you think the advent of social media, smartphones, and 24/7 Internet have changed communication in relationships?

6. What are your thoughts about older women who date younger men? Are you Team Cougar?

7. How do you deal with office drama when it comes your way?

8. What's the best way to ask forgiveness from a significant other?

9. Clearly, both Christina and Steven had trouble letting go of the past and trusting. What advice would you give to them moving forward?

Don't miss Michele Grant's *White Mocha* in

CRUSH

In stores April 2011

Turn the page for an excerpt from *White Mocha*. . . .

1

It All Starts with a Sip

"You need to do something," my assistant, Kim, said from the doorway of my office, propping a hand on her hip.

I glanced up from the report I wasn't really reading. "What do you mean?"

"Girl, you are dragging."

"It's eight o'clock at night." I tried to justify my sluggishness.

She pursed her lips. "Um-hmm, but you looked like this at eight o'clock this morning."

I reached back and lifted my hair off my neck, kneading the knotted muscles there. I sighed, knowing she was right. I'd been lethargic, restless, and listless for days. I hadn't been sleeping well either. "I don't know what's wrong with me. Maybe I need some vitamins, a protein injection, some caffeine or something."

She laughed. "Oh, you need a protein injection all right—how long since you and Say-It-Ain't-So Joe broke up?" The lovely nickname she had for my ex, Joseph.

"Nine months."

"And since then?"

I sighed again. "No one."

"No one." She shook her head in disgust. "Not a peck on

the cheek or a hand grazing your hind parts. Jayla, get some, already!"

I laughed. "Kim, there's more to life than sex."

"How would you know? You have no sex nor life to speak of."

"That's harsh. I'm career focused. I am woman, hear me roar."

"Ya lonely and cranky. Fix it."

"So you want me to just jump on the next guy I see?"

She turned to leave on her crocodile stiletto and smiled at me over her shoulder. "There's an idea!"

"Yeah, right—that is *so* me. . . ."

"Seriously," she called out as she strode toward the elevator, "a little spontaneity wouldn't kill you."

"That's what people say to excuse rash behavior."

"Nothing wrong with cutting loose every once in a while. You don't have to make it a lifestyle choice. And don't stay here all night—you cannot snuggle up to income projections when you're old!" Her final words caused a few of the other late-night stragglers to stick their heads out of their cubes and offices to see who she was addressing.

"Good *night,* Kim."

" 'Night, boss."

The thing of it was—she was right. Since Joseph and I split (okay, since I kicked his lying, cheating, wallet "borrowing" ass out), I had funneled all of my energy into my career and little else. I stopped into the coffee shop every morning (specialty mocha and zucchini muffin), I visited my grandmother once a week, I went out with friends once a month. Everything else was work related.

I had been working at a nonstop pace for months. And I was well on my way to being the youngest chief financial officer this company had ever seen. Granted, BeniCareCo was a small, independent health insurance company, but I was making my mark. As the assistant vice president of financial operations, I was two steps away from my goal. But I was tired. Maybe the listless, restless thing was my body's way of telling me to slow it down.

Slow down for who and for what? What was I in a rush to get home to? Most of my friends were either married or on the same crazy, cutthroat corporate merry-go-round I was. I was too restless to curl up with a book. Maybe I'd watch a movie, soak in a long bath. Irritated with myself, I closed the folder that was in front of me and turned away.

As I swiveled my chair toward the window, I looked out into the late summer night. Chicago was on the tail end of a heat wave. Downtown Chicago was full of people enjoying the balmy, breezy weather. Across the street, I saw a couple coming out of the new coffee shop on the corner. The couple looked happy and carefree, clutching each other with one hand and their coffee with the other. The sign reading JAY'S COFFEE CAFÉ bathed them in an electric blue and green light.

Suddenly I wanted what they had: their togetherness, their apparent happiness, a shared carefree moment. I sighed. You have to give to get. You have to look to find. And I hadn't been doing much of either lately. Maybe I couldn't get that happy-couple vibe right away, but for now I'd settle for their coffee.

I packed up my desk, sliding what I needed into my purse and laptop case. By the time I got downstairs, crossed the street, and entered the door, there were no other customers in the coffee shop. Actually, looking around—there didn't appear to be any workers there either.

"Hello?" I called out.

"We're closing up," a deep voice called out from the back.

I was inexplicably disappointed. As if the promise of that carefree moment could truly be found in a cup of coffee. "Story of my life," I said to no one in particular, and pivoted back toward the door.

"Excuse me?" The voice sounded closer.

I swiveled back around and stopped dead in my tracks. A

flash of pure heat passed through me, awakening nerve endings and receptors that had been long dormant. In front of me stood a specimen of maleness that could only be described one way: hotness. The kind of hotness that burned right through common sense and rational thought.

In the many times I had visited this coffee shop, I had never seen him. And believe me, I would have remembered. He was gorgeous in an oh-my-God-where-did-you-come-from kind of way. The kind that takes your breath away. He was a beautiful exotic blend of European and African-American descent, had a Derek Jeter kind of vibe without all the unnecessary polish. Raw, earthy, and did I say brutally hot? Light green eyes framed with thick lashes, wavy brown hair closely cropped to his head, full lips set into a square jawline currently softened with a smile. He was a solid block of a man, just at six feet tall, with the muscles of a gym regular. Flat-front khakis and a navy polo imprinted with the shop's logo stretched easily across his frame. He had the look of what I'd call a man's man, even while wearing a bright pink apron and clutching a purple mug decorated with green hearts.

The longer I studied him, the more he studied me. I knew what he saw: a curvy woman, busty, with hips that could politely be called generous—a true hourglass figure, no matter how hard I fought against it. I was taller than average, with caramel-colored skin, and thick wavy hair of the same color curling past my shoulders. A rounded face often referred to as cute, with wide, light brown eyes and a pouty mouth with no gloss left on it from this morning. And there we both stood, somewhat intrigued by instant chemistry, that urban legend. After thirty-three years of living, it was happening to me. That primal spark calling out from male to female and back again.

I stood staring at him as though he were the last shrimp on the buffet table and I hadn't had fresh seafood in a while. Clearly I was deprived of far more than sleep when the mere presence of a male made me jittery and breathless. *Get a grip, Jayla* I told myself sternly, determined to raise my eyes above his waist and act like I had some good sense.

When I finally lifted my gaze back up to his face, his eyes had gone from casually friendly to heatedly curious. It wasn't until the drool was literally pooling at the corners of my mouth that I regained any semblance of composure. "Oh, I'm sorry, long day," I lamely explained. "I'll just get out of your way so you can close up." I smiled sadly, tentatively, as I turned back toward the door. Was I so starved for male attention that I manufactured chemistry with the coffee guy?

"Hey," he said softly, his voice deep, velvety and smooth.

I looked back. "Hey?"

"I can always make just one more." He smiled with a flash of pearly white teeth that sent a tingle straight up my spine. "Do you mind if I make you my last customer?"

I don't mind if you make me your concubine. "No. No, that's fine. I appreciate it. I'm sure you're ready to get out of here."

His look was pensive. "Don't worry about it—you're a customer."

Right. Customer, here to buy coffee. "Well, thanks."

"Not a problem. Will it make you uncomfortable if I lock up?"

"Not all at, do what you need to do." I stood primly, clutching my case in front of me.

He brushed past me to lock the door and switch the OPEN sign to CLOSED. He slowly circled the store, pulling down shades and closing the drapes. It suddenly felt like a close and intimate space rather than a storefront. Walking back, he paused beside me, close enough that the scent of him wafted to me. I took a deep breath. He smelled like coffee, cinnamon, chocolate, soap, and some sort of spicy musk. "So what'll you have?"

You, on a platter, please . . . I looked up at him and saw by the slight glint in his eyes that he heard me loud and clear, even though I hadn't said it out loud. Okay, maybe the chemistry wasn't so manufactured after all. "What's your specialty?"

"White mocha." Two words, innocent words at that, but I instantly shivered and flushed. His nostrils flared and his jaw tightened as he watched me.

"I'll take it extra large, extra hot." After the words left my mouth, I realized how it sounded. I was a little bit out of control.

He swallowed and blinked, as if he wasn't sure he heard me correctly. "I beg your pardon?"

I took a step back and grabbed the last remnants of my composure. "The white mocha, extra large, extra hot. To go."

He stepped back as well. "Oh, okay. Will that be all?" He started to move away.

I paused. What if I did what Kim suggested? What if I decided to be a little spontaneous, proposition the first guy I saw . . . this guy? Not ask his name, not care what his circumstances were, just ask for I wanted in this moment, for right now. I trembled a little just in contemplation.

He saw the tremble, stopped walking, and looked me over from head to toe. Those ivy green eyes clearly missed nothing, noticing my tension, my fluttering pulse, and my parted lips. Green eyes heated to laser intensity gave me a clearly appreciative look. He raised one brow, saying slowly, "Is there *anything* I can get you to go with that mocha?"

"Would you mind terribly if I had it here after all?" I said breathlessly, almost panting with anticipation and nervousness. I've never propositioned a barista before—okay, any stranger. What if he said no? Oh God, what if he said yes?

"The mocha?" He tilted his head and gave me a look that said *if you want it, ask for it.*

"Yes, the mocha and . . ." I set down my purse and my laptop case and stepped to him in my black, figure-hugging sheath dress and peep-toe heels. "Listen, you don't know anything about me or what I'm going through, and I don't know anything about you—"

"I do know something about you," he interrupted, meeting me until we stood toe-to-toe. "I know you are sexy and beautiful and you like coffee. I know you don't hook up with strange men often."

"Ever. I don't hook up with strange men ever," I corrected him. "And how do you know?"

He reached down and touched the fluttering vein pulsing at the base of my neck, caressing the area in soft strokes. "Because you're nervous and unsure. It's cute, sexy."

Cute. Sexy. I nodded, with no clue what to say next. *Should I, shouldn't I?* I had reengaged my brain and it was getting in the way of what the rest of me wanted.

He grinned at me. "Let me get you that coffee."

Coffee. Yes. That is what I came in here for. I stood there and continued to argue with myself. Was I really going to make a move on some strange guy at the coffee house? I mean, really? I sighed. I was bold, but I wasn't that bold. Tonight, the only craving I was going to assuage was for flavored, expensive caffeine. I watched while he measured beans, steamed milk, and mixed syrups in a cup. I could watch him all day and feel it was twenty-four hours spent productively. I sighed again.

He looked over at me with a look that sizzled. "So . . . just the coffee?" He was giving me every opportunity to make a move.

Wimpy Jayla beat Wanton Jayla down. I shrugged. "Just the coffee."

With a final stir, he capped the beverage and handed me the cup. "Tell me what you think."

I took a sip, my eyes slid shut, and I moaned. It was the best white mocha on the face of the planet: sweet, fragrant, hot, rich, and strong. The chocolate flavor didn't battle the coffee; it was a heavenly marriage of taste, texture, and spice. I took another sip and enjoyed the flavor of it exploding on my tongue and sliding down the back of my throat. "Oh my God." When I reopened my eyes, his face had taken on a predatory gleam. "What?" I asked him.

"Your face when you drank the coffee . . . that was a look I'd like to see again. And again."

I took a shaky breath and vowed to maintain some semblance of control.

"It's okay, you know."

"What's okay?"

"I'm not going to do anything you don't want."

Ha! If he only knew . . . "Thanks."

"Do you work around here?"

"Across the street. Are you new here? I haven't seen you before."

"I'm just helping to close tonight. I'm usually at one of the other stores."

I nodded. "This is the best white mocha I've ever had. There's something different about it. It's not like the others I've had here."

"I added a little something extra. It's my own private formula."

"Is that right?"

"Indeed."

"What would a girl have to do to get the formula?"

"What would a girl be willing to do to get it?"

I let a slow smile spread across my face. This guy was trouble. In all caps and bolded. I liked it. I took a final sip of the brew and set the cup down. "What do I owe you?"

"It's on the house."

"I can't let you do that."

"Come back and see me. That's payment enough."

I flashed a grateful smile and gathered up my things. Nothing like stellar coffee and harmless flirting with a good-looking man to reinvigorate you. He came around the counter to unlock the door for me. As I walked past I said, "Thanks. For everything."

"You're welcome." He took a step toward me and leaned down to whisper in my ear. "Just so you know . . . I would've given you anything you asked for."

I paused midstep and shifted toward him a little. "Anything?"

"Absolutely."

I lifted my eyes to his and we shared a smile as though we knew far more about each other than we really did. I nodded. "Good to know." I moved forward.

"Have a nice night."

"You do the same." I strolled out into the night, wondering if I'd just dodged a bullet or missed out on something potentially great. Only time would tell.